3800 18 0042403 2

HIGH LIFE HIGHLAND

# THE SHOP WINDOW MURDERS

'THE DETECTIVE STORY CLUB is a clearing house for the best detective and mystery stories chosen for you by a select committee of experts. Only the most ingenious crime stories will be published under the THE DETECTIVE STORY CLUB imprint. A special distinguishing stamp appears on the wrapper and title page of every THE DETECTIVE STORY CLUB book—the Man with the Gun. Always look for the Man with the Gun when buying a Crime book.'

**Wm. Collins Sons & Co. Ltd., 1929**

Now the Man with the Gun is back in this series of COLLINS CRIME CLUB reprints, and with him the chance to experience the classic books that influenced the Golden Age of crime fiction.

# THE DETECTIVE STORY CLUB

# THE SHOP WINDOW MURDERS

## A STORY OF CRIME

### BY

## VERNON LODER

WITH AN INTRODUCTION BY
NIGEL MOSS

COLLINS CRIME CLUB

An imprint of HarperCollins*Publishers*

1 London Bridge Street

London SE1 9GF

www.harpercollins.co.uk

This Detective Story Club edition 2018

First published by W. Collins Sons & Co. Ltd 1930

Introduction © Nigel Moss 2018

A catalogue record for this book is available from the British Library

ISBN 978-0-00-828298-1

Typeset in Bulmer MT Std by Palimpsest Book Production Ltd,
Falkirk, Stirlingshire
Printed and bound in Great Britain by
CPI Group (UK) Ltd, Croydon CR0 4YY

MIX
Paper from
responsible sources
FSC® C007454

# INTRODUCTION

VERNON LODER was a popular and prolific author of Golden Age detective mysteries and spy thrillers. He wrote 22 titles during the decade from 1928 to 1938. Subsequently Loder has been out of print and largely overlooked. Fortunately, the tide is turning. In 2013/14, two noted crime fiction commentators, Curtis Evans and J. F. Norris, championed a number of early Loder titles, the latter in a series of enthusiastic reviews. A flurry of e-reader versions of Loder stories followed. But it was not until 2016 that Loder made his first return in print since the 1930s with the re-issue of his first novel *The Mystery at Stowe* (1928) as part of the Collins Detective Story Club reprint series. In the original Preface, the Club's Editor, F. T. (Fred) Smith had welcomed Loder as 'one of the most promising recruits to the ranks of detective story writers'.

*The Shop Window Murders* (1930) was Loder's fourth novel, after *The Mystery at Stowe* (1928), *Whose Hand?* (1929) and *The Vase Mystery* (1929). It was published by Collins in the UK, and with the same title by Morrow in the USA. The storyline is intriguing and unusual, with one of Loder's more ingenious plots. The setting is Mander's Department Store in London's West End (loosely modelled on Selfridges in Oxford Street), owned by Tobias Mander and famous for its elaborate window displays. Early on a Monday morning, the crowds of passers-by pause to watch the window blinds being raised on a new weekly display, but the onlookers quickly realise that one of the wax figures is in fact a human corpse, shot and placed among the mannequins in the window display. Shortly afterwards a second victim is discovered, and this striking tableau begins a baffling and complex mystery tale. Was it murder and suicide, or double murder?

Loder draws a wide cast of diverse suspects, each with a motive for the killings. To a toxic mix of jealousy, fear, panic and anger, he adds further colour to the story with a proliferation of bizarre circumstances and enigmatic clues, displaying some fiendishly intricate plotting.

The case raises a fundamental question: why did the perpetrator of the killings leave so many signs and clues? Did it show a confused mind? Or was this a deliberate and clever attempt to confuse the police by leaving a trail of red herrings and different angles which implicated more and more characters and made proof of guilt harder to determine?

The police investigation is led by Inspector Devenish of Scotland Yard, who makes his sole appearance in Loder's canon of detective novels. Devenish is intelligent, workmanlike, tenacious and indefatigable. He displays a strong moral compass, giving short shrift to those who lie when questioned, particularly a suspected blackmailer. He remains firmly in charge throughout, pursuing the case with impressive diligence and total absorption; though his superior powers of ratiocination are largely by dint of effort. In these qualities, Devenish perhaps resembles Freeman Wills Crofts' famous series detective, Inspector French. He does not have any of the eccentricities which Loder bestows on some of his other police detectives: for example the likeable Superintendent Cobham in *Whose Hand?* (1929), who deliberately lulls suspects into a false sense of security by pretending to be an absent-minded blunderer (similar to the TV detective Columbo), and who often hums while investigating, alternating between opera arias and music hall tunes. Loder describes Devenish as 'tall and thin, dark hair, dark eyes, and a swarthy complexion; he might have passed as a southern Italian'. Beyond this, we learn nothing of Devenish's background or personal life, not even his first name. There is no amateur sleuth on hand to rival or potentially embarrass the police. Devenish works alone, assisted by Detective-Sergeant Davis and reports to Mr Melis, an Assistant-Commissioner.

Melis is debonair, suave and ethereal, with the air of an amateur actor. But his ideas on the case often turn out to be perceptive and seminal, providing the germ from which Devenish produces workable theories.

The denouement is surprising, and not easily foreseen. But it is plausible and makes sense, even though partly speculative. It shows the plot to have been solidly clued for the reader who can follow the hints. Loder often shows villains falling prey to their own scheming and he does so again here. There is also a pervading sense of tragedy, almost tragi-comedy, affecting those directly involved. One of the killings involves a variation of a method of dispatch seen in other Loder novels. The other foreshadows the murder setting in *Drop to his Death* (1939), co-authored by John Dickson Carr (writing as Carter Dickson) and John Rhode.

*The Shop Window Murders* is an entertaining and richly plotted example of the Golden Age deductive puzzle novel. The unusual and bizarre crimes make it one of Vernon Loder's best mysteries for bafflement and ingenuity. The narrative is direct, brisk and lively, and the complex storyline is absorbing, well-constructed and moves at a swift pace. Loder pays close attention to carefully worked-out and intricately structured plotting. But his skill in creating clever, insightful 'good lightning sketches' of characters, a feat praised by Dorothy L. Sayers in her review of *Murder from Three Angles* (1934), is also evident—Melis being a good example. The combination of subtle witty observations and good humour help to leaven an otherwise dark tale. Here is Loder describing Mander's older female admirer: 'She did not look an amorous type, though she was obviously endeavouring to hold her fugitive youth by the skirts'. Overall, the novel shows Loder writing with assurance and maturity as a crime fiction author.

Of particular interest to Golden Age aficionados will be the striking similarities between *The Shop Window Murders* and *The French Powder Mystery* by Ellery Queen, also published in the US and UK in 1930. It was only the second Ellery Queen

Mystery, a year after the successful debut of *The Roman Hat Mystery*. The book begins almost immediately with a murder: a model inside the main shopfront window of French's Department Store in downtown New York City is demonstrating some modern furniture and accessories on display, with a crowd watching from outside. When a button is pushed to reveal a concealed wall folding bed, out tumbles the murdered body of the wife of the store owner. The similarities continue: the owner has a private apartment above the store which the victim visits late one night when the store is closed. There are bizarre and unexplained clues, strange discoveries of unusual items found where they should not be, and a plethora of alibis and motives. The plot is ingenious, almost to the point of being overly complicated and involuted. Each small fact and clue is examined, discussed and (mostly) discarded with impressive deductive logic and reasoning. The rigorous intellectual approach is indebted to the popular Philo Vance mysteries of S. S. Van Dine. The climax is generously praised by the eminent critic Anthony Boucher as 'probably the most admirably constructed denouement in the history of the detective story'. Following the trademark Queen 'challenge to the reader', it comprises 35 pages of tightly worded explanation, with the identity of the murderer only revealed in the last two words of the novel. Ellery Queen was the nom-de-plume of Fred Dannay and Manfred Lee, two cousins from Brooklyn. According to their biographer Francis M. Nevins, the novel was inspired after one of the cousins passed a Manhattan department store display window and stopped to look at an exhibit of contemporary apartment furnishings which included a Murphy bed. It is not possible to say whether Loder or Queen first conceived the idea of the store window murder, but the similarities between the two stories and close proximity of publication dates are certainly a remarkable coincidence.

Vernon Loder was one of several pseudonyms used by the hugely versatile and productive Anglo-Irish author Jack Vahey

(John George Hazlette Vahey), 1881–1938. In addition to the canon of Loder titles between 1928 and 1938, Vahey wrote initially as John Haslette from 1909 to 1916, resuming writing in the 1920s as Anthony Lang, George Varney, John Mowbray, Walter Proudfoot and Henrietta Clandon. Born in Belfast, John Vahey was educated in Ulster and for a while in Hanover, Germany. He began his working life as an architect's pupil, but after four years switched careers and sat professional examinations with a view to becoming a chartered accountant. However, this too was abandoned after Vahey took up writing fiction. He married Gertrude Crewe and settled in the English south coast town of Bournemouth. His writing career was cut short by his death at the relatively young age of 57.

The Loder novels were all published by Collins in the UK, and from 1930 his detective works were published under their famous Crime Club imprint. Several of his early novels (between 1929 and 1931) were also published in the US by Morrow, sometimes with different titles. The publisher's biographical note on Loder, which appears in *Two Dead* (1934), mentions that his initial attempt at writing a novel (apparently never published) was during a period of convalescence in bed. Various colourful claims are made of Loder: he once wrote a novel on a boarding-house table in twenty days, serialised in both England and the US under different names; he worked very quickly, and thought two hours in the morning quite enough for anyone; also, he composed directly on a typewriter, and did not ever re-write. Whether these claims are true—or indeed laudable—is a matter for conjecture.

Loder had several recurring detectives. Inspector Brews and Chief Inspector Chace were each quite contrasting characters, the former a stolid local policeman with an emphasis on the importance of routine, the latter a highly efficient new breed of Scotland Yard CID detective. Brews appears in *The Essex Murders* (1930) and *Death of an Editor* (1931); Chace is found in *Murder from Three Angles* (1934) and *Death at the Horse*

*Show* (1935). In his later espionage thrillers—*Ship of Secrets* (1936), *The Men with the Double Faces* (1937) and *The Wolf in the Fold* (1938), published under the separate Collins Mystery imprint—Loder's protagonist was Donald Cairn, a British secret service agent involved in a series of thrilling adventures combatting continental spies in the lead-up to the outbreak of World War 2.

Loder never quite achieved the first rank of detective novelists, and has received scant attention in commentaries of the genre. Nonetheless, he was a popular, dependable author in the 1930s, and better than many; perhaps a paradigm of the English Golden Age mystery writer. The original Collins dust wrappers show that he was warmly reviewed: 'The name of Mr Loder must be widely known as a reliable and promising indication on the cover of a detective story' (*Times Literary Supplement*); 'Successive books by Vernon Loder confirm the impression gathered by this reviewer that we have no better writer of thrill mystery in England' (*Sunday Mercury*); '. . . just the effortless telling of a good story and meticulous observation of the rules' (Torquemada in the *Observer*). And in 2014, J. F. Norris wrote: '. . . keep your eyes out for any book with the Vernon Loder pseudonym on the cover. They make for fascinating reading and are as different from the standard whodunits of his colleagues as champagne is to soda water.'

Since the 1930s Loder has remained out of print, and his works have largely been the purview of Golden Age book collectors, among whom he has a following, with scarce first editions commanding high prices. This welcome re-issue of *The Shop Window Murders* and earlier *The Mystery at Stowe*, should help Loder, deservedly, to be rediscovered and enjoyed by a new wider readership.

NIGEL MOSS
March 2018

# CHAPTER I

MR TOBIAS MANDER'S new stores in Gaffikin Street had been a public wonder from start to finish. From the moment that this almost unknown man from the west country had visualised the idea of a store that would beat all other stores for cheapness combined with luxury, a highly-paid press-agent had seen to it that the country should join vicariously in the building and equipment.

The plans had been published in the front sheets of all the prominent newspapers, and every stage of the immense building progress had been reported with diagrams, portraits of the (titled) architect, and descriptions of all the eminent firms that had contributed to the material elegancies and equipment of the famous Store-to-be.

But Mr Tobias himself had remained unphotographed and unfeatured throughout the campaign, and no one from the outside world had even guessed accurately at the manner of man he was, until the Store was opened with a flourish of trumpets, and a luxurious house-warming.

To that function everyone of importance went. People who were wont privately to sneer at trade, forgot their principles, and crowded to the show; even titled actresses (notoriously exclusive) were among the throng.

When Mr Tobias Mander first burst upon the world, the world saw him as a man who might have been a prosperous stockbroker, a genial bookmaker, or a retired Smithfield merchant. He was of medium height, with a very fresh colour, and roving blue eyes; inclined to stoutness, always dressed in trousers with a very black stripe, a morning-coat and vest, with a white slip, and a monocle that never by any chance went into his eye.

1

The connoisseurs among the men called him a 'cheery bounder', but the women's votes were mixed. Some thought him charming, if vulgar; and others vulgar if charming; while a few, who had encountered his roving blue eyes with a twinkle in them, declared themselves fascinated.

There was one detail in which he differed from most men of his kind, and that was in the fact that he lived on the premises. To call the very luxurious flat on the top floor 'premises' is modestly to understate facts. But undoubtedly Mr Mander had taken up his residence within the walls of the store.

One of the stunts with which he had taken London, some months after the store opened, was a new gyroplane. No one knew the inventor's name, but there was trouble one day when it sailed over London, and landed with the greatest precision on top of the flat roof that covered the store. 'The Mander Hopper' it was called, yet that particular hop was frowned on by the authorities, who were not convinced that any aeroplane was quite safe among the roofs of a city. But the necessary prosecution provided further *réclame* for Mander and his store, and, later, those were not lacking who said they had heard aero-engines at night, and professed to believe that the great man sometimes landed after dark on his own roof.

There was no reason, beyond out-of-date regulations, why he should not have done so, for the 'Mander Hopper' proved to be the gyroplane for which the world had been looking, and the department which stocked and sold the 'Plane you fold up in a room; and land in a tennis-court' was one of the most paying in the whole Store. The 'Hopper' was, as one ancient pilot said, 'The plane that put the F in safety.'

The windows of the store were enormous, and each window was changed weekly. There you did not see wax figures disposed in solitary state, but naturally disposed in a room, with an appropriate stage-setting, so to speak. And the contents of each window were announced in the Sunday papers, so that an avid public would know where to look for a novelty when the blinds were drawn up on Monday morning.

The store did not believe in a constant, all-night electric-lit display. Mr Mander, with the turn for quaint originality which had helped him so much in booming his business, explained to a reporter (and he, in turn, to a delighted world) the reason for this.

'It's my house, you see,' he told the man. 'I make it a rule to put business out of my head when business is over. At night, and during the weekends, the Store is my Store only in name, and you do not pull up the blinds, and keep the light on, in private houses during the night.'

During the first week in November, the Sunday papers had spoken of the season of fancy-dress, and the writers had artfully proceeded from the general to the particular, and mentioned that the principal window in the chief bay of Mander's Store would 'feature' the next day a marvellous selection of fancy dresses, carried out by British workers, in British materials, by British designers.

There are always in London, at any hour of the day or night, sufficient people with no visible occupation, and an intense curiosity about anything novel, to form a crowd on the pavement. At five minutes to nine, there was a line of spectators three deep before Mander's Stores, which was continuously being added to by fresh arrivals. Many of them, it is true, were not of the class likely to wear fancy-dress, but all kept intent eyes fastened on the immense blinds that cloaked the splendours within from view.

At nine precisely, a man inside set in motion the mechanism which raised the blinds, and there was the instant '*Oo-er!*' of vulgar appreciation, mingled with the more polite enthusiasm of the cultivated.

The floor-space inside the window was dressed as a ball-room, even to a waxen band that sat in a recess at the back. The moment portrayed was a pause between dances, and at least forty couples in the most novel costumes stood about the floor, or leaned against the walls in *dégagé* attitudes that were almost lifelike.

But there was an exception to the rule, and, while most of the crowd outside were in ecstasies over the originality displayed, it was left to a commoner, a little bricklayer with ginger hair, on the outskirts, to discover it.

'Lumme!' he said contemptuously. 'Mebbe it's a novelty for the likes of 'im to work, but t'ain't what I would call novel!'

'It's supposed to be a motor-mechanic,' said someone next to him.

'Wat if it is?' he demanded firmly. 'Moty mechanics isn't novel!'

The figure in blue overalls to which he referred at once drew every eye. It was not elegant or elegantly disposed, as were the others in that window. And there was something else about it that provoked a sudden shriek, and a flop, from someone in the crowd.

Most of the spectators now concentrated on giving the fainting one as little air as possible. The few who remained at the window gasped and stared, or shivered. For there is a difference between even the best wax model and the appearance of a dead man beside it.

While they shuddered and debated, the bricklayer darted across the road to a policeman and spoke to him energetically. Then, with the policeman at his heels, he hurried in through the principal door of the great stores. Someone in the meantime had removed the public nuisance, who had fainted, and the rest of the crowd surged back to see the horror.

By the time a few more people had fainted and been duly removed, those next the window saw a door panel open at the back, and the blue-coated policeman pass through it. He was followed into the 'ballroom' by an alarmed shopwalker, and, when they had passed through, the supererogatory figure of the bricklayer was framed in the doorway.

There was a hush outside as the constable advanced to the figure in blue overalls, reached out a long arm, and gripped its shoulder. There was a scream as the figure overbalanced and fell down, while the mask came off, and where it had been there was disclosed a face that was quite white, but had no other visible relation to wax, and bore a striking likeness to that of Mr Tobias Mander.

Then the shopwalker turned and bellowed something, and, like the safety curtain at a fire in a theatre, the blinds came down with a rush, and blotted out every trace of the tragedy from the public view.

The constable was one of those very superior policemen who have joined up since the war. He recognised Mr Mander, and he recognised the nature of the wound which had put an end to that consummate commercial impresario. He unbuttoned part of the blue overalls.

'Gunshot wound,' he said slowly. 'Let's have some more of those electrics on, and get to the telephone, and ring up our people quick as you can—Mr Mander, isn't it?'

'It is,' said the horror stricken shopwalker, who looked as if he were going to be sick. 'It's murder, that's what it is!'

'Maybe,' said the constable. 'Now get your manager, and send for our people. They'll bring a surgeon with them.'

The shopwalker rushed for the door at the back, ejected the bricklayer from it, and closed the panel behind him. The constable, left alone in that scene of empty and now tragic grandeur, let his eyes wander round the ballroom, and suddenly brought them to rest on something that lay on the floor beside one couple of static dancers. He looked at that first searchingly, and then at a figure of a young woman, who sat huddled back in an empire chair, just concealed from the general front view by the dancers at rest already mentioned.

The young woman's figure wore a balloonish skirt, covered with what looked like painted diagrams of the 'Mander Hopper'. She wore over that a loose circular cloak which had something about it suggestive of a red parachute. On her head was fixed what looked like an aeroplane propeller with red silk trimmings, and over her face a black crepe mask, while her right hand wore a kid glove.

Taking the utmost precaution to disturb as little as possible, the constable walked over to the first object, and bent down to look at it. It was a Mauser automatic pistol. From it he approached the figure of the young woman. He looked at it hard. Then he extended his index finger, and gravely pressed it against the figure's shoulder. With that he started, bit his lip, and seemed uncertain what to do. Finally he went back to stand by the sliding panel which formed the door to the 'set', and waited there for someone to come.

The manager of the store, Mr Robert Kephim, a smart man of middle-age with a very stolid cast of countenance, suddenly entered. He looked at the constable.

'Mr Hay tells me there is something suspicious here, constable,' he said. 'I—'

And then he stopped, and looked very uncomfortable and unhappy. He was not the type of man to feel sick or faint, but the sight of his employer lying on his back there gave him a dreadful jolt.

'Do you recognise him, sir?' asked the constable.

Mr Kephim swore, then he nodded. 'Why, what has happened? That is Mr Mander—I can't understand it.'

The constable thought that a mild remark. 'I think the gentleman has been shot,' he said, 'and I shouldn't be surprised if there isn't another one gone west too.'

Now Mr Kephim did really go pale, and made incoherent noises in his throat.

'That young woman in the chair over there looks too natural to be true,' went on the constable, 'and there is a pistol on the floor. But we must wait till they send the inspector round before we have a look at that.'

Mr Kephim switched his eyes unwillingly to the woman in

the chair. His eyes went from her head to her feet, and there remained, while they appeared to grow rounder and more glaring, and his body trembled to such a degree that the constable gripped him in a friendly way to lend him support.

'Now then, sir, steady!' he said.

'The shoes—her shoes, said Kephim thickly. 'But it can't be—it can't!'

A curious look came into the constable's face. He stared at the man beside him, and put a sharp question.

'Whose shoes, sir?'

Kephim gulped. 'It must be a mistake. Of course it is. They aren't really uncommon—they must sell hundreds of them.'

'Very good, sir, but perhaps you would like to tell me to whom you are referring?'

Kephim shook his head. 'Not just now. I may later. But I don't think it will be necessary. How soon do you think your people can be here?'

'As they are just round the corner, they may be here any minute,' said the constable, and went over to look at the shoes in question.

They were not evening shoes, but walking-shoes of brown leather, with a strap decorated with a serpent whose eyes were the buttons. He was still looking when the panel slid back.

Inspector Devenish, who had just come in, accompanied by a detective-sergeant and the police-surgeon, was tall and thin. He had dark hair, dark eyes, and a swarthy complexion, and might have passed as a southern Italian. Leaving the sergeant to close the panel behind them, he approached the constable, after a dry glance at the white-faced and trembling Mr Kephim.

'What's up here?' he asked the constable, who saluted.

'Looks like murder and suicide, sir,' said the policeman.

He pointed out the body of Mr Mander, and then indicated the sitting figure of the young woman. Inspector Devenish bent over the body of the dead man, examined it cursorily, and then left it to the surgeon.

'Now let's see the other,' he remarked to the constable, quite well aware that Mr Kephim had not concerned himself at all with Mr Tobias on the floor, but had continued to stare at the figure in the chair.

Devenish went over, and gently drew off the circular cloak and the mask from the huddled figure of the young woman. Then a thud behind him made him turn quickly. Mr Kephim had fainted, and fallen.

# CHAPTER II

A SMALL army of officials had taken charge of the ballroom in the main bay of Mander's Stores. There were many detective officers of various ranks, and two photographers. Leaving them to their routine work, Inspector Devenish had gone upstairs in the lift to Mr Mander's flat, in the company of Mr Mander's chief of staff.

Kephim still looked ill, but he was more composed now, and as they entered the lift, he was explaining in a low voice the arrangements his late employer had made to ensure privacy for his own apartments, and his comings and goings out of business hours.

'He had a private door, and staircase at the back, inspector,' he said; 'there was a landing that gave access to a door in the hall of his flat. Then this lift takes you to another door, also opening in his hall, though at another side.'

By this time the lift had taken them to the top-floor, and they got out. Devenish stared at the door before him, then swept the floor with a swift glance.

'I see. Now if we take it that Mr Mander did not descend into the shop during the weekend, was there any other means than this lift by which he could have been taken down?'

'But he must have gone down,' said Kephim, biting his lip. 'The pistol down there—'

'I know,' said the other impatiently, 'but were there other ways?'

Mr Kephim hesitated for a moment before he replied. 'Yes, there are, of course, more than a dozen lifts used for parcels and goods from the store-rooms that are on this floor. But Mr Mander's flat is cut off from that section by an unbroken wall.'

Devenish nodded, and rang the bell of the flat. In a minute

9

the door was opened by a man-servant, a stout and dignified fellow of about fifty. Mr Kephim hastily explained the matter to the man, who looked as upset and frightened as any experienced man-servant can do, and hurriedly voiced his horror and regret.

Devenish nodded. 'Very natural. Now take us to your master's drawing-room, please. I shall interview you later, and also the other servants. How many are there?'

'There's Hames the footman, sir, Mr Mander's valet, cook, two housemaids and a parlour-maid.'

'It's a large flat then?'

'Yes, sir. There are ten rooms, and our rooms.'

'The servants' quarters are also quite cut off from Mr Mander's part of the flat,' explained Kephim.

'Quite?'

'I mean except for one communicating door, inspector.'

'Very well. When I ring, I shall want to interrogate the staff one at a time.'

'I understand, sir,' said the butler, intelligently showing them into a vast and expensively furnished drawing-room, and left, closing the door gently behind him.

Devenish sat down, and motioned his companion to a chair.

Kephim sat down, biting his lip, and obviously very ill at ease. The inspector did not add to his embarrassment by staring at him, but surveyed the drawing-room from end to end as he put his first question.

'Now, Mr Kephim, you saw what happened below. Mr Mander died from a shot-wound that entered the groin. The young woman had been stabbed in the back, with some thin-bladed, pointed weapon. Perhaps you will explain to me the reason why the discovery of the woman's body proved a much greater shock to you than that of Mr Mander?'

Kephim's eyes filled with tears. 'I—we—were engaged to be married,' he said in a very low voice. 'A week ago,' he added.

Devenish looked sympathetic. 'I am sorry. That is indeed a

tragic thing for you. Take your time, sir, and try, if you can, to let me hear a little about her. I won't keep you any longer than I can help.'

Kephim pulled himself together with a visible effort. 'Her name is—was Effie Tumour, inspector,' he said. 'She came here from Soutar's, where she was second-buyer in the millinery. Mr Mander made her chief-buyer.'

Devenish had heard of Mander's methods, and nodded. 'Promotion, of course. I suppose he did not know her prior to making her this offer?'

'I am sure he didn't, inspector. She would have told me. I have known her for three years.'

'She seems to have been a very handsome girl,' said Devenish, looking at him thoughtfully.

Kephim coloured, and looked slightly indignant. 'She wasn't that kind of girl, and Mr Mander wasn't that kind of man,' he snapped. 'Mr Mander was mad about aeroplanes. He has a kind of laboratory and workshop up here in the flat.'

'I'll have a look at that presently,' replied the detective. 'I am making no aspersions, remember. Only it seems rather odd that Mr Mander should have had two entrances, one from the rear.'

'Three entrances,' said Kephim; 'there's the stairs down from the flat roof, where the gyroplane landed the other day.'

'Ah, the new gyrocopter,' said Devenish. 'But let us get back to Miss Tumour, if you please. In spite of Mr Mander's absorption in aeroplanes, it is pretty obvious that she must have visited Mr Mander here during the weekend.'

'She was up the river with me yesterday,' replied Kephim, and drew a long shuddering breath. 'I left her at eight o'clock at her flat.'

'Where is that?'

'No. 22 Capperly Mansions, Pulsey Street.'

'Thank you. You left her at eight last night. After that she must have come here.'

'I—yes. I suppose she must.'

Devenish got up, and crossed the room to ring the bell. The butler presented himself a minute later.

'Did you wish to see me now, sir?' he asked.

'Yes. Did you admit anyone to this flat after, say, a quarter-past eight last night?'

'No one whatever, sir. I am sure of that. Mr Mander had been at Gelover Manor, his country place, during the day. He came in at half-past seven, and dined at eight. He was alone, sir, and had no visitors that I know of last night. I never come in here after ten, unless I have special instructions.'

'But you heard nothing during the evening, nothing during the night? Nothing out of the common I mean?'

The butler reflected. 'Unless you mean that engine kind of noise, sir, I didn't. But then this part is sound-proof from our part.'

'What do you mean by the engine sound?'

'Well, it was just like the noise that gyro thing made, sir; when it dropped on the roof, and there was so much fuss about it.'

Devenish nodded. Kephim stared.

The butler went on. 'Do you want to see the rest of the staff now, sir? I may tell you, that when I lock the communicating door from our part at night, I keep the key under my pillow.'

'Oh, you lock it from your side?'

'Yes, sir, but Mr Mander generally shoots the bolts on his side as well.'

'Awkward, if he lies late?'

'Well, no, sir. He had a button by his bed, and if he presses it, a mechanic withdraws the bolts.'

'Thank you. That will do. I'll send my sergeant up presently to interview the staff.'

When the butler had gone once more, Devenish looked at Kephim. 'I wonder, sir, if you are the gentleman who figures so well at Bisley every year?'

Kephim's jaw dropped a little. 'I am fond of rifle shooting; yes.'

'I thought so, sir. Your name is not a common one. But now we'll go through the flat, and end up on the roof.'

'Do you believe anyone could have landed on the roof last night?' Kephim demanded quickly, as he rose.

'It seems to be a possible thing,' said Devenish.

With Kephim looking on, he made a rapid but careful survey of the big drawing-room, then passed on to a dining-room that opened out of it. There was nothing in either to suggest a crime, or to hint that a woman had visited it lately. From there they entered the billiard-room, and a study. But Devenish did not linger long at any particular spot. His assistants, when they had finished below, would make a minute search, and photograph whatever was necessary for the exposure of finger-prints.

Then they visited four bedrooms, and ended up in a room, with two windows facing to the rear of the Store, one of which was fitted up as a workshop, and the other as a sort of store for metal and spare parts. In the workshop proper, there was a lathe, two benches, various band-saws for cutting metal, and an aero-engine of a rather unusual kind.

'Is it possible that the engine noise the butler heard was made by one of these saws, or the lathe running?' asked the detective.

'I don't think so, replied Kephim. 'There are dynamos, I think they call them, in the basement. Mr Mander used power from them to work his machines here, but you wouldn't hear them so far up.'

Devenish looked at a large switch-plate on the wall, 'I suppose not. But what about this engine. It seems as if it had been strapped—fastened down for a bench test. It may have been that the butler heard.'

Kephim approached. 'I don't think so. Look here—there are

three sparking-plugs missing. I know a little about cars, if not about aeroplanes.'

The inspector agreed. 'Couldn't fire without those, of course. Well, my people will go over this presently, and I think we had better have a look at the roof.'

A stairway led from the flat to the roof, the door let in to the panelling. It was unlocked, and Devenish put his handkerchief over the handle and turned it gently. Then he prepared to mount the stairs.

'Seems to be the only way up,' he remarked. 'Anyone else wanting to get there would have to land from the sky.'

The flat roof of the Stores was a hundred and twenty yards long by fifty wide. It was covered with a rough-surfaced material, to enable an aeroplane to draw up more easily on landing, and, about thirty feet from the parapet at either end, there were banks of sand about two feet high, that had the appearance of emergency buffers.

'By the way, Mr Kephim,' said the inspector, as they walked slowly across the roof, 'November is rather an off month for the river.'

Kephim looked at him resentfully. 'I did not say we went boating. I meant up the Thames valley in my car. You can check that, I think.'

But Devenish seemed suddenly to have forgotten the point. He looked down at the roof, and raised his eyebrows.

'Speaking as a layman, those look to me remarkable like the tracks of an aeroplane, which took off from a rather clayey field,' he said.

Kephim stared at the tracks indicated. 'That is odd. We have, as you know, had wonderfully dry weather for the past fortnight.'

Devenish went down on his knees, and carefully collected some of the dry clay with the blade of his pen-knife. When he had collected enough he put it in a little box he took from his pocket.

'It will be interesting to know when that was deposited here,' he said. 'I think we shall go down to the workroom again.'

They descended, locked the door behind them this time, for the key was still in the lock, and visited the other room where were the stores of metal and spare aeroplane parts.

'Ah, here we are,' said Devenish, going to a large table in a corner, and pointing to two rubber-tyred wheels that lay there, 'I take it that these belong to a gyrocopter, and we shall be able later to compare their tracks with those above. I shall have the whole of Mr Mander's part of the flat locked up. No one must enter until we have given permission.'

'I shall see to it,' said Kephim. 'We shall probably pay off his servants, later on, and close the flat.'

Devenish led the way out, locked the door of those two rooms, and put the keys in his pockets. He went back to the drawing-room, and now Kephim was beginning to show signs of restlessness.

'Well, sir, I suppose, since you are here, you can tell me what your movements were from eight last night until you arrived this morning in your office?' said the inspector.

Kephim sat down gloomily. 'That's an awkward question to answer,' he said abruptly.

'I am afraid I must ask it, sir,' said Devenish calmly.

Kephim bit his lip. 'I left Miss Tumour, and had supper at my flat in Baker Street—I have dinner in middle day on Sundays. I read a book until ten, and then sat and smoked, and tried to work out a crossword puzzle till eleven.'

'And after that, sir?'

'Well, that is the annoying part. I didn't feel sleepy, so I went out at about a quarter-past eleven, and walked up to Regent's Park. Mr Mander was a great man for novelties, and he had asked me to try to think of a novel advertising campaign. I always find my brain works best in the open air. At any rate, I did not get back till about two. I let myself in, and went to bed. My trouble is that I am afraid I did not see anyone who could identify me. I suppose that is what I should have had?'

'It would seem better,' Devenish replied mildly, 'but think

again, sir. Surely there was a policeman? They are more or less trained observers, and notice people at night. Or there might be lovers somewhere about. Take your time, sir.'

'I saw various people, but no policeman,' said Kephim, 'but I did not see anyone look at me, and I was not always under a lamp.'

'A policeman in the shadows may have seen you, sir. They do sometimes see without being seen. I'll make inquiries, if you give me a sketch of your route.'

Kephim repeated from memory what he thought had been his route. He looked weary and dejected now, and Devenish was about to dismiss him, when someone rang the bell of the flat, and on opening it they saw the detective-sergeant who had accompanied Devenish to the Stores.

'I beg your pardon, sir, but something rather important has been discovered,' he said. 'It's one of the goods lifts. Seems to have traces of the murder.'

Kephim started. The inspector nodded. 'We can't apparently get to it from this floor, and I don't want to examine it below. Have it sent up to the floor below this. Now Mr Kephim, how do we get to the floor below?'

'We take this lift, inspector. One floor down, we can get along a passage to the goods-lift landing.'

They got into the lift together. The sergeant let them out at the next stop, and then descended in the lift to carry out his instructions.

The inspector was in plain-clothes, and no one took any particular notice of him as he walked at the manager's side.

As they turned into the corridor, running parallel with the back of the building, and clear of the selling departments, Devenish turned to his companion.

'I am sorry to speak of it again, sir, but could you tell me how Miss Tumour was dressed when she left you yesterday evening?'

Kephim was very pale, and began to tremble again, but he found voice to reply.

'As—as we saw her just now, inspector.'

Devenish nodded. He did not say what both of them thought; that Effie Tumour might have gone almost straight from her flat to the flat above them—just waited, perhaps, for her lover to go out of sight!

# CHAPTER III

As they approached the lift, Devenish suddenly thought that it was sheer cruelty to take his companion with him any farther.

'You have had a horrible morning, sir,' he said to him, noticing how he now dragged his feet. 'If I were you, I would go out and get some air; and have something to pull you together.'

He had already given instructions to the policemen on the various doors to follow any member of the staff who had been allowed to leave the premises, and felt quite safe in letting the manager go. Kephim thanked him weakly, and left. The detective advanced to where two subordinates stood before an open lift, in a recess at the back of the building.

One was his sergeant, who had brought it up to this floor, and he made way for Devenish, and pointed silently to a tiny spot of dry blood on the floor of the lift itself. The other man handed him a long and slender knife, the handle carefully wrapped in tissue paper, with the information that he had found it lying in the corner by the bloodstain.

Devenish examined the knife most carefully, then returned it. 'Pack it with the other exhibits, Corbett,' he said. 'Where was this lift when you first saw it?'

'It was down in the basement, sir.'

'But it can be brought automatically to any floor, can't it?— It can? Is it a very noiseless lift, or not?—Wonderfully quiet, eh?—Right. It is hard to say whether anyone was brought down in this, or simply came up in it.—Sergeant, I want to see the night watchman who patrols this section of the store. Send him here.'

The sergeant having gone off on this errand, Devenish knelt carefully on the floor inside, and fixed the exact position and dimensions of the blood-spot.

'It seems to me a useful bit of evidence,' he remarked, as he got up again, 'but here is the watchman. Carry on! I am going to question him, but farther along the corridor.'

'This is Mann, the night watchman, sir,' said the sergeant.

Devenish nodded to the respectably dressed man of forty who had come up, noted that he looked like an ex-soldier, and motioned him to move a yard down the corridor.

'Now, sergeant, I have a few jobs for you,' he said. 'First you must see the assistant-manager, and he must telephone to a director, if needs be, to have the Store closed. We can't carry on with people trampling over the place; and if it remains open any longer, we shall have a drive of pressmen harrying us.'

'But what of the assistants, sir?' asked the sergeant.

'My dear fellow, we can't interrogate thirteen hundred odd men and women today. It doesn't look like a job that one of them would do either. We must keep those in executive positions for the moment, but get the rest away, and the place closed.'

'I'll see to it, sir. Anything else?'

'You must visit Mr Kephim's flat in Baker Street, and Miss Tumour's—I'll give you both addresses. Find out all you can, and particularly when Miss Tumour left home last night. Also discover at what hour Mr Kephim went out and returned.'

'Very well, sir.'

When the sergeant had gone, Devenish walked over to the waiting witness. 'What exactly is your usual round when you patrol this section of the stores at night, Mann?' he asked, while the ex-soldier kept a steady eye on his face.

'I come on my shift at ten, sir,' was the reply. 'I walk round once, and see that it is all O.K. I have a box to sit in between rounds. They're every hour, sir.'

'How long does it take you to get round?'

'Fifteen minutes. That is as I do it now, sir. But then I have only been here two months, and never seen anything suspicious.'

'Then I may assume that you set out on your rounds at a quarter-past ten, a quarter-past eleven, a quarter-past—'

'No, sir, it is an hour after finishing each round. I start the second round at a quarter-past eleven, and have it done by half-past eleven. I set out on the third at half-past twelve, and so on, sir.'

'You are an ex-soldier, Mann—what branch?'

'Finished as a sergeant, sir. I was an old regular, discharged unfit 1924.'

'A man of method apparently, anyway,' said Devenish. 'Now, did you see or hear anything suspicious last night in the Store?'

He took out his note-book as he spoke.

'Nothing at all, sir.'

'No noise like a lift going up or down, no sound that might suggest an aeroplane engine?'

'I didn't hear any lift, sir, but then they are uncommon quiet. I did hear a faint sound like an engine up above, but I often hear that weekends, so I don't count it suspicious.'

'The dynamos in the basement were running? Why don't these people take current from the mains?'

'I don't know anything about it, sir. I do know Mr Mander used to tinker with machines up above. I thought he was at it again last night; though it didn't last long.'

Devenish nodded. 'Let me see where this box of yours is, Mann,' he said, and called softly to the detective at work in the lift, 'I say, Corbett, run that lift up and down a bit for the next three minutes, will you, while I am away.'

Receiving an assent from his subordinate, he accompanied the watchman along the corridor, and down another at right angles, which ended in a sort of cabinet. This cabinet contained a seat, a switchboard and telephone, and the bell of a burglar-alarm. Devenish seated himself in the chair, and looked down the corridor. 'You don't see much of the Store from here,' he remarked thoughtfully; 'only a corner of it.'

'So I'm not seen, either,' replied his companion. 'If I put on my torch, I might frighten any thieves, and if I keep the place dark I can't see. But, dark or light, I can hear better than anyone else.'

Devenish smiled dryly. 'You must have very acute hearing indeed, if you can hear slight sounds in a place as big as this, with partitions to cut sounds off or blur them.'

'It isn't that my ears are specially good, but this ear here, sir,' said the man, with a quiet smile, and pointed to a tiny horn, like a gramophone-horn, at the level of his head, which projected slightly from the wall of the cabinet. 'Mr Mander was great for the latest dodges. I just switch on this microphone here, and every sound comes my way. More than that, sir. There's a kind of selective attachment to it, and it tells me from what quarter the sound comes, so I can take action.'

'Royal Engineer?' asked the detective gently.

'Signals, sir. But you see what I mean.'

'Turn on the switch now.'

Mann obeyed, then looked puzzled. The detective did not look so puzzled, but faintly startled.

'Someone's been monkeying with your buzz-saw,' he murmured. 'I don't hear any of the noises magnified now.'

Mann had obviously some mechanical knowledge. He examined the horn and the switch, then looked at the electrical connections, and swore.

'Cut a lead here, sir,' he said.

Devenish took out his magnifier, and examined the thing closely, then he dusted the panelling in the region of the lead, and scanned it for finger-prints. None showed. Someone had interfered with the microphone, but he had left no traces while doing it.'

'He must have been here while you went on one of your rounds. Did you not notice that there were no sounds coming through as loud as you would expect to hear them?'

'I didn't, sir, but you know how it is. I didn't suspect anyone was here, and you aren't so sharp after nothing has happened for two months on end.'

'An unfortunate but truly human failing,' agreed Devenish,

'but I must admit to defects myself. For example, I have not been listening for the sound of the lift going up and down. I must get my man to keep it working.'

He went away, to return again in a minute, and raise a hand to command silence. It may have been the noises from the Store, but he could hear nothing of the moving of the lift, and realised that the experiment could not be made until the place was empty and perfectly quiet.

Explaining this to the watchman, he went off, and found himself in a couple of minutes in the shop window with the blind down, talking to his superintendent, who had just arrived from the Yard, and the surgeon, who sat smoking a cigarette, and watching the last efforts of the lower ranks, as they measured and surveyed and plotted the big space. When he had finished explaining what he had done, Devenish was rewarded by a nod of approval from the superintendent.

'Any sign of the bullet yet, sir?' he asked.

'None at all,' said the big man stolidly. 'High-velocity bullet, Dr Grindley thinks.'

'*Knows*,' said the surgeon, puffing. 'I saw enough of them during the war. Steel-jacketed, I should say.'

'Not that Mauser?' asked Devenish gently.

'I ought to have been a gunner,' said the surgeon, smiling. 'I know all about 'em—all kinds. That Mauser is new, been fired once. But I think your experts will agree that it was fired with blank. I won't swear, but that is my opinion.'

'Possible,' murmured Devenish. 'A man who would take the trouble to set up his victims as specimens in the window here wouldn't leave the gun on view.'

'Was the shot fired at close quarters?' said the superintendent.

'I should say not. Not very close anyway.'

'How long should you say he had been dead?'

The surgeon reflected. 'It isn't so easy to answer that as some people imagine. I should say roughly between twelve to fourteen hours, but I may be sadly out.'

'And the young woman?'

'Less, I should say, but I can't tell you how much less. In neither case does the bleeding seem to have been extensive—a sporting bullet with a more or less soft nose would have been different. The other wound was made by a weapon that did not—'

'Wait a moment,' said Devenish. 'If she was killed after him—'

'Then he didn't do it,' said the surgeon. 'I admit that! I don't think either of them did it to each other!'

Devenish smiled faintly. 'Well, you'll have the P.M., and then we shall know more. I thought, superintendent, of going to see the man in charge of the aeroplane department. I see you have cleared most of the people out of the Store, but the executives will be here.'

'I asked them to stay in Mr Mander's private office,' said the other. 'I am going to have a talk to them. But if you care to see one alone—'

'If he would come to me in his department above, sir,' said the inspector, 'I will go there now.'

The superintendent nodded. 'Very well. I'll send him.'

The inspector nodded to the surgeon, and went away. Taking one of the automatic lifts, which had upon a board outside 'To Sporting and Aeroplane Departments', he found himself on the first floor, and presently arrived in an immense room looking over a street at the side of the Stores building. Housed in this department (some ready for flight, and some in the various stages of folding that made the Mander Hopper such a boon to the private pilot without a hangar) were about six machines.

Devenish lit a cigarette, and walked round them thoughtfully until the sound of someone approaching told him that the manager of the department was arriving for his interview. He came in, and greeted the detective briefly. Devenish saw that he was an alert and handsome young man of about thirty, rather of a military cut, and obviously intelligent.

'I was up on the roof just now, sir,' the detective told him.

'There were tracks that made me rather wonder if a machine had landed there lately.'

'This is a pretty filthy business, inspector,' said Mr Cane in reply. 'Hardly bargained for a Wild-West shooting here. But what was that you said? A machine landed on the roof? Most unlikely, I should say. We had enough of that sort of thing a month ago.'

'A certain amount of trouble, but also a good deal of advertisement, sir! I should like to have a list of purchasers of the "Mander Hopper".'

'The first purchasers. But suppose they had been resold?'

'No doubt we could trace them, said Devenish, offering his case to the young man, who took a cigarette and lit up.

'I suppose you could. I'll get you a list.'

'Are these heavy machines?'

'Yes, they are heavier than machines would be which were not fitted with the gyrocopter device, inspector.'

Devenish approached a machine which was ready for flight. 'The tyres on the landing wheels are naturally wider when the machine rests on them than when they are removed,' he said.

Cane grinned. 'That is what "Punch" would call "another glimpse of the obvious", inspector. I might even go further, and suggest that, at the moment when a machine lands, the impact makes the track even wider than that!'

'Quite what I thought, sir,' replied Devenish innocently. 'Now could we get one of the wheels to make some sort of track here?'

Cane thought it over. 'I might chalk the treads of the two tyres, and we could push the 'bus a bit along the floor, if that is any good to you.'

'Splendid, sir. While you are doing that, I might be looking at your books, and taking down some of the names of purchasers of these machines.'

'Come to my office in the corner there. You'll find pens and paper, while I get the books out of the safe.'

There had been perhaps fifty purchasers of the 'Mander

Hopper' since it had been put on the market, or rather, there had been promise of delivery of that number of machines. Devenish took down the names and addresses, and had completed his list when Cane called to him.

'Palaver set, inspector.'

Between them, they pushed a machine along the floor, and the inspector not only measured the whitened track made by the tyres, but also the width of the treads pressed out by the weight above.

'That will do nicely, sir,' he said when he had finished. 'Now I want to ask you a question about Mr Mander. He was interested in machines and aerodynamics, wasn't he? I saw some sort of a laboratory, or workshop, above.'

Cane laughed a little. 'He did tinker a bit, I believe; but I really know nothing about it. He said he always gave full charge of a department to a man, and never interfered.'

'But who invented the machine here that is called by his name?'

'It is assumed that he did.'

'Well, didn't he?'

'Can't say. He patented it, I know. I was only once up in his workshop, and he didn't like that much. What I saw there of the jobs he did struck me as elementary. A fellow who invented this had to be a swell at other things than mechanics.'

Devenish's eyes lit up. 'You mean that he did not seem to you capable enough?'

Cane nodded. 'I mean that, when I had to talk to customers once or twice before him, he never said a word. Can you imagine any chap who could invent a perfect gyrocopter standing mum while you were fiddling with his subject? I can't! I know inventors. Perfect pests, poor devils, and ready to jaw your head off! That is about the only satisfaction they get out of their inventions.'

'But someone must have invented it?'

'Obvious again. But isn't there just a hint that the man who did might have been on his uppers, and beam-ends, and so on, and been told he could get a purchaser if he kept his mouth shut?'

'Ah!' said Devenish heavily.

Then he thanked Cane for his help, and left him to go on the roof again, where he made fresh measurements and comparisons, emerging half an hour later, and going towards the lift, when he met a man he had not seen before, a pompous stout man, with a bald head, who introduced himself as the assistant-manager.

'The Stores are now completely cleared, inspector,' he informed Devenish. 'Is there any way in which I can help you?'

The detective reflected, then: 'Is this a private company?' he asked.

'No. Mr Mander was the sole proprietor.'

'Really. But this is a very big organisation. Do you mean that he financed it himself?'

'So far as I know. I can't say.'

The interview got no further than that, for a constable came hurrying up to say that Mr Melis, an Assistant-Commissioner from the Yard, was in Mr Mander's private office, and wished to see the inspector.

# CHAPTER IV

THE staff had been turned out of Mr Mander's room, and Mr Melis sat there in state, a cigarette between his long fingers, and his brown, humorous eyes fixed on Inspector Devenish's face.

'Doesn't seem anything very tangible to take hold of so far, inspector,' he was murmuring in an agreeable voice, 'unless it is this business of the gyrocopter.'

'What interests me more, sir,' replied Devenish, 'is the person who financed Mr Mander. I can't make that out. He seems to have sprung up suddenly from nowhere, and even if he was a genius at this sort of thing, where did he get the money?'

'Ah, that,' said the assistant-commissioner, laying down his cigarette and smiling very faintly at some thought, 'that is not so difficult as it looks. But being simple—at least I think it is, if gossip counts for anything—it does not interest me.'

'Then you know, sir, who was behind him?'

'I don't exactly know, inspector; but one picks up things as one moves about; doesn't exactly know if they are authentic, you see, but wonders if they may not be.'

'Then, sir, if I may ask, who do you think, or wonder, may have been behind here?'

Mr Melis began to toy with his cigarette again. 'Frankly, Dame Rumour hints that Mrs Peden-Hythe was the goddess from the machine. She was the widow of that fellow, you know, who had the shipping company in Buenos Ayres.'

'About forty-three, and rather handsome,' said Devenish. 'I have seen her photographs in the society papers. But why pick on Mander, sir?'

Melis shrugged. 'Mander was managing-clerk to the country solicitors at Volbury, where her place, Parston Court, is. Fancy is an errant thing, inspector.'

'So it is, sir,' replied Devenish. 'That does put another face on it. But you spoke of the gyrocopter, sir, what is your view about that?'

'Mine? I thought it was yours. The wide track and the narrow track, you know. It quite seemed to me that you regarded the idea of the machine having landed on the roof last night as more or less—shall we say—a plant?'

Devenish thought that over. 'You see, sir, it looks like an inside job. Someone who knew Mander and the place thoroughly. But I wouldn't bank on it all the same. Naturally, it did strike me that the gyrocopter, if it did land on the roof, would make a wider track with its wheels than the track up there. Also, a man who took so much care over the job would hardly leave muddy wheel-tracks.'

'Since pilots who can fly gyrocopters are rare, and easily identified,' Melis agreed, 'the only trouble is the mud. Was that brought in?'

Devenish shrugged. 'We must find out what kind of mud it is, and where it rained last night, if anywhere. The man would not rise out of a marsh. As a start, I shall inquire if it was wet near Mr Mander's new country place last night.'

Melis took up the telephone on the desk before him. 'We'll get that from the weather people straight away.' He gave a number, and turned again to Devenish. 'You have an idea about those spare wheels in Mr Mander's workshop, eh?'

'A man could have pushed them along the roof, if he had muddied them first, and cleaned them after, sir. We must remember that, once up in Mander's flat, the fellow could do anything without being heard or disturbed.'

Mr Melis nodded quickly, then spoke into the telephone.

'A heavy shower for three-quarters of an hour, eh? At what time? Half-past ten? Thank you. That is all I want to know.'

He looked at the inspector. Devenish looked at him. 'Just a faint hope?'

Devenish pursed his lips. 'Who invented this new machine?

That is what I want to know. I saw Mr Cane just now—manager of that department—he seems to think Mander's experiments and workshop-trifling a sort of pose.'

'Oh, does he? And why should he suggest it? Is he an expert, by any chance?'

Devenish frowned. 'I wasn't really thinking of him, sir, but now I do remember reading about him in the paper, when they were advertising this store at first. Well-known flying man to be in charge of aeroplane department, wasn't it?'

'I think it was.'

'Inside the building, been once in Mander's flat and workshop,' murmured the inspector, 'if there is any other link, I ought to look into it.'

Melis smiled. 'I saw a fat man just lately, who was, I think, the assistant-manager. He is probably a good business man, but he struck me as soft otherwise; sort of fellow we might pump.'

'Shall I have him in, sir?'

'May as well.'

Devenish went out, and came back presently with the assistant-manager, Mr Crayte. The man at the desk asked him to sit down, offered him a cigarette, and smiled at him amiably.

'I am sure you are a very busy man, Mr Crayte, but I know you will help us. We want a little brains on the civil side, and won't keep you long. It's just a formal matter of getting a little insight into the relations between the staff here—I mean the executive staff, really. The sooner we get the routine work over and done with, the sooner we can come to grips with the case.'

Mr Crayte was all complaisance. 'I shall be happy to tell you what I know.'

'Good! Then we'll get to it. Mr Kephim now, the manager; I suppose he and the late Mr Mander were on good terms?'

Mr Craye scratched his head. 'Oh, yes, quite. I should say very good terms. We are, on the whole, a happy family here.'

Mr Melis raised his eyebrows. 'On the whole? Much as one

can expect, I suppose. Can't expect a dozen different men to be absolutely soul-mates, can we?'

Mr Crayte laughed. 'But what little friction there has been was nothing to speak of; flashes of temper, no more. You understand that running a big place like this is bound to make one nervy at times.'

'But it seems to me rather strange,' said Melis, with his head on one side like a bright bird, 'rather strange that one of the higher staff even should presume to exhibit temper to his—er—chief.'

Mr Crayte hastened to explain. 'Oh, they wouldn't dare to with Mr Mander. I meant among ourselves.'

'May I ask the names of the antipathies?'

'Well, it is all over now, but there was rather a scene between the manager of the shipping department and the manager of the furniture. A strictly departmental quarrel, if I may put it so.'

'Apart from that, may we take it that the rest of the executive staff are good friends?'

'Well, no. Friends is another thing. Outside our business relations, there may be a certain amount of hostility. I mean to say, men thrown together, as we are, don't necessarily like each other.'

'For example?'

Crayte looked at him cautiously, but Mr Melis's expression was so bland and ingenuous, and his own love for gossip so keen, that he went on to amplify his statement. 'Kephim and Cane have never hit it off. But I can understand that. Mr Kephim worked up. He has a fine salary now, and is worth it, but he worked up. I will say Mr Cane is a bit of a snob—I mean to say, he rather showed by his manner that he looked down on Mr Kephim.'

'When, officially, he should have looked up,' murmured Mr Melis, with a quick glance at Devenish; 'but after all we are only here to inquire into the murder of Mr Mander. Mr Cane was not on bad terms with the deceased, was he?'

'Oh, no. Quite the contrary. Mr Mander was rather proud of having a D.S.O. in charge there, and Cane was always pleasant with him.'

Devenish put in a question: 'Who flew the gyrocopter that time it landed on the roof here?'

'Who flew it? Let me see? Oh, it was the mechanic who helped Mr Mander with his experiments in the country. What was the name—Wepkin—Weffin—No, Webley. I remember the man very well, since I asked him to explain the way the thing worked, and he appeared to me appallingly stupid.'

'Although he was able to fly this difficult type of machine?' said the inspector.

Melis laughed. 'My dear fellow, when I was in West Africa, I had a negro chauffeur. He was an expert driver, but a complete fool. Some very brainless people have a genius for mechanics. He turned to Crayte, and added: 'Well, we are very much obliged to you. By the way, do either of these receivers communicate with Mr Mander's flat above?'

'This one,' said Mr Crayte, raising it.

'Would you mind asking his butler to come down here?' said Melis. 'Ah, thank you. Then we shan't keep you any longer.'

Mr Crayte rang up the butler, told him to come down, and then left the room. Melis stared at Devenish.

'Now is that a link, or isn't it?' he asked. 'Departmental quarrels apart, we have Cane and Kephim the only dogs that bark and bite.'

'I can imagine,' said Devenish thoughtfully, 'I can imagine that, if it wasn't for the girl in the case, sir. A man might want to murder one fellow and put it on another he disliked, but he wouldn't kill a girl to top up, and he couldn't know that the other fellow hadn't an alibi.'

'But suppose the other fellow is Kephim?' said Melis. 'And Cane had means of knowing that Kephim was coming here last night. No; that is out of the question, for Kephim wouldn't be likely to come on a flying machine, and if those marks on the roof do not denote an actual landing, they were put there to suggest that the murderer arrived by air. But, say Kephim determined to do the deed and put it on Cane. Would that go better? As you say, Kephim is a crack shot.'

'There is still the girl,' said Devenish. 'Why kill his fiancée?'

Melis leaned back in his chair, lit another cigarette, and half-closed his eyes. He was a good amateur actor, and carrying that art into official life was the only thing his subordinates had against him.

'There is a psychological side to this crime that does not seem to have occurred to you, inspector. If it has, I apologise. To put a murdered man and woman in a shop window, where they would inevitably be exposed to the public gaze, what does that suggest?'

'Revenge; with something personal and bitter in it,' said Devenish. 'Not a murder for gain. I see what you mean, sir.'

Melis nodded. 'Mander is top-dog. With him are promotions, and increased emoluments. He seems—I only say he seems—to have fascinated one wealthy woman, while he was still in a subordinate position. To a poorer woman under him, he might assume the aspect of a little god.'

Devenish bit his lip. 'The evidence tends that way, sir, but—'

The butler knocked and came in, to apologise for his tardiness. Melis told him to sit down, then bent, picked up a despatch-box, and took from it a slender weapon, the handle covered with tissue paper, and laid it on the table.

'I suppose there is no chance that this came from your master's flat?'

The butler suppressed a slight shudder. 'Excuse me, sir. May I look at it closer?'

Melis nodded, and gently exposed the handle, being careful not to touch it with his fingers. 'Well?'

I remember it, I think,' said the butler. 'I do believe it was the sample Mr Winson showed him one evening at dinner.'

Melis pressed for details, and the butler gave them. A famous

Birmingham manufacturer had dined at the flat one night. He and Mander had discussed a contract for a half a million 'Eastern daggers', to be made in Birmingham, and sold in the Oriental department for trophies, and paper-knives. The manufacturer had brought a sample with him, and laid it on the table. Mr Mander had kept it, and—

'Then run up, and see if it is still there,' said Melis.

'I'll go up with him, sir,' said Devenish. 'I have locked that part of the flat up. Evidently this telephone connects with the servants'—'

'With my pantry, sir,' said the butler, getting up.

'Where did Mr Mander keep the dagger?' asked the inspector, as they ascended a minute later.

'On the ormolu table in the drawing-room, sir.'

Devenish nodded, took the keys of the flat from his pocket, and the lift stopped.

The butler led the way into the drawing-room a few moments later, crossed to the ormolu table, and gave a little cry: 'It's gone, sir! It was here yesterday, when I came in after lunch to see that the fire was lit.'

'You are sure you recognise it?' said Devenish.

'I am sure I do, sir. I had an oppportunity to see it on the table, and I saw those curly marks on the blade, and the odd-shaped handle.'

Devenish nodded, and let the man out, telling him he could go back to his quarters. Then he relocked the flat, and went back to the assistant-commissioner.

Mr Melis raised questioning eyebrows, was told that the knife, or dagger, had indeed gone from the flat above, and rose. 'Well, Devenish,' he said, 'I have an appetite for lunch, and an engagement afterwards. Come along and report this evening, will you?'

'Yes, sir,' the inspector replied. 'I sent the sergeant to inquire at Miss Tumour's flat. I think I shall go round myself, after I have had something to eat.'

'Do!' said Melis, with his best amateur actor's air, picked up his gloves and hat—he never wore an overcoat—and walked out.

For some time after he had gone, Devenish sat drumming his fingers on his knee, and thinking hard. He was still at it when his sergeant came in, saluted, and approached.

'Miss Tumour went out last night at a quarter to ten, sir,' he told Devenish, 'but she didn't say where she was going, so the porter at the flats told me.'

'And Mr Kephim?'

'Mr Kephim, they think, left after eleven. But no one heard him come in again.'

'Any night-porter at those flats?'

'Yes, sir, but he did not notice Mr Kephim return. I thought it would be best to come back and tell you, without waiting to make any more inquiries.'

Devenish nodded. 'Quite right. The times are important—one of them, anyway. I am going over myself this afternoon, so don't trouble again. I want you to go carefully over the ground here, and make me a plan of the route which the murderer might have taken if he carried one, or both, of the bodies into the front window space from the lift.'

'The goods-lift where the dagger was found, sir?'

'That's it. After you have done that, I want you to make inquiries about the night watchman. Go to Mr Crayte for the address. I don't want the man to know. By the way, have you seen Mr Kephim anywhere in the building?'

'No, sir. I think he did not come back.'

# CHAPTER V

BETWEEN the Victorian shop and the twentieth century modern store there is a great gulf. It is widest perhaps in the matter of salaries paid to the higher staff. So Inspector Devenish was not much surprised to find that the late Miss Tumour occupied a rather luxurious little flat in a very nice quarter. It is true that she had only moved in there since she got the post at Mander's.

It was to the porter that the detective first applied for information, and before he could come to grips with the problem he had to endure a small instalment of the man's curiosity with regard to the crime. He cut that as short as he could, and asked if there was anyone in the flats who had an acquaintance with the dead woman.

'No one, yet, sir, and aren't likely to have now,' said the porter, with rather mordant humour. 'You see, sir, this was the first time they had anyone like her here. I don't know who it was blew the gaff, but the others—'

'I see,' said Devenish, who knew very well that the man was referring to a certain snobbishness on the part of the other tenants. 'So it's no use my asking any of them about her. But you may have seen some of her visitors come in from time to time.'

'She hadn't many, and that's a fact,' said the man, 'but one came regular lately, and another used to come with a car.'

He described the regular visitor, and Devenish recognised him as Mr Kephim.

'Now what about the man in the car?' he said.

The porter approached a wink. 'I never saw him, sir. He used to come late sometimes in a closed car, and always sat back.'

'But I should have thought you would go out to open the car door for him.'

'It wasn't ever necessary, sir. His chauffeur used to get out and stand in front of the door, till she came out and got in. I had always to speak up the tube to tell Miss Tumour a car had called for her.'

'So you have no idea of the visitor's appearance?'

'Not a bit. He never went in neither. I'd have got into trouble if I'd gone and looked in at him.'

Devenish looked thoughtful. 'It won't have any bearing on the case, I am afraid,' he said, 'but could you tell me how long the second man has been coming?'

'Came first a week after she had been in here, sir.'

'Thank you. Did all her furniture come in from her former house?'

The porter blinked reflectively. 'No, not all of it. Two lots came from Warungs ten days after she come, and then some went out to a sale room.'

'I suppose the two visitors never came on the same day?'

'No, they didn't. When Miss Tumour went out with the other one she was always togged up gaudy—regular swell.'

Devenish procured the master-key and visited the flat itself after that.

In a search through Miss Tumour's papers and correspondence, of which there was no great abundance, he found nothing in the nature of a clue. He finished up with her telephone, and took a note of the numbers in pencil on the pad. There were just five.

Getting on to the exchange, and explaining who he was, he made inquiries about the five numbers. One was Mr Kephim's, one belonged to a Mrs Hoe in Bester Street (whom he determined to interview later), two were the numbers of her hairdresser and chiropodist respectively. The fifth number was Mr Mander's, the number belonging to his flat telephone, and not that which would go before the switchboard operator at the store.

That in itself was not conclusive proof of any intimacy between the dead man and woman. It might be useful for her to have her employer's number, as she held a responsible position at the Store.

Devenish looked at his watch. It was dark early at this time of year, but that did not matter. He would go down to Gelover Manor and satisfy himself with regard to the 'Mander Hopper' that was kept down there.

He caught a train from Paddington, and was walking up towards the biggish house on the outskirts of Gelover an hour later. It was now dusk, but, as he went up the drive, he could see the outlines of the Queen Anne house against the sky, and to the left of it, in what looked like a paddock, an aeroplane hangar, which would easily have housed four of the new machines. This hangar was built alongside a small but pretty thatched cottage, and a light sprung up in a window as Devenish glanced that way.

The conjunction of the two buildings hinted to him that the mechanic of whom Mr Cane had spoken might be the occupier of the cottage. He changed his mind about going direct to the manor, and turned towards the place where the light showed.

He knocked at the cottage door, and it was opened to him after a short delay. The man who opened it was respectably dressed, and had somewhat the appearance of a valet. His face was long and clean-shaven, his forehead high, but he did not look very intelligent, in spite of that clever brow.

'I am a detective-inspector from Scotland Yard,' Devenish opened. 'I suppose you have heard about Mr Mander's death?'

The man had. In a blundering fashion he expressed his sorrow, and when he invited Devenish into the lighted parlour it did seem from his looks that he was really cut up by the news.

Devenish offered him a cigarette, lit one himself, and sat down.

'Are you the mechanic who had to do with the new gyro-copter?' he asked.

'That's me,' he said; 'Webley's my name. What about it?'

'I want to know if Mr Mander kept one of the machines here, and if so, did he or anyone else use it yesterday—I mean after half-past seven in the evening?'

Webley grunted. 'No. No one did, nor yesterday morning either.'

'But Mr Mander was down here.'

'No, he wasn't.'

'You are sure?'

''Course I am sure. I'd have seen him if he'd been here. As for the machine it is here, and you can see it if you like, and you can ask anyone in the house if it went out.'

'They might not know.'

'The engine doesn't work without any noise,' said Webley impatiently. 'Any fool would know that. You ask 'em.'

Devenish laughed. The man was apparently not at all servile, or frightened at this visit. 'I see. Now can you tell me if it rained here yesterday?'

Webley stared. 'It did. It rained hard for an hour or so—first we've had for some time.'

'Is your taking-off place liable to get marshy and cut up with use after rain?'

Webley stared again. 'Of course not. Mr Mander, he got money, and he wouldn't leave it like a plough. Go out and look at it. The machine takes off in a very small bit, being what she is, and that bit is laid out like a hard tennis-court.'

'Not hard clay?'

'Clay, no. Cinders; fine and well rolled.'

Devenish began to see that his first thoughts might be the best guide. If the gyrocopter rose from a cinder ground it would not be likely to reach London with mud on the wheels—unless it had had a forced descent on the way.

'May I see the machine? I have to make sure,' he asked.

Webley laughed. 'Come along. It's your business, not mine.'

They left the cottage, and Webley opened the hangar with

a key he kept in his pocket, and switched on about half a dozen arc-lamps that made the interior of the building almost as light as day, and whitened the asphalt floor which was laid there. In the middle of the garage one of the famous 'Mander Hoppers' stood ready.

Devenish walked over and examined it carefully, while Webley lounged near the doorway, puffing disinterestedly at his cigarette. The aeroplane was as clean as a new pin all over, but that of course might merely mean that Webley had spent his day on it.

As Devenish was going to return to the man, he looked down and noticed that there were nine or ten cigarette stubs on the floor near the machine. He dropped his own half-finished cigarette, and contrived to pick two of the others up as he bent. One was a cheap packet-cigarette called 'Twix' and the other was a fine Turkish brand, of a flat shape. Out of the stubs on the floor at least six were of this brand.

Webley was apparently a quick smoker. He had finished the cigarette given to him, and lit one of his own from the stub of it as Devenish rejoined him. The packet which he replaced in his pocket was labelled: 'Twix—the cigarette that has a kick.'

'Look here,' said the detective, his eyes fixed on the man's face, 'I believe Mr Mander was here after all. I see a lot of Turkish cigarette ends on the floor.'

'He only smokes Russian,' said Webley, spitting on the floor with an air of contempt. 'What else?'

'I should like to know who else was here then?'

'Expect you would. It isn't your business though.'

'Now, Webley, you needn't be hostile. That is silly. I have come here just to investigate Mr Mander's death.'

'And that's silly, for Mr Mander wasn't here yesterday, and them cigs aren't anything to do with him.'

Devenish reflected. Anyone who put mud on spare wheels to suggest that the gyrocopter might have been flown from Gelover must have known that it had rained at Gelover. On the other hand, if that were so, he must be a man who was not aware that the taking-off place there was covered with hard-rolled cinders.

'At any rate you had a visitor?' he said.

'That's right,' said Webley. 'I had a visitor—a pal you may say, or you mayn't—just as you like. I don't make no mystery of it. If you'd asked me I would have told you.'

Devenish forced a laugh: 'Yes, I brought it on myself. But now, if I ask you nicely, I don't suppose you will object to telling me who your visitor was?'

Webley considered that for a few moments. 'It was Mr Cane, if you want to know, that's all. He's in charge of the planes at the Store, he tells me.'

Devenish concealed his satisfaction. 'I suppose he didn't have a trip on the machine? No, I remember you said no one had. May I ask the nature of the errand he had here?'

'Just came down for more details, that's all. He said the guv'nor was complaining that the machines cost more to build and advertise than they were worth; to make a profit anyway. The guv'nor told me that before, so it was no news.'

'Why, it seems to me, from all I hear, to have been a wonderful invention,' said Devenish. 'The find of the century.'

Webley's eyes lighted up, and his surly expression faded. Some inner enthusiasm seemed to be eating him up as he replied that it was the best thing flown. He moved over to the machine as he spoke, and began eagerly to explain its points in technical language that passed for the most part over Devenish's head. The change in the man from a surly and rather unintelligent boor to a clever and keen technician was really remarkable, and struck the detective, who listened for a quarter of an hour in silence. Then the man stopped, scratched his head, and instantly relapsed into the dull, morose being he had been before a mention of the gyrocopter struck a spark in his brain.

'When did Mr Cane come here yesterday?' the detective asked.

'About six o'clock, sir. He caught the seven train.'

'Had he ever been here before?'

'No; I never saw him before. He came straight to this place, and went direct from it.'

'He did not ask you about the landing ground, or look at it, eh?'

'It was dark when he came. He didn't ask.'

Devenish thanked him, and went away to the manor. There he was admitted by an elderly butler, a man Mander had enticed from Lord Valley's service, and was assured that Webley was right. Mr Mander had not been there on the Sunday.

The butler had heard of the murder. Mr Kephim had rung him up (at this news the detective frowned). Mr Mander had been a generous master, and all the staff were greatly worried about the tragedy. Mr Kephim had said he would come down to settle what should be done about closing the Manor, but they had heard nothing since.

Devenish heard in addition that Mr Mander had not stayed a night in the house for the last month.

'Did any of you hear the aeroplane go up on Sunday?' he asked. The butler shook his head.

'We'd have heard it if it had.'

Devenish nodded. 'Right. Now, may I ask if Mr Mander has made any friends down here?'

'Not yet, sir. The county people are, as you may say, stand-off,' replied the man. 'More than in most places I should say.'

'So Mr Mander did not entertain?'

'Not here, sir, though he may have done so in his flat in town.'

'He never brought anyone here from town then?'

'Not to stay, sir. None at all, unless you count the young lady came here with him once about five weeks ago.'

Devenish started. 'Was she anything like this?' he asked, and described the dead woman as well as he could.

The butler bit his lip. He was obviously wondering if he

ought to disclose anything about his master's guests. 'That might not be unlike the lady, sir. Of course I did not look at her closely.'

'Did she lunch or dine here?'

'No, sir. She just came down in the car he keeps in town. He was in the car too. He showed her the gardens, and the house a little, and then drove off again.'

'Did he say where?'

'No, sir. He never told me.'

'I can get that from his driver in town,' Devenish said to himself, as he left the house, and started for the station.

## CHAPTER VI

DEVENISH had a hasty meal in a café when he returned to town, then went off to Gandy Mews to see the man who had been Tobias Mander's London chauffeur.

Robinson had been hanging about home all day, expecting a visit from the police, and he had made his mind up to take himself and his wife to the cinema, when Devenish suddenly descended on him.

He was a sleek, meek-looking fellow, and the first of Mander's servants who was not openly much touched by his master's death. It had startled without shocking him very much, and he was quite composed when he replied to the inspector's questions.

Yes, he said, he had called several times at the block of flats where Miss Tumour lived. He did not understand why the guv'nor went there, but understood that Mr Mander was in the habit of having business inspirations during his leisure hours, and might then want to consult the head of this or that department. He said this with the air of a man who does not believe what he is saying but obediently presents the excuse his master has given him.

'Where did you drive them?' asked Devenish, noting all this.

'Sometimes up the river, sir, and sometimes to a hotel restaurant.'

'Surely that would have been commented on by the paid gossips in the papers?'

Robinson shook his head. 'We always went to the Sangrado Hotel, sir.'

Devenish knew of it; a small hotel where the cooking was very good. But it had not been taken up by the Bohemians in society, and it was quite possible that Mander had not been noticed there.

'Right,' he said. 'Now we'll take yesterday. Mr Kephim was under the impression that Mr Mander had been at Gelover Manor.'

'He was going, sir,' replied the chauffeur, 'but he got a telephone message, and I drove him to Parston Court. We were there till the evening.'

The inspector nodded. Parston Court was Mrs Peden-Hythe's country place, where her son, Jameson, lived most of the year.

'Was Mrs Peden-Hythe at home?' he asked.

'Yes, sir; it was her the guv'nor went to see.'

'Was Mr Jameson Peden-Hythe there too?'

Robinson's face underwent a slight change. It expressed at once a general knowledge of the relations between the Peden-Hythes, mother and son, and Mr Tobias Mander.

'He bolted off as soon as we came, sir.'

Devenish looked at him reflectively. 'You mean to say that Mr Jameson, the son, was not very friendly with your master?'

'If looks are anything to go by, he couldn't abear him,' replied the chauffeur. Not that he's any great shakes himself, I should say. Looks as if he couldn't get very far away from a bottle if he tried.'

When Devenish left the mews it seemed to him that Mr Mander's movements on the Sunday had been less mysterious than they had seemed at first. What more natural than that the woman behind the business should wish to see the man she was financing? He returned at once to Scotland Yard, to report to Mr Melis. But Mr Melis had left a note saying that he was going out of town.

Devenish determined to do another job before he wound up for the night. He had a hasty talk with two or three of his subordinates, and then learned that the Mauser automatic pistol found in the ballroom at the Stores had been taken from the sports department.

'Then you had better go round at once, and impound all

the rifles they have of a similar bore. .303 high-velocity ammunition was used, I believe.'

It was now nine o'clock, but he set out to see Mrs Hoe in
Bester Street. But first he took the precaution of ringing up
and making sure that she would be at home. She expressed her
horror at the tragedy, felt quite stunned by it, she said, and was
ready to answer any question.

The Bester Street address turned out to be another flat, a
very small but cosy one this time, and Mrs Hoe a woman journalist. After a short talk, Devenish discovered that she was one
of the paid propagandists of the Stores, and had met Miss
Tumour in that way, and taken a liking to her.

Devenish studied the pretty face of the little woman opposite
to him with appreciation. She spoke clearly, explained lucidly,
and was very intelligent. It struck him that she was a woman
whom it would be hard to impose on.

'Now, Mrs Hoe,' he said presently. 'You and I know enough
of the world to understand that the character of the person
murdered often gives as clear a clue to the tragedy as that of
the murderer. I know you were a friend of the dead woman.
Could you throw any light on the situation from that angle?
What sort of woman was she?'

Mrs Hoe screwed up her eyes a little. 'She was charming,
and a great pal. But I don't think she was very warm-hearted
really, and I feel sure she would be ready to sell nothing for
something. I know that sounds catty, but it isn't. She was born
so. I didn't like her less for guessing the truth about her.'

'You can only put it at "guessing",' he replied. 'But what you
say may be important. As you will realise this business of being
found in the Stores during the weekend will suggest to many
a possible intrigue.'

She shook her head. 'I don't believe it. Not of that kind—if
you mean that kind. If she was going to marry, it was because
she was conventional. I mean to say she was the sort of woman
who had to have a husband and house—an establishment. She

would have hated to be an old maid, because old maids are sometimes stupidly looked down on. But I don't think she would have made love her whole existence. I'm not sure that she was in love at all.'

He nodded. He was glad he had come. 'You mean she was temperamentally cold?'

'Yes, I am sure she was. She wouldn't go anywhere for adventures. She wasn't that type.'

'But undoubtedly she did go to the Stores yesterday.'

She shrugged. 'I see you are wondering where Mr Mander came in? She never mentioned him to me except in connection with business, but if he was infatuated with her, he would stand a lot, wouldn't he?'

'"Faint yet pursuing",' quoted Devenish, thoughtfully; 'well, that sort of thing has happened. But if he was infatuated with her, and her engagement to Mr Kephim was announced, would it help her? You are hinting so far at an ambitious but cold woman who might lure Mander on to improve her own position.'

'That's how I see her. But did Mr Mander know that she was engaged to Kephim?'

He bit his lip. 'That is a point. But it would be bound to come out.'

Mrs Hoe offered him a cigarette, and lit one herself. 'That may be the trouble,' she said. 'Don't you think so?'

'You have met her fiancé, Mr Kephim?' he asked, letting the other question slide.

'Several times. It struck me that he was a nervous man, and rather in awe of her.'

'I suppose you could not say if he was likely to be a jealous man?'

'Let us say "guess", inspector. You corrected me before on that. I should certainly say he—guess he—might be jealous. He was very much wrapped up in her. But then you would have to prove he was there—'

Devenish shrugged.

'We don't know where Mr Kephim was last night.'

She stared. The journalist in her made her avid for details, though she had no intention of selling them. It was not her line, even if she had not remembered Kephim; timid and affectionate, one of those weak men that some women naturally like and despise at the same time.

'Has he no alibi?'

Devenish did not say yes or no. He simply told her one of the bits of stock knowledge a detective-officer is bound to pick up.

'Ah, that's one of the layman's ideas,' he said lightly. 'We generally find that only a lunatic fails to provide an alibi of some sort.'

She smiled. 'He is a well-known rifle shot, but, if you will forgive me saying so, the idea of a rifle is absurd. Where's the bullet? Why use a rifle at all? Why use a knife, and then a rifle? And where is the rifle? Can't you fire a high-velocity bullet from an automatic?'

'A certain length of barrel is necessary for high velocity, I believe,' he replied; 'the Mauser pistol is one of the few automatics sighted to a fairly long range. For that reason, you can have a skeleton shoulder-stock fitted to it. But there are technical reasons why we don't think the bullet was fired by a Mauser.'

'Then why the Mauser?'

'Because, perhaps, it is long-ranged, and sighted to a thousand yards. To give an impression that it had been used, you see. But I must get away soon, and that question doesn't come up here. It is one for experts. I wonder if you would be good enough to tell me—out of your journalistic knowledge—anything you know about Mrs Peden-Hythe?'

Mrs Hoe crushed out her cigarette on an ashtray, and screwed up her eyes again.

'I've seen her at crushes where I went to pick up pars, inspector. Fifty, dressed thirty, a woman who looks greedy for sensations. That is what I thought. Of course it was whispered that she was the power behind the Stores,' she smiled whimsically. 'I think she was. Mr Mander went up like a rocket, and she had the powder, hadn't she?'

'If so, I shall be hearing soon from her, or her lawyers,' he replied. 'Do you know anything about the son?'

'Guesswork only. He lives in the country; it is said because his mother thinks he isn't safe in town. But I suppose his wine merchant has means of transport! But that's libellous. Shall I say he looks a weed who survives by stimulation?'

Devenish nodded. 'We'll take it at that. He's mostly at the country place; she mostly in town. I suppose he is the heir. Must be as the only son. And one couldn't imagine him quarrelling with an investment in the Stores. He wouldn't lose anything in the end.'

Mrs Hoe pondered. 'Ah, that's just the question! All of us on the Press are supposed to know a bit of everything. I don't; but I have a man pal who is on the financial side of the *Argus*. He seems to think Mander has been cutting it too fat—that is how he put it. The idea that a shop that sells a lot makes immense profits, isn't always safe. You may over-advertise, or pay too much in salaries, or too much for the site, and too much for the building. Then there is the question of Jameson Peden-Hythe's father.'

'I thought he was dead.'

'So he is, but Jameson is his father gone to seed. He's a gentlemanly wastrel. Peden-Hythe came of a good family, and married beneath him. His son has all the qualities atrophied, but a real prejudice against the commoner left a born snob.'

This fitted in with what the chauffeur had said, and Devenish mentally marked down the young man for inquiry.

'The stock, of course, one buys on credit,' he said thoughtfully. 'There is no difficulty about that. But I should say there was more than a million to be got. If she gave it to him, and pulled him up out of a country solicitor's office, it suggests an infatuation. And an infatuation where a middle-aged woman is concerned is likely to be indiscreet. Did you ever hear any rumour of a possible marriage between Mander and the lady?'

'Heaps of times. Gossips's slanderous throat, of course. It did strike me once or twice that, if I were a young man, and saw my mother making a fool of herself about a Mander, I might feel nasty about it. And with his prejudices he was bound to.'

Devenish thought he had never met a witness who had given him so much food for thought in such a short time. He got up, thanked her warmly for her help, and went home. People with whom he came in contact officially often put glosses on their evidence, but none saw his points before he made them.

'She's put a couple more in the pot though; worse luck!' he said to himself, as he put on a pipe, and sat down with a pad before a fire to make a few notes. 'It's going to be fine confused feeding unless I am careful.'

He scribbled at once: '—*Kephim*, fiancé, and rifle shot. Possibly jealous.—*Miss Tumour*, calculating, ambitious. Not always liable to give value for value received.—*Mr Cane*, frank, perhaps too frank, and with some little game on.—*Wembley*, my greatest paradox so far. Looks like a fool, but talks like a mechanical angel. Wonder if he is really the inventor of the "Mander Hopper"?—*Mrs Peden-Hythe*, infatuated, and may have got wind of a Mander-Tumour complication.—*Mr Jameson Peden-Hythe*, who hated Mander, and all "upstarts"; inhibitions perhaps weakened by drink. Must have seen the way the wind blew.'

Devenish next planned out the following day's work, and that of his subordinates. He felt that he was going to do best on the human side, leaving the mechanical details to the others under him. Even a detective-sergeant at the Yard is a highly skilled expert, and for the business of taking finger-prints, examining clues and making inquiries can hardly be improved on.

'I should like to tackle Mrs Peden-Hythe herself first,' he thought, as he got ready for bed, 'but, if she should approach me, it would be better. People seem naturally hostile when you have to start the questions.'

Cane he must certainly see, though it would be unlike an aeroplane expert to fake a landing on that roof without suggesting that the gyroplane had come to rest against the sandbanks piled at both sides of the roof to slow up a machine on landing, or at worst, prevent it from diving over the edge.

A real or a fake landing would have been set for darkness. It is one thing, even for an expert with a marvellous gyrocopter, to land on a confined space during the day; but at night, with no flares on the roof to outline the extent of the space, he would be a lucky pilot who could calculate on landing in the middle.

On the whole Devenish decided that if Cane had faked a landing, he would have shown the wheel-tracks in the sand as well as on the bare roof. If the thing was a fake, then there was the presumption that the man who had staged it was not an expert.

# CHAPTER VII

WHEN Devenish reached Scotland Yard next morning, he found some rather surprising news awaiting him. Sergeant Davis had been very busy at the Stores during the previous afternoon, and one of his jobs had been a thorough and minute inspection of all the goods and passenger-lifts, including that which gave access to Mr Mander's flat.

Each of the passenger lifts was fitted with a square of fine deep-pile carpet, laid upon a square of thick cork lino. In one lift, when the carpet was removed, there were traces of blood. Curiously enough, though the cork lino was deeply stained, only the underside of the carpet bore stains, and those of no considerable kind.

It was impossible to believe that anyone could have used a rifle in the lift, and there was no trace of a rifle-bullet having struck the framework, or the lino, or embedded itself anywhere either in the lift or in the shaft. In these circumstances, the puzzle was made the subject of a police conference, attended by the superintendent, the police-surgeon and the sergeant.

The view of the surgeon was that Miss Tumour had been killed in the lift. The hæmorrhage in her case had been slight; which he explained technically, demonstrating the nature of the wound and the species of slender-bladed weapon used.

'Then it makes us more muddled than ever,' said Devenish, when he had heard this. 'If she was killed in the passenger lift, the man must have gone up in the goods lift. But why did he take the knife up with him, and then throw it down in the goods-lift? Did he go up and kill Mander in the flat, and bring him down by the goods lift? I suppose you have examined all the walls of the rooms in the flat?'

'Every one, sir, and there was no sign of a bullet. And I

examined the servants closely, and don't think any of them had a hand in it. The bullet beats me. It must have gone somewhere.'

'Quite,' replied the inspector dryly. 'Now, let me see, is there a possibility—it can be no more—that some windows or ventilators were open, and that the bullet chanced to fly out that way?'

'I examined every opening, sir. As for the windows, none were left open, except one in the flat. That was the window of Mr Mander's drawing-room.'

Devenish smiled faintly. 'The prosaic fact is that the bullet either flew out of that window or was stopped by something. So far as the investigations go, it was not stopped by any of the walls of this building, but we shall have to go over them from top to bottom before we can decide that finally. We'll put more men on that job at once. There is a third possibility, and it's remote, but we must consider it. It would require two men to be in the case, I think, and I imagine Mr Mander would have been gagged, if it was done that way. I mean a metal plate held behind the victim might stop the bullet, though very likely there would be a richochet and the bullet glance off.'

'But why take all that trouble, sir?'

'I don't say there is anything in it,' remarked Devenish, 'but that faked landing might be intended to convey the idea that Mr Mander was not shot in this building at all.'

'But he returned here, and dined—I mean to his flat, sir.'

'Yes, but the faking intended to prove that a machine landed on the roof and that the man from the machine did the murder. If that man was supposed to be the mechanic and gyrocopter pilot, Webley, it might be assumed that he had seen his employer, and perhaps taken him for a short flight, then shot him while in the air, descended with the body, and disposed of it. That would seem to account for there being no bullet visible.'

'But what could be his motive, sir?'

Devenish shrugged. 'At a venture, we could find a motive. I have a strong idea that Webley is the inventor of the gyrocopter, and I know from him that Mander said it wasn't profitable to sell; though I think that suggests the financier cheating the humble inventor, as has often been done before. Webley, outside his speciality, is an ignorant sort of fellow. He might have been very glad to get someone to finance his pet toy. Then, as I know, Mr Cane in the Stores went down to see Webley on Sunday evening.'

'And perhaps said they were making a good thing out of it?' said the sergeant. 'He might get wild if he found that out.'

Devenish nodded. 'In any case I am not building on that theory. I merely make sure that we neglect no alternative. Did you get all the rifles out of the sports department?'

'Yes, sir. There were three sporting rifles firing a .303 cartridge. But these were all clean and unfouled.'

'There can't have been continuous processions up and down in the lifts,' said Devenish, 'but the night watchman ought to have heard a shot, even if his microphone device was out of order.'

'As regards that, sir,' said the sergeant, 'I had one of our experts in, as you suggested. He says the connection must have been cut by someone with a little knowledge only. The thing could have been put out of order much more simply.'

The desk-telephone rang as he spoke. Devenish lifted the receiver and listened, then said: 'I'll go round at once,' and replaced the instrument. 'That's good,' he said, 'Mrs Peden-Hythe's butler had just rung up from Curzon Street, asking me to come round to see his mistress. Well, get back to the Stores, see that the walls are most carefully examined—everywhere. If Mr Kephim turns up, tell him that I hope to see him there at two today.'

The sergeant saluted, and went. Devenish put on his hat and coat, and started for Curzon Street.

Mrs Peden-Hythe's town house was not very large, but it was most luxuriously and expensively furnished. The walls of the room into which Devenish was shown were hung with pictures that could not be bought for a song; Courbets, two pictures by Maris, some by Anton Mauve, and others by the now costly French impressionists. And this was only a little room that was rarely used. Mrs Peden-Hythe collected pictures, and was said to buy simply by price; so that you did not see the Coopers or Goodalls that might be expected to shine in the collection of a woman who had no artistic standards. But she had bought lately, when all the 'picture-tells-a-story' school had fallen into the price doldrums.

Every man who rises to inspector's rank in the detective force is something of an elementary psychologist and accustomed to judge character from the faces of witnesses. But when Mrs Peden-Hythe came into the room, he found himself rather at a loss to decide the category into which she fell.

She was obviously lacking in distinction, in spite of her fine clothes. She did not look an amorous type, though she was obviously endeavouring to hold her fugitive youth by the skirts. She was very pale, rather handsome. Her mouth was large, and her lips full. She bit her lips constantly as she talked, and made them look fuller and redder than ever.

She bowed, then bit her underlip viciously. 'I suppose you wonder why I asked you to come, inspector? The fact is, I financed Mr Mander. Had you heard that?'

He nodded. 'I thought it was so, madam.'

'I was horrified to hear of his death,' she went on rapidly, 'and of that—that woman's death.'

'It must have been rather startling to you, since he had been lunching with you that day,' said Devenish.

She gave him a quick glance. 'Who told you that?'

'His chauffeur.'

'I see. Well, of course, I have nothing to hide. I may as well tell you that he came down at my request,' she remarked coolly. 'My solicitors had heard some disturbing rumours, and as so much money was concerned it was up to me to look into it.'

'Rumours of what, madam?'

'Well, a suggestion that the business was not paying as it

should. There was a great deal coming in, of course, but too much had gone and was going out. I asked Mr Mander down to give me his views.'

'Why did your son not see him, and save you the trouble?'

She bit her lip again, and seemed slightly resentful. 'My son has no knowledge of business.'

'But I presume he can confirm your account of what passed between you and Mr Mander that day, madam?'

'No, he went off for the day. He went to stay the night with some friend in town.'

Devenish nodded. 'And what did Mr Mander say?'

'He reassured me. He admitted that we were not making profits, but he said that we mustn't take the first year's expenses as an annual "overhead". When the Stores were established finally, the various appropriations could be cut down greatly.'

Devenish was struck by her knowledge of business terms, and the fact that she spoke as if she understood them. 'That was the last time you saw Mr Mander? When he left Parston Court?'

She seemed surprised now. 'Of course. After dinner I had people in for bridge, and we did not stop playing until one o'clock.'

'Mr Jameson Peden-Hythe did not return?'

She drew herself up. 'I beg your pardon—I don't quite see what my son has to do with this.'

'I am making no suggestions, madam. But I have heard it hinted that your son had a hearty dislike for Mr Mander. The chauffeur said he "bolted" when Mr Mander arrived at your house.'

'I am afraid I cannot accept a strange chauffeur's word about my son's prejudices,' she countered. 'There was no reason why he should like or dislike Mr Mander. Our relations with him were strictly those of business.'

Now why did she think it necessary to say that, or to stare him hard in the eyes as she said it? Devenish wondered, as he went on. 'I see that, madam. But may I hear with whom Mr Peden-Hythe spent the night?'

She shrugged, and bit her lips again. 'He said he was going to see Sir William Lefort. But all this is beside the point. While the Stores are shut up, very serious damage is being done to the business. I do not blame you for that, of course, but I should much like to know when it will be possible to open again.'

Devenish reflected. Mrs Hoe might be a too facile character-reader and have made a mistake here. Was Mrs Peden-Hythe greedy, but for money, not sensations? She had a vast fortune, but that said nothing. Those who have one fortune are often apparently avid for two, and no doubt the audacious lawyer's clerk had not lured her into risking a million without proving to her that proportionate or disproportionate profits would be made.

'They are holding the inquest today,' he said. 'I shall have to go there just now. But I see no reason why the premises should not be put at your disposal—or shall we discuss that with your solicitor?'

'Mr Hay will communicate with you about it,' she said. 'At our disposal, when?'

'Tomorrow,' said he. 'Of course we may have to pay further visits, and I suggest that the flat above should be kept locked up until we conclude our investigations. Otherwise, tomorrow.'

'Have you any clue?' she asked composedly.

'The hearing today will be purely formal,' he replied. 'There is nothing to go upon so far.'

She nodded, bit her lip again, and then frowned a little. 'Who was the young woman? Mr Mander always struck me as wrapped up in business. Was she very attractive?'

Devenish rose. 'She was decidedly pretty.'

'I suppose the motive was jealousy?'

He smiled dryly. 'If we knew the motive, madam, we should get the man.'

'Then you think it was a man?'

He did not think she was frightened or upset, but wished he could be sure. Her questions might be merely curiosity made manifest, or they might have a more personal spring.

'I am afraid our people discourage loose thinking,' he said. 'A little evidence is more important. So we may expect to deal with your solicitor in the matter of the Stores.'

'With Mr Hay—yes. I'll telephone to him now.'

She dismissed him with a nod, and he went out.

'If Mrs Hoe hadn't been so attractive, I mightn't have thought her so clever,' Devenish said to himself as he made his way to a telephone call-box, *en route* to the inquest. 'Mrs Peden-Hythe is greedy, but I am beginning to wonder for what.'

He rang up Scotland Yard a minute later, and gave instructions to a detective-officer. 'I want you to find out where Mr Jameson Peden-Hythe was on Sunday night. I hear he went to stay with Sir William Lefort. Go round there and find out what you can.'

# CHAPTER VIII

THE inquest had been a brief and formal business. Evidence of identification had been put in with regard to the dead man and woman; the doctor had given the results of his examination; and then the police asked for a fortnight's adjournment, which was granted.

After a late lunch, Devenish went to the Stores.

At two, punctually, the manager entered. He looked less haggard and overcome than on the previous day, but his mouth was hard and his eyes grim. Devenish got the impression that the man was now more bitter about the revealed connection between Miss Tumour and Mr Mander (whatever the nature of it might be) than grief-stricken at his loss.

He made the manager sit down, and then asked him if he had announced his engagement to Miss Tumour to his employer.

'No,' said Kephim, dourly. 'I did not.'

'No doubt you meant to do so?'

'Of course, but it had nothing to do with him; or I thought it hadn't.'

'So that, as far as you are aware, Mr Mander did not know that you were engaged to the dead woman?'

'So far as I know, he did not.'

Devenish looked down. 'Are you aware that Miss Tumour had been visited by Mander for some time before his death? I mean that he called for her, and took her out in his car?'

'I know it now. I went round to her flat yesterday after I had left you.'

'She never told you about it?'

'It is not,' said Kephim, with a fierce look, 'the kind of thing she would tell me about.'

'Can you account for her visiting Mr Mander on Sunday night? I mean would there be any business explanation of it?'

'I don't think so.'

Devenish looked him in the face. 'Have you any .303 ammunition in your possession, Mr Kephim? You can answer that or not as you like.'

Kephim did not look surprised. 'I have perhaps twenty cartridges of that calibre,' he replied dully. 'If you care to come round to my flat, you can see them, and my match-rifle.'

'I shall go with you at once, if it is convenient. You use match-rifle ammunition, not the ordinary Service issue?'

'That is right. But you shall see for yourself.'

Devenish rose, and they went out together. A taxi took them to the flat. It was large and well-furnished, though not luxurious. Kephim made Devenish sit down in the drawing-room while he went upstairs and returned with a match-rifle, fitted with a telescopic sight, and a box containing some ammunition.'

'These are all the cartridges I have,' he said quietly.

Devenish examined the rifle closely, and then the cartridges, one of which he kept. 'I want this one to examine more carefully,' he said. 'By the way, would you mind shouldering the rifle and allowing me to make some measurements?'

If Kephim was the guilty man, he showed no signs of discomposure. He got up, and levelled the rifle.

'Just point it a trifle below the level of my groin, sir,' said Devenish. 'Mr Mander was about five feet seven. I should say you were five feet nine.'

'Ten, inspector.'

Devenish took out a tape-measure and made several marks on the wall while Kephim lowered the rifle and watched him. He asked the manager then to aim at the marks in turn, and took perpendicular and lateral measurements, and once went behind the man with the rifle to look down the sights over his shoulder.

'You need not assist me with these experiments unless you wish,' he explained as he worked. 'I want you to understand that.'

'I have not the slightest objection, inspector,' replied Kephim.

'The point is this,' said Devenish, rolling up his tape at last. 'You do not need to be a tall man to shoot a man in the groin so that the bullet takes a slanting course downwards. But the police-surgeon in this case says the slant was more or less vertical, which hints at an assailant of more than average height.'

Kephim put down the rifle. 'I should say, inspector, that you have not only to look for a tall man but also for the kind of man who was able to carry Mander some distance,' he remarked. 'Anything else?'

'Do you object to my making a search of your flat here? I have no warrant.'

'I have no objection to your doing anything in reason. It is not amusement to you any more than to me.'

For the next hour he was busy going over the flat. He found nothing with the slightest bearing on the case, however. Kephim was helpful throughout. When the inspector had finished, he offered him tea, but Devenish refused.

'No, thank you, sir. I must get on with the job. I am much obliged to you altogether.'

Kephim shrugged wearily. 'That's all right. Good-day, inspector.'

When he left the flat, Devenish decided to take Mr Cane next. He had heard from the men at work at the Stores that Cane had not turned up, so went off at once to the young man's rooms in Caister Street.

Cane happened to be in, and having tea. But he did not invite the inspector to join him; only offered him a cigarette, and appeared quite cheerful and at ease.

'Still barging round on the quest?' he said. 'Anything fresh?'

'Nothing, sir,' said Devenish. 'May I ask, sir, where you spent the evening of Sunday last?'

'Sunday last?' Cane drank some tea, and nodded. 'Yes, rather.

But am I supposed to be the villain, inspector? Mustn't answer that, eh? Oh, on Sunday afternoon I went out in my little car, and had a good drive round. Covered a hundred and twenty miles before half-past five. On my way back I found myself near Gelover, so I turned in there and renewed my acquaintance with the mechanic pilot of our Hopper. Brainy boy for his type, but I still contend that it is only in one line. He was quite shirty with me because I said I wondered if he was the inventor.'

'You think he was?'

'He's quite capable of it. Anything more?'

'What time did you get back here, sir?'

Cane pushed his cup away and sat back. 'Let me see. It was half-past nine I think. I had left my jigger in the garage. I have to put it up with Bale's, for there's nothing nearer here. But, wait a moment, did you say when I returned here?'

'I meant to town, sir.'

'Then that's right. Then I turned in at a cinema near there, and was home here about half-past eleven.'

Devenish noted that. 'And did your people here (I see you have rooms, not a flat), did they hear you come in, or let you in?'

Cane laughed. 'Good old alibi, eh? No, they did neither, as far as I know. But I had better make sure if they heard. Old Haines and his wife here were servants with my people in the old days. I'll have Haines up.'

Devenish sat silent till Cane had got up and pressed a bell.

'You have a latch-key, then?'

'They trust me with one!' Cane smiled as he resumed his seat. 'They were country people, and they aren't used to late hours yet.'

A minute later, an elderly man with the look of a retired butler entered the room.

'You rang, Mr William?'

'I did Haines. This gentleman wants to know if you heard me come in on Sunday night, and if so when.'

Haines gave the inspector the sort of half-suspicious, half-resentful glance reserved by trained servants for dubious callers.

'No, Mr William, we did not either of us hear you come in. You said at breakfast next morning that it was about half-past eleven.'

'Wonderful memory for facts,' said Cane. 'All right, Haines, that will do.'

There is always the possibility that a man who mentions the times of his goings and comings after the event is anxious to impress those times on his hearer. But Devenish made no comment one way or the other.

Cane smiled at him quizzically, and went on, as Haines left the room. 'English law and order, they say, are achieved by the wonderful and unique co-operation of police and people, inspector,' he said. 'As one of the people happy to be able to collaborate with you, I invite you to have a look over my rooms. I can't promise you the sight of a hidden armoury, or anything romantic like that, but we may as well get it over.'

Devenish remained unmoved by this banter. 'Very well, sir, since you suggest it, I will.'

He made his search, found nothing, and returned with Cane to the sitting-room. 'Do you remember, sir, anyone who sat next to you at the cinema?' he asked. 'Anyone next, or near you?'

'I don't clearly, my dear fellow. I go to the cinema to look at the horrors on the screen, not those next to me. I have a vague idea of peppermints on the right and chewing-gum on the left. The man with gum might be a soccer professional. I believe they are addicted to it.'

Devenish shrugged. 'Ah, then that is all I wish to ask you at the moment, I think.'

'Don't worry on my account. I am interested,' said Cane. 'By the way, someone said the police-surgeon swore the Mauser could not have fired that bullet. Now what the dickens does he know about it?'

'He appears to be an amateur in ballistics, sir,' said Devenish, dryly.

'*Ne sutor ultra crepidam*,' quoted Cane. 'I hate to see perfectly good surgeons posing as experts. My own theory is that Mander stabbed Miss Tumour, and then shot himself with that pistol.'

'Where did the bullet go?'

Cane frowned. 'Oh, that is the trouble, of course. But suppose someone else was in the flat; I won't say whom. Suppose he came to polish off Mander, and found that the deed was done already. Not liking to be found in the flat with two bodies, he carried them down to the ballroom below, to make it appear the murder and suicide took place there.'

'Why didn't he make himself scarce in any case?' asked Devenish. 'If he could enter the flat, he could get out again.'

'I don't believe he went out again by the way he got in,' said Cane. 'It's my idea that the murder was committed by Mander when he heard Miss Tumour was engaged to Kephim. I think she came up the stairs to the flat from the back, which opens off the lane only used by us for vans and loading-banks. No one would be about there on Sunday.'

'And this hypothetical man who also entered?'

'By the same way. When he found the bodies, he might believe that the servants had heard the shot and would look out into the lane. I think it's quite likely he hid in the shop, and went out when the shoppers crowded in on Monday morning.'

'Rather fantastic, when you remember, sir, that there was no sign of the bullet in the flat either. And why should two bodies worry the man more than one? If he was tried and convicted wrongly, he could be hanged for a single murder.'

Cane laughed. 'I am really afraid I should not make a good detective. I forgot those points. Will you have a drink?'

'No, thanks,' said Devenish. 'I must go now.'

He had all along suspected that the surgeon was attempting a too hasty diagnosis in the matter of the Mauser pistol, but naturally he had not considered the matter carefully. Scotland Yard does not accept expert conclusions from anyone save experts, and the Mauser had been submitted already to a rifle-maker.

When Devenish left Cane's room, he went straight to this man and asked him if he had come to any conclusion about the pistol.

'Absolutely,' said the other. 'Your surgeon wouldn't give a verdict on a case without studying it scientifically, but he seems to have glanced through the gun and then fired away.'

'They say famous fiddlers always want to be composers, and authors want to pose as business men,' remarked Devenish, smiling.

'That's about the size of it, inspector. We inspected the rifling under a brilliant light, and it shows undoubted signs of having fired a bullet.'

'Oh, good. But not a lead one, or soft-nosed?'

'No, steel-jacketed sure enough. But you may take it from me that it was the gun used—that Mauser.'

'We can't find the slightest sign of the bullet. I take it that the pistol was held by a taller man than Mander, or else Mander was in a crouching or sitting position. Unless it was deflected by a bone or something, as does not seem to have been the case, it ought to have entered a wall, or flown out through some aperture about eighteen inches from the floor.'

'Have you examined all possible ventilators?'

'Yes. The only hope we have is a window that was open in Mr Mander's drawing-room. But unless Mander was sitting on the sill, I don't see how it could have gone out that way. If he was sitting on the sill even, as people do sometimes—though rarely in November—the murderer would have had to be about seven-foot six in height for the bullet to have struck at the angle it did.'

'I can see you have a job before you,' remarked the other.

Devenish nodded. 'A nasty one. But there is always this to

remember. A bullet goes somewhere. If it is not found to have penetrated any surface in a building, then it was not fired in that building. It's like a man telling you how a crook escaped from a locked room without going through the door, the walls, the floor, or the ceiling; or up the chimney. You know he did go by one of those ways, however it may appear to the narrator. Once my men have cleared up that point, I shall be able to narrow things down.'

'That's right. But they'll have a devil of a business in that vast place.'

# CHAPTER IX

INSPECTOR DEVENISH had had a man shadowing Cane, and another Mr Kephim, while a third had gone down to Gelover to keep an eye on Webley. Assistant-Commissioner, Mr Melis, had apparently gone down on his own to the vicinity of Parston Court and interviewed a couple of friends of Mrs Peden-Hythe's. Both had independently stated that they had been members of that Sunday bridge party and that their hostess had not left them for more than ten minutes during the evening.

Remained Mr Jameson Peden-Hythe. Devenish had dinner and returned to the Yard, anxious to know something of that young man's movements on the Sunday. The detective-officer he had detailed for this duty came in a little later to communicate his discoveries.

'The gentleman did not go to Sir William Lefort's,' he said. 'I heard that from the butler, as Sir William has gone to Scotland. I looked Mr Peden-Hythe up in a book of reference, and found he had two clubs. I went to one of them, but no trace of him there. At the second, they said he had a bedroom, and stayed there Sunday night. He came in at twelve o'clock and went to his room.'

'Has he gone back?'

'I believe not, sir. But I thought you might prefer to interview him yourself.'

Devenish agreed, left for the club, and was there within a quarter of an hour. It was a free-and-easy club mostly frequented by young men with sporting proclivities, and the standard of membership was not too high.

When the inspector asked if he might see Mr Jameson Peden-Hythe, he was asked to wait. The messenger returned to say that Mr Peden-Hythe was in his bedroom and had had tea sent up to him about six.'

Tea seemed a strange drink at six o'clock to a man who was reputed to be addicted to alcohol. But it turned out that the young man had gone to sleep and only waked at six. He was still lying down, clad in shirt, trousers and a gorgeous silk dressing-gown, when Devenish entered the room.

He was very tall, very thin, and very pale, but not unhandsome. He had a sulky air, and was very terse in his remarks too. Either he had been drinking heavily or had slept little during the past few days.

Devenish stated his business, and added that he had been told that the young man had stayed the night of Sunday at Sir William Lefort's.

'So I did,' was the reply. 'Take a gasper!'

'You are sure of that, sir?'

Jameson stared, murmured to himself, and shook his head. 'No. I didn't. Thought of it, that's all.'

'You spent the night here instead?'

The young man raised himself on his elbow, peevishly. 'What are you up to?'

Devenish looked stern. 'You must know, sir, that official inquiries like mine are meant to be taken seriously. I shall be obliged if you will think carefully before you reply.'

'Carry on!'

'I want to know your movements last Sunday, sir. I am aware that Mr Mander visited Parston Court, and that you left when he arrived.'

'So I did—Beastly bounder!'

'Nominally, to go to Sir William's,' said Devenish. 'But where did you actually go?'

'Came here—do take a gasper! Smoke your own if you don't like mine.'

Devenish shook his head. 'Not at present, thank you.'

'Then would you mind ringing the bell? I want a drink.'

'Excuse me, sir, but you must really concentrate on my questions.'

The young man felt for his cigarette-case and matches, and lit up, 'Go on!'

'Where did you go after that?'

'Took this room here, then went into the park.'

'For how long?'

'Back at six. No; I went to see a fella. Left him at seven, and had to see another fella. Then I had dinner here.'

'And after that, sir?'

Mr Jameson Peden-Hythe looked exceedingly wise. 'Damned if I know.'

'But you must surely know?'

'Surely don't! Both fellas hospitable, and all that, and I had a spot or two with my dinner. Went somewhere after, and had a spot or two. I was damn spotty I must say.'

'Drunk, you mean?'

'Stewed! What do you think?'

Devenish frowned. 'I am rather anxious to know where you were on Sunday evening, all the same,' he said slowly. 'Can't you think back? No one seems to have noticed that you were as drunk as that, when you came in here that night.'

'Perhaps no one saw me,' said Jameson exhaustedly.

Devenish dropped that; tried him from a new angle. 'Perhaps you can give me some idea of Mr Mander's character. I know you disliked him—'

'Like hell!'

'And that being so, I must discount a certain amount of prejudice.'

Jameson Peden-Hythe sat up suddenly, and delivered himself of the longest speech of his life. 'That fella! I ask you—what was he? Jumped-up lawyer's clerk, gift of the gab, cunning as monkeys—I say, he could talk a cook into doing a twelve-course dinner on her evenin' out. The trouble is that the mater's impressionable. Damn good business woman; but impressionable. He had a programme, all cut and dry. He convinced her—what? That swab; getting away with it, hocussing her from top to bottom. And no use me talking! I'm not a business man. What do I know about it? Nothing! Wasting the family substance in riotous livin'!—Me? No, not me; Mander. But, as I say, it was no use talking.'

He lay back on the bed, exhausted, and inhaled deeply, staring up at the ceiling.

Devenish had nothing to go on here, and knew it. 'Very well, sir,' he said, rather contemptuously. 'You can't remember.'

'That's right.'

Devenish went down to the hall-porter, and asked the man if he had noticed the condition in which Mr Peden-Hythe had come in on the Sunday night. He showed his card, and the man whistled.

'Nothing out of the ordinary, inspector,' he replied.

'What is the ordinary?'

'I should think he had had a few, sir, but nothing to speak of.'

'It wouldn't have struck you that he was incapable, or anything like that?'

'No, sir. He seemed in a bad temper, but that was about all.'

'Did he come in a taxi?'

'I don't think so, sir, though he may have paid one off near at hand.'

There was an inconsistency somewhere, but even that did not prove that Peden-Hythe was connected with the case. It was obvious that he did not wish it to be known where he was on the Sunday evening, but a dubious visit somewhere and association with a murder are not necessarily linked.

Jameson evidently suspected that Mander had been swindling, or about to swindle, his mother out of some money, and naturally resented this large wasting of the family funds. On the other hand, would he have spoken so strongly against the dead man if he had been concerned in his death? There was no convincing answer to that question. A guilty man will sometimes find it to his account to do something the rules suggest he would not have done.

Devenish thought it all over while he had supper in a restaurant. There appeared to be nothing subtle about Jameson, but you never knew. That idle, weedy, debilitated sort of man was sometimes as tricky as the devil.

When he had finished his meal, Devenish hurried back to the Stores, and this time collected Sergeant Davis, and went straight up to the flat. They sat down in the drawing-room and smoked, while Devenish talked over the evidence with his assistant.

'Since there were no holes or slits in the costumes the two wore, we can be quite sure they were dressed up after death,' the inspector began, 'but we want to know where those things came from.'

'The dongarees, I mean the blue overall, was one he used to wear when he was tinkering in his workshop up there, sir.'

'I suspected that. It fitted him too well to be a chance find. But there were an even number of wax models in that window—all paired off. Since Mander was not in fancy-dress, Miss Tumour was odd one out. Did you find where the fancy cloak she wore came from?'

Davis nodded. 'Up here, sir. It seems the designers submitted ideas and models to Mander. That was one which he turned down, but the butler knew it. He said Mander left it lying about.'

Devenish frowned. 'Very well. That places both up here. Now there is that wound the woman had. I am not very satisfied about it. Did it seem to you—I mean to say, if you were going to stab anyone, would you choose that spot?'

The sergeant considered. 'No, sir, I don't think I would. The instinct would be to strike either at the throat or down between the shoulders—I wondered too.'

'Push up that window and sit on the sill, looking this way,' Devenish commanded.

Davis got up and obeyed. Devenish went through the

pantomime of shooting, tried his assistant in various positions, and sighed.

'This place is so much higher than any building near at hand,' he said. 'Still, we had better be thorough and go through with it. Fired at this angle, the bullet would hit somewhere within a radius of a thousand yards at most, whether Mander was sitting or standing. We must inquire at every building near. A broken window, or chipped plaster or stone, would show. We might also get some photographs from here with a telephoto lens and see if they show anything. See to that tomorrow, will you?'

Davis assented, and sat down again, after shutting the window to keep the damp cold air from the dark beyond.

'I can't help thinking, sir, that there is something fishy about Mr Kephim,' he said tentatively.

'Why do you think so?'

'There was a pretty young lady came to see him today, sir. Corbett saw her go in, looking pretty serious. She stayed over an hour, and he says she came out again smiling, as happy as anything.'

Devenish laughed. 'If that is all, Davis, a good many men in town are suspect.'

'Oh, it wasn't only that, sir, her going to see Mr Kephim. But Corbett followed her home, and made inquiries, and it seems she was a great friend of Miss Tumour's.'

The inspector started. Could this have been Mrs Hoe? She knew Kephim, of course, but could she be getting materials for the Press, or was there a personal motive behind her visit?

'There may be nothing in it,' he replied, 'but have an eye kept on Mrs Hoe—if it was she. I interviewed her, and she impressed me favourably; but gave me an idea that she was not as fond of her friend as she wished me to believe.'

'I will keep an eye on her, sir,' said Davis, 'but there is another thing I wanted to know. That gadget at the Stores, to let the watchman hear anyone moving about the departments at night, was cut by Mann perhaps. I wonder what he did it with.'

'It is easily cut,' said Devenish; 'what interests me is the fact that it is cut so that it would not be seen if the microphone attachment was only cursorily inspected.'

'Yes, sir, that is true.'

'Well, there is a job for you. The man may be a sleepy devil, who wanted to snooze between whiles. That microphone would make a beast of a noise if cars passed in the street too.'

'There is that,' the sergeant agreed. 'Quite a lot of them look on a night job as easy money.'

'Then please have another talk with him, and also find anything you can about him round where he lives. Also see if Mr Kephim or Mr Cane, or anyone in this show, was in touch with him. Now I am going on the roof. Got your torch?'

'Yes, sir.'

As they went up the stairs, Devenish remarked that the missing sparking plugs puzzled him as much as anything.

'If it wasn't the gyrocopter descending, it was the engine on the bench in the workshop that made the noise,' he said. 'If it was the engine in the workshop, then the murderer removed the sparking plugs after he had done with it.'

'I don't quite follow you, sir,' said Davis.

Devenish shrugged. 'If a gyrocopter didn't land here, and yet there were wheel-tracks on the roof, it was to give the impression that a landing had been made. But, to help out that impression, there would have to be the sound of an aero-engine, wouldn't there? So the murderer must have run it to make the sound, and then removed the sparking-plugs to prove that the engine on the bench couldn't have made it.

He took a torch from his pocket as he stepped out on the flat roof. Davis also switched on his.

'All the evidence we have in the way of bloodstains suggests that the two people were killed below,' said Devenish, 'but we have against that the missing bullet, and that, to my mind, is the real crux. Now, up here, we have all the apparatus necessary, and I want to go into it. I may be wrong, but I have a feeling that we are warmer here than down below. How many men are there in the Stores now?'

'We have seven on various jobs below, sir.'

'Right. Bring them up here quickly. No, send a couple of them into the hardware department first, and let them scrounge a sieve apiece. These sand-buffers for the aeroplane landing would be the very thing to stop a bullet.'

'You're right, sir,' said Davis, starting. 'I never thought of that.'

Devenish pondered. 'It's a chance. The bullet went somewhere. Get off now, sergeant.'

Davis hurried down the stairs. Devenish approached one of the long piles of sand at one end of the roof, and focused the beam from his torch upon it.

'If it was here, it narrows it down a bit,' he said to himself, pulling up the collar of his coat against the chill night air, 'but what the dickens would they be doing up here in winter?'

He was leaning against the parapet, smoking and thinking, when the sergeant returned, with seven men. He had had the foresight to scrounge torches as well as sieves, and there was plenty of light on the sandbanks when the men set to work.

The sandbanks were deep and thick, and torches gave out and were replaced with others from the Store as time went on. It is a long job sifting and inspecting tons of sand, and two hours had passed before Devenish was satisfied that the first bank contained nothing to interest them.

At midnight he went down to the flat and asked the butler to make them some hot coffee while they began to tackle the second bank. Ten minutes rest, while they drank the coffee, and they went at it again with fresh zeal.

But Devenish as he saw the bank being gradually worked through began to feel pessimistic. His conviction had been strong that the sand might cover the secret of the murder, and the reaction was all the greater when they had sieved one bank, and half of the second, without any results.

'Short cuts don't save distance it seems,' he remarked to Davis.

As he said that, a detective to his extreme right gave an excited cry.

'Look at this, sir!'

# CHAPTER X

'THERE is no doubt that it is blood,' said Devenish, after he had examined the red stained sand pointed out to him by the detective. 'But leave that bit, and the rest of you stop work till we have a better look. Davis, do you think we had better leave it till daylight? I mean this part. I intend to have a look for the bullet the other side of the bank.'

Davis nodded. 'I think it might be better, sir. This blood is on the inner side, and if Mander was killed by a bullet fired from a little distance, then the firer must have stood on the inner side, not the parapet side.'

'And the bullet would pass through a certain amount of sand before it was stopped,' Devenish nodded. 'Here, you fellows, get round to the parapet side, opposite where I am standing now. I just want two of you.'

While the surplus men concentrated their torches on the bank, and two moved round the sandbank, Devenish stared at Davis.

'Do you remember if there was any wind on the night of Sunday?' he asked. 'I think there was a breeze when I went to bed. Of course we can soon settle the point if you are not sure.'

Davis nodded.

'Yes, sir. There was a strongish wind from the west.'

'That would blow across this roof then?'

'It must, sir.'

'I shall have to inquire how a gyrocopter lands,' said Devenish half aloud, and turned again to the men who waited. 'Sieve the sand very slowly and carefully for about six feet on your side, taking my position as the centre, and working inwards. Don't move the bank generally any more than you can help.'

All the torches were now concentrated on the sandbank, and

75

the two men went very carefully to work. Devenish told them to be very thorough, then went down with Davis to the flat below and, opening the door communicating with the servants' quarters, got the butler, and asked him if he had any lamp oil.

'We want more light up there,' he explained.

The butler proved useful. He explained that he had heard there were some new petrol lamps on show below, and, as there was a daily demonstration, no doubt the lamps would be filled.

'They're the new, safe kind, sir,' he said.

Devenish despatched Davis to bring two lamps up, and returned to the roof. He was thinking as he went that the secrecy which Mr Mander's manoeuvres required had not only made it easier for the murderer to operate, but also fogged the path of the law. This private staircase, and the care Mander had taken to see that no one spied on his actions, enabled the murderer to take his time over the job, replace the sand over the blood, and clear up before he left.

'There is one thing that may help,' he mused. 'If anyone concerned in the case tries to leave London in a hurry, we may get a clue. If I gave it out that the sand was to be cleared from the roof, it might provide a scare, but I'll leave that for the present.'

Davis had returned and set up the lamps before either of the two detectives with sieves made another discovery. But, five minutes after fresh light had been thrown upon the scene, the bullet came into view.

At once all work was stopped. Devenish took the bullet in his palm and produced a pocket magnifier, while his assistants stood round, eagerly staring.

'That's the ticket,' said Devenish. 'Just the kind of bullet we were looking for. Now then, two of you loot the Store again and bring up tarpaulins, or dustcloths; anything you can get suitable—waterproof sheets would be best, perhaps. And one of you had better stay here on guard till four, when another man will relieve him.'

'Are we closing down for the night then, sir?' one of the subordinates asked.

'As regards this; yes. I want the superintendent and Mr Melis to see this when it is light. It must be covered up now as it stands, and not touched. By the way, no one outside is to hear that anything has been found on the roof. Do you understand?'

Having made that clear, he and Davis went back to the late Mr Mander's drawing-room and sat down to examine the bullet in turn. When they had both stared at it closely, Devenish put it away.

'Now how do you think an aeroplane lands?' the inspector asked his sergeant.

'Head to wind, sir, I believe,' said Davis. 'Just as a bird does.'

'That was my idea, and I think it is correct. Now if the wind was westerly on Sunday night, that is blowing across the roof, and the gyrocopter did land here, how does it come that the tracks of the wheels lie running between the sandbanks, lengthways?'

'But we thought it did not land here, sir. That that was a plant?'

'True, but even a badly arranged fake may give hints. Say a sailor was trying to make it appear that one of the other sailors had bound a man with rope. He would use the best knots sailors are expert at, wouldn't he?'

'Naturally, sir.'

'Whereas a landsman would not know all the tricks of the trade. If a man who did not know much about aeroplanes faked a landing here, he would not think of any difficulties made by the direction of the wind that night.'

'No, sir.'

'Then the presumption is to my mind that an aeroplane did not land, but that a man who was not familiar with the machines tried to prove one had. That would let out both Webley and Cane.'

'But Webley, being the man who could pilot this particular

kind, the murderer must have tried to put it on him. But who would have a grudge against Webley?'

'That I don't know,' said Devenish, getting up. 'Now I am just going to see that the man is posted above, and the sandbank made snug, and then I shall take a few hours sleep. I advise you to do the same, Davis.'

'Very well, sir,' said the sergeant.

The superintendent did not come in next morning, but Mr Melis arrived, looking more eager and interested than usual, and explained that the superintendent was having an interview with Mrs Peden-Hythe's lawyer, Mr Hay.

'Mr Mander's sins have been finding him out a bit,' he added. 'Mr Hay and the auditor grabbed what books they could yesterday, and started making hectic inquiries. Looks as if Mander had been raising some coin on the security of this show, and generally piling up a little mammon while the sun shone. There is no doubt he had a kind of genius for initiating big enterprises, but I imagine he wasn't a stayer.'

Devenish pursed his lips. 'Really, sir? Preparing for a bolt, eh? I wonder if he was making a proposal to take Miss Tumour with him?'

Melis shrugged. 'I don't suppose we shall ever know now. But let us have a look at your walrus-and-carpenter job upstairs.'

They ascended the stairway to the roof and approached the sandbank, which was now sheeted over. Davis and a single detective were up there, and at a word from Devenish they took off the covering most carefully. Melis went over to look at the red-stained sand and then raised his eyebrows.

'You didn't see anything out of the way when you first saw this stuff on Monday, inspector?'

'No, sir. Whoever did the job did it thoroughly. He must have removed the body, taking care to leave it there till all bleeding had stopped. Then he must have set to work to make the bank as tidy as before.'

'Ever lie down in the sand at the seaside, inspector?'

Devenish smiled faintly. 'I must have done when I was younger, sir.'

'You found sand in your boots and your clothes after, I'll bet. I suppose it is your theory that Mander was either sitting or standing beside this bank—wait a moment! Taking the line of the bullet, he must have been sitting, unless the murderer was standing on the parapet opposite to get height?'

Devenish reflected. 'There is another way it may have happened, sir. Mander would not sit down for fun on a sandbank on a November night. That's obvious. Isn't it quite possible that he knew a man with a gun was after him, and backed slowly across the roof, until he fell over the bank—fell over the edge of it, and sat down I mean—as the shot was fired?'

Melis nodded approvingly. 'That's a good idea. Mander wouldn't shout for help, of course. He would know that he was shut away from help by his own silly private arrangements. He would hope the other man would not shoot. But why should the other man not have fired at first—why wait till he got as far as that? If you suspect Kephim, it was a crime of jealousy. A jealous man does not think out a plan.'

The inspector nodded. 'I can see two possible explanations, though both are speculative. The parapet round this roof is four feet high. Was the murderer driving him back, hoping he would try to climb to safety and fall over? That would, if it came off, suggest that Mander had committed suicide. Or was he a calculating ruffian, who knew that the best place for Mander to fall was on the sand, where the stains could be easily hidden for a time, and the bullet stop out of sight.'

Melis laughed.

'And make it difficult to decide on the manner and method of the murder for a little while till he got away?'

Devenish bit his lip. 'We still have the stray sand difficulty you mentioned. I quite see that. Our only help is our knowledge that the murderer may not only have been in the building for some considerable time, but may even have concealed himself till the store opened next day. That is to say, he had seven to eight hours to clear up the mess. It was only when he was actually in the lifts, or the departments below, that he was in danger of being seen.'

Melis hummed a disjointed tune for a few moments. 'Then if Mander fell in the sand here, the other fellow must have taken considerable trouble to clear the clothes of the grains. His own clothes would not matter so much. He could shake those out at home.'

Devenish stared about him. 'That is true, sir. Let me think— There are all kinds of gadgets about in the flat below. Do you mind if we go below, sir?'

Melis assenting, they descended to the flat, and rang for the butler.

'Got a vacuum-cleaner up here?' Devenish asked.

'Certainly, sir,' replied the man, with a puzzled air.

'Use it lately here?'

'No, sir. You see, you gentlemen locked up the flat, and—'

'I know that, but don't you use it for your own quarters?'

To the amusement of both, the butler disclosed a fact that they might have known; that domestics, if left to themselves, often cherish a foolish grudge against labour-saving appliances. It appeared that the vacuum-cleaner was not used by them.

'Where is it kept then?' asked Devenish.

The butler took them to a large built-in cupboard in a passage and produced an electric vacuum-cleaner.

'This is it, sir.'

Devenish promptly lifted and detached the bag which contains the dust collected. 'It isn't full, sir,' he said to Melis.

'I emptied it, of course,' said the butler.

'But not since Sunday,' remarked Devenish. He took out his pen-knife, dismissed the butler, and carried the bag into the dining-room where he laid it on the table.

'I may be wrong, sir,' he said, 'but it seems to me that this thing would clean clothes more effectually than any amount of brushing, and it wouldn't scatter atoms of sand about as a brush would. I think I had better open it.'

'Bright idea, my dear fella,' said Melis. 'Dissect the bag by all means. Any grains will show on this nice polished mahogany table.'

Working very carefully, the inspector slit up the bag, all round the seams, and decanted its inconsiderable contents on the table. Then he shook it lightly, and laid it on a corner of the mahogany.

'Not quite a beach, but sand enough,' said Melis, patting him gently on the back. 'There is half an ounce here with other matter.'

Devenish looked eager now. 'That's right. It is sand, and some of it reddish, too, sir. Have a look at it through your magnifier, while I see what some of the other stuff is.'

Melis studied a quantity of the sand, and Devenish, after a survey of the mixed dust and fibres from the bag, left him and made a tour of the other rooms of the flat, coming back to find Melis sitting smoking and reflecting at the table.

'Putty medal for you, Devenish,' he said as the inspector came in, 'but what made you hop up just now?'

Devenish sorted the dust again, and put apart from the rest a few fibres of wool.

'Though Mr Mander went to lunch with Mrs Peden-Hythe that day, sir, we know that he was dressed in tweeds and had not dressed for dinner when he came back. Now the kind and colour of these wool-fibres suggests his suit. An analysis will probably show that they came from it. With the sand here, I think we can be pretty sure of this point.'

'Callous devil,' said Melis. 'Just sat down as if he were going to tidy up, but, oh, help! Where does the girl in the lift come in?'

Devenish sat down, and went over that point. 'Ten to one the cleaners on Saturday night took up the square of carpet in the lifts and did their job. Evidently they replaced the square that night, or we should have heard of the bloodstain sooner on the Monday.'

'I see that.'

'But the carpet square was not down in the lift when the girl was killed there—if she was killed there. If it had been, the stain would have been on, *not under* the square.'

'Solomon,' murmured Melis, 'I am with you in your judgment—carry on.'

'Which suggests to me that she was not killed in the lift,' said Devenish. 'I cannot imagine the murderer lifting the square, asking the girl to step into the lift, and then killing her.'

'Then the stain was put there to confuse us? Maybe. It could be worked, for though this was not a very bluggy business, Devenish, it was to a certain extent. But all along, as you and I both agree, there is the jealousy feature in this case. We can't get away from it. A murderer did hold his victims up to obloquy by sticking them in fancy-dress in the window. If killing Mander was the job intended, and the girl only an accidental victim, there would be no reason to put her there too.'

Devenish nodded. 'There is this chance, sir, that Mander and the girl were lovers. Also, if Mander was meditating a bolt, either because he foresaw eventual failure for this place, or had intended all along to scoop a pile and get off, he may have fixed it with her to go with him. Wasn't there something in the papers about Mr Mander going to South America to look into the possibilities of starting another establishment there? I think there was. At any rate, for one reason or another, Miss Tumour came here to visit Mander.'

'I'll grant it. Go on!'

'Say she is in this flat when a bell rings. It would have to be the bell either of the door at the back or the one opposite the lift. It would certainly not be one that would call the butler.'

'Not at night—no.'

'Well, Mander perhaps tells Miss Tumour to hide out of the way. He goes down, or goes to the other door on this level. Say he meets at the door a man with a gun. This man makes him open under threat of firing. Mander has to admit him to the flat. They have a parley up here, probably a scene.'

'Very likely, if it ended in shooting.'

'Very well, sir. Either Mander takes his visitor up to the flat roof, or bolts, and tries to escape up there. He is followed, and Miss Tumour, hearing the noise of the altercation, and the running footsteps, comes out, and follows. When she gets up there, Mander has backed on to the sand, and falls over it. The man shoots him. Perhaps the girl gives a cry, and the murderer knows he is discovered. He gives chase, and stabs her. In the dark he might strike at random, lower than a man would in daylight—as we know in the small of the back. If he is the jealous lover, he would then discover who Mander's visitor was, and that would account for his later action in sticking both in the window.'

'I believe you did it yourself, Devenish,' said Melis. 'If we can trust our writers of detective fiction, detectives are a most dangerous and deceitful lot!'

# CHAPTER XI

THE afternoon of the day that found Mr Melis and Inspector Devenish on the roof of Mander's Stores also found Mr Kephim taking tea in Mrs Hoe's flat. The Stores, at the request of Mr Hay and the auditor, had not been reopened that day, as promised by Devenish, but were not to begin business again until the following Monday. Everyone agreed that the establishment would lose nothing by the tragedy, for half London was determined to shop at the first opportunity in the place which had witnessed the event. 'Mander had such a genius for *réclame* that he couldn't help advertising the Stores when he died!' said a minor wit.

Whether it was that his love for the dead woman had turned to hate, or that Mrs Hoe's attractive sympathy was helpful, Mr Kephim seemed to be in better spirits that day, though he was actually disturbed in mind.

'A man is watching me everywhere,' he said fretfully, as he ate a little cake.

'I have a strong suspicion that a woman is doing the same for me,' she replied, smiling faintly, 'but I suppose it is part of the routine.'

He looked almost resentful. 'Do you mean to say that they are justified in thinking I may be guilty?'

'Not guilty—no,' she nibbled a cake too, and dropped her long eyelashes as she spoke, 'but they have to do it, you know. Everyone connected with the Stores—'

'But you're not connected with them,' he interrupted.

'I was a friend of Effie's,' she said.

He laughed bitterly. 'I was a—friend of Effie's.'

'And they're watching you, aren't they? It's natural.'

Kephim asked her if he might smoke, and lit up. 'I might have been jealous if I had known.'

'Didn't you know, suspect even a little?' she remarked.

He stared at her. 'No, I didn't. What an odd thing to say.'

'I don't think I was a friend of hers, or of yours,' said the little widow solemnly. 'I did suspect once or twice, but I said nothing. Do you think I ought to have done?'

Kephim was not looking at her. Devenish, if he had been an invisible spectator, would have said that, if Mrs Hoe was not a friend of the man's, it was because she wanted to be something more—*was* already something more in mind and hope.

'I wonder,' said Kephim, puffing out a cloud of smoke and staring into it as it floated up, 'if she was like that; marriage wouldn't have helped. I am an odd fellow in some ways. It seems funny telling you, but this has killed it—killed it dead as dead,' he added rather vaguely.

'What?' she asked, absent-mindedly reaching for his cup and refilling it.

'I was madly in love with her. People knowing how I feel now—if anyone could know—would say it wasn't real love. Love, they say, goes on and on, even if you get smacked in the face, cheated and beaten—I don't believe it, I never did.'

'Oh, that's just convention,' she murmured, watching him. 'I don't believe it either. Most of the world is pacifist nowadays; in love and war. I admit I like to hit back. Even in the courts they ask if the witness is not vindictive. Vindictive? As if it was a crime. If other people kept off one's toes, one would have nothing to be vindictive about.'

He hardly seemed to be listening to her. 'No, when I heard that, and knew what she had done, it all went. She got what she was asking for. It sounds beastly to say it, but there it is. She got what she was asking for. I was ready to let her walk over me. She could have had everything she wanted then. Now I am not even sorry.'

'No woman is worth it,' said Mrs Hoe. 'Do you think she could have fooled someone else too?'

'Mander? But it couldn't have been murder and suicide. The police are sure of that.'

'But anyone else—someone you don't even know,' she persisted. 'I think it possible. For I don't know who could have killed her.'

He shrugged. 'I don't know either. But I think the police are making a mistake when they say they don't think that gyrocopter landed on the roof. How do they know? No one heard a shot, but there was a shot fired—'

'Hardly anyone lives in Gaffikin Street,' she said; 'you know that. If it had been the old days of living in—'

'I know. And then people think any bang is a burst tyre somewhere, but according to Cane there were marks of tyres on the roof. The inspector told him so. And an engine was heard running. Who can swear that fellow Webley didn't come over.'

She shook her head. 'He's rather a mystery, isn't he?'

'I don't know much about it. Cane says he is evidently a mechanical genius, though an ignorant man. You know what Mander did. He sucked people's brains. He would have let us all down later, as I see now. He stole what he couldn't get decently,' he added with bitterness.

'But this man Webley?' she hinted discreetly.

Kephim pursed his lips for a moment, then noticed the tea in his cup and drank it before he resumed. 'Mander couldn't have invented that gyrocopter. I often wondered about that. Just after I joined, he took me for a drive in his car to talk things over. We broke down, and I'm hanged if he knew what to do. He fiddled about a bit, and then got a man from the garage.'

'Go on,' said Mrs Hoe eagerly as he paused.

'Well, I mean to say, couldn't Webley have invented it?'

'What?'

'Why not. That's what I think. Cane thinks so too. Webley

would have no money for experiments. Mander could buy him cheap, and tell him to keep his mouth shut about it. He's not the first inventor choused out of a patent, and not knowing how to prove his claim. Mander would have seen to that before he took out patents.'

'Even then—' said his companion timidly.

'Someone did it,' said Kephim, as if in a sort of desperation. 'You see that. They may say there is an adequate motive in jealousy. Isn't there one if a man invents a famous machine and gets cheated over it? I should say there was.'

'I wish I had thought of that and told the detective when he came to see me,' murmured Mrs Hoe sympathetically. 'I shall if he comes again. Uneducated people are so, shall I say, unrestrained. They see red when we would keep control of ourselves.'

'There's only the question of—Effie,' said Kephim, looking at her furtively. 'Why should he kill Effie?'

Mrs Hoe blushed slightly. 'If it worries you to talk about her, do let us drop it.'

He reddened. 'It doesn't. I told you I had no feelings about her now. None! What I mean is this. I am worried about being followed. I suppose innocent people have been arrested before now. If I could only think of some way to explain why she was killed, it would relieve my mind. I wasn't doing any harm. It was she got me into this mess.'

'You? Why, you wouldn't kill a fly,' said Mrs Hoe.

'I wouldn't have killed her, though I suppose I should have felt like it, if I had been the man in the flat.'

'It couldn't have been another woman, I suppose?' she asked.

'Carried them down and put them in the window? But what do you think? If it was Webley who did it, as I think, what motive could he have?'

Mrs Hoe thought silently for a few minutes. 'Unless he was afraid he had been seen by Effie. She was in the flat, I suppose?'

He bit his lip. 'Yes. We can be sure of that. Curse Mander! He would get anything he coveted by hook or crook.'

'Does that idea help?'

He nodded. 'It seems simple, but I never thought of that. You mean that an eye-witness would have to be made away with?'

She looked at him narrowly. 'That is what I think. It's happened a good many times before. I suppose people think they may as well be hanged for a sheep as a lamb.'

He made a gesture of distaste. 'Don't talk about it.'

She looked sympathetic again. 'I was deceived about Effie,' she observed. 'Really, I never thought her capable of it. It makes one wonder why she accepted you.'

Kephim frowned. 'That is in my mind all the time. Was it rank cruelty or what? Now I remember, she asked me not to tell Mander at once. She said she would tell him later. It didn't strike me as odd at the time.'

Mrs Hoe pursed her lips. 'I can't explain it.'

'Look at the Stores—still shut up,' he said suddenly. 'There is some trouble. The auditor and Mr Hay were down. There's a rumour that Mander had made a tremendous bloomer and intended to bolt.'

Mrs Hoe started. 'That's funny. I remember now—I don't suppose it has anything to do with it—'

'What has?'

'A little while ago she asked me if I knew anything about South America,' she said softly. 'I thought it was just curiosity.'

'He was going there on a business trip,' said Kephim. 'South America! It's the place they do bolt to.'

'I couldn't believe that,' said Mrs Hoe.

'That's it,' he said, rather shrilly. 'I had got her to half promise to marry me a year ago. She hadn't met Mander then. Naturally I was keen and eager. I wanted her to fix it up. I suppose she just did it to keep me quiet at last.'

'You really think she would have gone with him to South America?'

He looked convinced. 'What can I think? But if anything

was wrong, and he was going out there, I do believe it. I expect they were both laughing in their sleeves at me.'

He scowled into vacancy, and then mopped his forehead with his handkerchief. Mrs Hoe spoke soothingly.

'I shouldn't worry too much. It can't affect you. After all, you were in Regent's Park that night. It's a pity you can't get a witness, of course, but in any case, how could you have got in? I am thinking now of what the police would say to themselves.'

He nodded. 'I suppose one could have got in, but I didn't.'

'How?'

He reflected. 'Mander must have had the flat all to himself. If anyone rang, eh? He would have to ignore it, or come down. Say it was an important telegram. And there are no people living in the buildings at either side of the back lane where we load.'

'But he wouldn't let anyone in who was dangerous,' she said, her eyes fixed curiously on his face.

'Well, what could he say if it had been me?' Kephim asked. 'I'm not supposed to be dangerous. I'm not dangerous, if it comes to that. Or, if it was a dangerous man, he might threaten.'

She nodded. 'What are you going to say if you are questioned at an inquiry?'

'I can only tell them what I did. It wasn't my fault that I saw no one.'

She leaned closer. 'It was lucky that Mr Mander never invited you to the flat. I mean if you had been known to go there—'

'I've never been in it until I went in with that inspector.'

'I thought you knew all about it?'

'I did in a way,' he said hurriedly. 'Cane told me, and I had heard something about it when the place was building. 'It is all second-hand my information, I can assure you.'

Mrs Hoe looked relieved. 'I hope you will come and see me whenever you feel hipped,' she said.

'If I stay in town, I shall be glad to,' he replied, 'but no one knows what will turn up next. If there is anything wrong, they may make a change. I suppose Mander's death breaks contracts. Mine was with him, not with a backer, and, as you know, there was no company.'

'What would you do in that case?'

'I might go abroad,' he said. 'I had an offer to go to Hildred's in Buenos Ayres before I got the offer from Mander.'

'South America too?' murmured Mrs Hoe.

He looked at her uneasily. 'Don't say anything about that. I see what you mean. But, hang it all, I am not going to bolt. When I go, everyone will know about it.'

'Of course it's quite different,' she agreed, as he got up, 'but don't forget your promise.'

'You have helped me a lot,' he said, smiling again as he shook hands. 'I must remember what you said about a possible eye-witness. Ought I to put it to Devenish too that I never suspected what was going on? You have no cause for jealousy if you don't know.'

She pressed his hand warmly. 'Of course you should. But it is absurd—to think that they would suspect you, in any case.'

Kephim nodded. She seemed to have cheered him up. 'That's what I think. Well, *au revoir*.'

Mrs Hoe showed him out, then came back to sit down. She looked a little puzzled, and a little worried at first. Then her face cleared, and she smiled.

# CHAPTER XII

MRS PEDEN-HYTHE arrived at the Stores on the afternoon of the day Melis and Devenish had their first conference. The auditor had come and gone again, but Mr Hay was there, and he vouched for the lady to the policeman on the door, and led her into Mr Mander's private room.

'Another conference, Devenish,' said Melis, who had again been helping Devenish attack the problem of the roof. 'I really should be back to deal with the work which is my job, but this is too attractive.'

'What do you think she wants here, sir?' the inspector asked as they took a lift down.

Melis laughed and shrugged. 'She may be anxious about her precious son, or, as you hinted lately, about her money. We'll tell her, I think, the tip we got from the passport office today.'

With Mr Hay, a dry anxious little man, at the head of the table, and Mr Melis at the other, Devenish modestly faced the wealthy woman across Mander's expensive piece of furniture. Melis languished a little, as was his habit. Devenish waited for a lead. Mr Hay, after a glance at all the faces, gave a dry cough.

'I am afraid we have established the fact that Mr Mander was—ahem—speculating outrageously,' he said. 'There is quite a considerable sum that we cannot account for.'

Melis woke up. 'We hear today that Mr Mander recently procured two passports. The first was quite in order. I mean it was said openly—announced that he was going on a business trip to South America.'

'He told me so,' said Mrs Peden-Hythe. 'He made it rather clear that there was a profitable opening there for another Store.'

'Too clear,' said Melis, leaning forward, 'but, as I say, that was all right. The second passport was made out in the name of Miss Linkton, his secretary—'

'But Mr Schofield—' she began.

'Absolutely,' said Melis. 'Mr Schofield is his secretary, and there is no Miss Linkton employed here.'

'But surely he wouldn't have dared do that?' cried Mrs Peden-Hythe.

'I don't know that there was much daring required—only a certain amount of expedition. Our passport office, though from the passport formulæ one would imagine it almost fatherly, is not much interested in us as travellers. I cannot believe them aware, for example, that Miss Tumour, a buyer here, might go as Miss Linkton—a secretary.'

Mrs Peden-Hythe reddened. 'Then it was that woman?'

Melis nodded. 'A really satisfactory passport photograph for once. One could have recognised her from it. There does not seem much doubt that Mr Mander had arranged to vanish—and not unconsoled.'

Mr Hay nodded. 'Fortunately for us, I think we may be able to trace and recover most of the money. I hope so indeed. It is an ill wind that blows nobody any good,' he added, with his best bromidic manner.

For the last minute Mrs Peden-Hythe had been looking at Devenish. 'The inspector here,' she said with slight acerbity, 'has been worrying my son, Jameson.'

'As little as possible, I am sure,' remarked Melis blandly. 'Devenish is one of my most respected aides, I assure you.'

'But why at all?'

Melis smiled. 'We put everything in our show down to "information received". We hear that Mr Peden-Hythe has a strong dislike for the dead man. That's nothing out of the way, of course. A dozen people may have hated him. But having set on foot a modest inquiry, Mr Jameson Peden-Hythe appears to have forgotten where he went last Sunday night. I hope you don't think that we attach too great a significance to the fact?'

She looked at Devenish. 'You saw him at his club, he tells me. I think he gave you a reason.'

'Yes, madam,' said Devenish.

'I should like to know myself where he went, but the idea that it could have any connection with Mr Mander's death is too preposterous,' she cried.

Tidings had come into the place that day, and Melis gently unfolded a part of them, while the inspector remained silent.

'We have an idea that Mr Jameson Peden-Hythe was in the laneway at the back of this place on Sunday night,' he said. 'That is of no importance in itself. But—' he felt in his waistcoat pocket and produced a silver match-box—'the initials are "J.P-H".'

She took the box, her lips tightening. 'I don't recognise this. Where did you say it was found?'

'In the laneway, where they load the vans.'

'And from which there is a stairway to Mr Mander's flat,' added the inspector.

She stared at him angrily. 'Even if this is my son's, it may be that he called, or thought of calling, to see Mr Mander.'

'May merely have thought of calling,' murmured Melis. 'That is my impression, but you see where this find leads us. Routine and general inquiries with us are like eggs-and-bacon at breakfast. We hardly take notice of them, as long as they remain routine. But whenever we come to the particular, much as we regret it, we have to take some action.'

She had courage, and did not wince. 'I am sure it can be explained.'

'I am sure it can. But you see our difficulty. Mr Jameson Peden-Hythe cannot remember where he went. I rather hope that you—knowing him so well, shall we say?—might help.'

Mrs Peden-Hythe got up. 'I shall see him at once. Will you come with me, Mr Hay? I think it could be put more strongly to him by you.'

'Certainly, if you wish it,' said the lawyer, rising.

Mrs Peden-Hythe returned the box to Melis, who pocketed it. She was pale now, but she put the best face she could on the situation and gave nothing away.

'Plucky woman!' said Melis when she had gone.

Devenish assented. 'She may get more out of Jameson than I could. It shows you how much he hated Mander, if she gets the wind up like that.'

'I wanted to see if she would,' said Melis, preparing to go. 'She had no reason to drag him in, but she did. Do you think, Devenish, that he really went up to the flat that night?'

'I couldn't say. He may have done,' replied the inspector.

When the assistant-commissioner had gone, he wandered down to the department where the sporting arms were kept. One thing had struck him from the very beginning: the fact that the Mauser pistol found below was only loaded with one shell, the one which had been fired. It suggested a man who was a crack shot, and very sure of his shooting, but even that could not be taken as proven.

Sergeant Davis joined him there presently, and found him hunting assiduously among boxes of sporting ammunition and taking the greatest care to replace everything exactly as he found it. Beneath a heap of other boxes and cardboard containers, he presently came upon a small flat case.

'This looks like it, Davis,' he said cheerfully as he withdrew the object. 'You can see there was not much sale for Mauser ammunition—dust of ages on it, what?'

'There's a box of cartridges under it has been broken,' said the sergeant.

'Oh, good! So it has. These are twelve-bore cartridges loaded with No. 6. They have sold a loose two dozen or so.'

'Twelve-bore wouldn't fit the pistol, sir.'

'No. And Mr Mander wasn't killed with a charge of small shot. You've made a find all the same, sergeant. If cartridges were sold out of the box below, how did they get out the box without knocking the dust off this pistol ammunition?'

Davis looked pleased. 'Never thought of that, sir. But surely that case is as sold by the manufacturers—unbroken?'

Devenish had been weighing the box on his palm, now he lifted it above his head, and pointed.

'Just room for one shell to slip out,' he said. 'It would be put down at the next stock-taking as damaged in transit, I expect. But that little hole was made by someone who knew the way the shells would lie in the box.'

'Then he must have put dust on the box,' said the sergeant admiringly. 'He seems to have thought of everything.'

'Except the fact that Webley wouldn't know his way about down here. It may be useful to fake one false clue, but it is overdoing it to fake two that don't agree. Pack this up, and have it sent for examination by our people.'

There was packing paper and string in plenty at their disposal, and while Davis carefully packed the find, Devenish put a question.

'Have you any news of Kephim?'

'Well, sir, he has gone to Mrs Hoe's flat again. I wonder if that woman is in love with him, sir?'

Devenish thought it over. 'Maybe. Bit catty what she said about her dead friend when I saw her. Still, I can't see her hand in this yet. Anything about the watchman?'

Davis tied the last knot. 'He's an old regular. He was apprenticed as a youth to a blacksmith, joined the Royal Engineers, and was in Signals when the war broke out. He was wounded in 1915, came home, went out later the same year, and had a good army record. There is only one thing about him that seems important—the nature of the wound he had. He was hit in the head by a bit of a bomb, and suffered from insomnia. From what I can gather he wouldn't have stayed in hospital as long as he did only for that.'

Devenish nodded. 'I see. It would be useful to get the opinion of his civilian doctor. Look that up, please. I can't believe that someone came and went on the Sunday night without his hearing a sound. Unless the after-effects of that wound of his make him suffer from drowsiness. The cutting of the microphone connection, if he did it, would be an attempt to give him a chance for a snooze between rounds.'

'Nice sort of watchman if he is like that, sir.'

'Quite. But if you and I could see *every* watchman *every* night I bet we should discover a fair percentage taking forty winks! I only see one objection to that. The murderer would not have taken the risk of bringing the bodies down, if he had not known of the watchman's weakness.'

'I expect Mann is on the "panel", and I'll make inquiries,' the sergeant agreed. 'Now what are we going to do about that sand upstairs?'

Devenish pondered. 'I think tomorrow we'll get Kephim and Cane and Webley here, and take them on the roof. You and the other fellows can uncover, but make it look as if you were just starting to work. A jog to the nerves sometimes helps to disclose things.'

Davis assented eagerly. 'That's a good idea, sir. Well, I'll take this to the Yard, and then get on with the inquiry about the watchman.'

'Do—but wait a moment. Any reports about Mr Peden-Hythe?'

'Nothing important. He goes about town as usual, and paid one call. That was to Sir William Lefort's. But he didn't stay there a minute. He came out looking black.'

'What is there at Sir William's to produce this blackness?' said the inspector, then: 'All right, Davis. Run along!'

But Devenish did not leave the department when his sergeant went. He looked thoughtfully at the broken box of sporting cartridges, and wondered.

'I don't know much about buying and selling,' he said to himself, 'but it seems to me odd that they should break a box of a hundred cartridges, sell some, and then replace the box under some stock that is not often called for.

He carefully removed the box, and detached the lid; starting slightly when he saw that the ammunition lay higgledy-piggledy, not arranged as the manufacturer's packers would have placed it. Taking it to a counter, he removed the cartridges and came suddenly on three sparking-plugs.

'The beggar must have been born in gloves,' he said, handling his find carefully. 'Still, he may have made a slip somewhere.'

He fished out a pocket insufflator, and dusted the surfaces of the plugs. Then he went in search of a man who was still painstakingly photographing in the building, and brought him in to take shots.

'N.G. I'm afraid,' he said, when the man had done, 'but develop those as quickly as you can, and we'll make sure.'

He had done as much as he could in that department, and was going to the lift giving access to the passage outside Mander's flat, when a policeman came up to say that a Mr Peden-Hythe wanted to see him.'

'Bring him here, please,' said Devenish, rather pleased with himself. 'I expected him to call today.'

Jameson Peden-Hythe looked much more alive than when Devenish had last seen him. The expression on his face was not one of alarm, but a mixture of resentment and sulky suspicion.

'Someone told me you'd got a match-box of mine,' he said without ceremony, when the policeman had brought him up, and retired again.

'At any rate a box with your initials, sir.'

'Found behind this bally show, eh?'

'Exactly, sir.'

'Why the devil didn't you tell me before, then?'

'Because it only came into our possession early this morning.'

Jameson glowered. 'What do you make of that?'

Devenish smiled. 'It looks suspicious, sir.'

'That's rot! At the most it means I was behind his place.'

'At the best, it means that, sir. But you see, you didn't remember where you had been.'

'Well I was in the lane behind.'

'Your memory is improving, sir. Pity you didn't say so before.'

'That's a silly remark! I didn't say I was in here. I said I had been behind here.'

'May I ask why?'

'Because I wanted to have a row with Mander, if you want to know.'

'You remember that too? Does it not strike you that in an inquiry your loss of memory would seem rather suspicious?'

The young man bit his lip. 'I rang his damn bell, and no one came. So I cleared out and went to my club.'

'I am afraid, sir, that after these details I can hardly take your word for it that you were too drunk on Sunday night to know what you were doing.'

'I'm not asking you to,' was the surprising reply. 'I don't want my private business shouted over the bally town, that's all.'

'We do not disclose the evidence of witnesses, unless it is necessary. You mean to say that you were somewhere that evening that you do not wish known?'

'That's it.'

'Where?'

'Sir William Lefort's.'

'With what object?'

Peden-Hythe reddened and then looked sheepish. 'Er—well, Sir William's daughter and I—' he stopped.

'Am I supposed to believe this, sir? The butler said you had not been there.'

'So he would. I told him to. Fact is, Sir William is a bit stuffy about it.'

There was something so genuinely shamefaced and incoherent and awkward about the young man that Devenish smiled involuntarily.

'Come along up to the flat, sir, and then you can sit down quietly and tell me about it,' he said.

Once in the flat, and ensconced in an easy chair, Jameson

began. He spoke in his staccato fashion, and often repeated the same thing, in ever more clumsy words, but what he actually wanted to tell Devenish was that he had fallen in love with Miss Lefort, and there had been something on her side too, he thought. Then, at Goodwood, earlier in the year, he had met some old pals and got 'squiffy', and Sir William and his daughter had happened to see him.

Sir William had forbidden him the house, and even the girl had appeared dubious about keeping the thing up after that. Being himself 'simply potty about her' he had not given up hope. On the particular Sunday of Mander's death, he had rushed up to town when that 'bounder' visited Parston Court. He knew Sir William was out of town, called at his house in the evening, and was told Miss Lefort was seeing some private show of pictures and would be back for dinner. He had announced to the butler his intention of waiting till she came, and had in fact declared that he would stay whether the butler objected or not. A fiver had helped, with a promise to the man that, if there was any subsequent trouble about the visit, he would say that he had refused to go.

But Miss Lefort did not return to dinner, and he suspected that the butler knew where she was, and had telephoned to her mentioning the name of the caller.

If the rest of his story was true, it proved that he entertained a fatuous affection for a girl who had already decided that his habits made him an impossible husband. It also proved that he was certainly tipsy when he visited the house. Not even the keenest lover in his sober senses would sit down in somebody else's house, and remain there till after ten o'clock in the hope that the girl would see him against her wish. A fiver had bribed the butler to silence about the visit, and no doubt the young man was soberer when he left the house than when he entered it.

'You left the house in a pretty bad temper. Where did you go then?' asked Devenish.

Jameson scowled. 'I ask you! Wouldn't you have been rampin' mad?'

'That may be, sir. But where did you go?'

'Go? I wanted to kick somebody, and Mander was the only fella I knew wanted kickin' badly. I went over, and rang his bally bell. It was dark as Hades in that lane, and I lost my beastly match-box trying to find the way to the door.'

'Did you keep on ringing?'

'You bet I did.'

Devenish looked at him thoughtfully. 'As your memory for details seems to have improved, perhaps you can tell me about what time this was?'

Jameson nodded. ''Bout eleven I should say.'

'And you saw no one, and heard no one?'

'Not a soul.'

Devenish excused himself and rang up Sir William Lefort's house. The butler replied, and asked who it was.

'Inspector Devenish of Scotland Yard,' snapped the other. 'Why did you not tell me that Mr Peden-Hythe called on Sunday evening?'

There was a short silence at the other end, then a chastened voice murmured that its owner hadn't liked to make trouble, as he had seen that the gentleman was not quite himself.

'How long did he stay?' asked Devenish.

'I couldn't get him to go, sir,' replied the butler. 'Sir William was away, as I told you, and Miss Anita was out, and it was rather difficult. At ten, sir, Miss Anita rang up. She said I was to tell the gentleman that she had gone away for the weekend. He called again since, sir.'

Devenish thanked him, and rang off. He knew now that there was some truth in the young man's story, though there might have been time for him to kill Mander between his leaving Sir William's and his arrival at his club.

'Well, sir, if you have been put to any trouble,' he remarked as he sat down again, 'it is your own fault.'

'I'm not blamin' you,' said Jameson, 'but, I say, what a rotten job yours is. I shouldn't care to spend my life spyin'!'

Devenish shrugged. 'Murder is a pretty foul affair. We don't take it so lightly at the Yard, as some people do.'

'No gyves for mine then?' asked Jameson with an air of relief.

'Not at present, sir,' said Devenish, 'but I should advise you to get rid of that pistol of yours, sir.'

This was sheer bluff, but it worked. Jameson started.

'It was the one I had in the jolly old war,' he said hastily. 'You think I had better sell it?'

'Much better, sir. Now I have a lot to do, so I will wish you good-day. You can take yourself down in the lift.'

When Peden-Hythe had taken himself off, Devenish went on the roof, and had a chat with the man on duty there.

Before he had left Scotland Yard, he had arranged that the police-surgeon, who had first examined the bodies, should meet him on the roof over the flat. He was still talking to the detective when the surgeon came up the stairs and greeted him.

'Well, inspector, what is it now?'

Devenish went across. 'You've heard that we suspect Mander was shot up here, tripped over that bank of sand, and provided the murderer with the means of temporarily covering up. That seems to work out all right, but the death of that girl bothers me—particularly the question of how that wound was inflicted. Did it seem to you one that required great violence?'

The surgeon lit a cigarette while he thought it over. 'Can't say that it did,' he replied at length. 'The blade was long and sharp.'

'Did it strike you that there had been any struggle between her and the murderer?'

'It seemed to me that she had been subjected to a certain amount of compulsion. There were bruises, not very extensive or serious, on both upper arms. They gave me the impression that someone had held her.'

'Standing behind or in front of her?'

'Behind. That is quite certain. The marks show that.'

'If a man wanted to kill her, why should he stab her in the small of the back?'

'I don't know. It would be a chancy business unless he knew his job. That kind of mark on both arms suggests someone pushing someone else before him, and taking care they went the way he wanted.'

'Do you mind trying it on the dog?' said Devenish, and motioned to the detective to come over. 'The doctor here is going to pin your arms from behind,' he told the man.

The surgeon took the man by the upper arms and gave him a push forward. 'Quick march, my good man! Where do we stop, Devenish?'

'Now, sir, if you don't mind,' replied the inspector, 'I'll tell you what your attitude suggested. It might be that the murderer got hold of the girl below and pushed her up the steps before him on to this roof.'

'That's my idea.'

'Or,' said Devenish more slowly, 'since we have to assume that she came here of her own accord, and was with her lover, it might be that she was used as a shield.'

The surgeon started. 'That sounds a posh idea, my dear fella. Only if you stab your human shield, you lose it! How do you get over that?'

Devenish nodded, and moved away to look over the parapet. He stood there staring into vacancy for two minutes, then came back looking happier.

'We'll stage the scene if you don't mind, doctor. Our friend here had better be Mander, as he can stand a fall better,' the detective grinned at that, and the surgeon laughed, 'and you will be the girl. Don't object, do you?'

'Not a bit, if it helps.'

'Very well. You must get a pencil or something for the knife—yes, that will do. Jones here must have that. He's Mander. And we'll have to use the other bank of sand for the fall. Now I am the murderer. I have an automatic. My torch here will represent that. Mander and the girl have retreated to this roof. I am coming up after. Mander funks it. Either he counts on the chivalry of the intruder, or he is so mad with fear he doesn't care who suffers as long as he escapes.'

'I begin to see my cue, Devenish.'

'At any rate, once up here, he gets hold of the girl by her arms, and presents her as a target for the enemy.'

'But she wasn't shot.'

Devenish shook his head impatiently. 'I know that. Mander, we'll say, has the knife or dagger. He can't hold the girl with that in his hand. He sticks it in his pocket temporarily. As he backs on to the sand, she wriggles free, and he whisks out the knife again. Let's have that.'

The detective promptly got behind the surgeon, dropped the pencil he held into his pocket, and gripped the man before him by the upper arms, and backed away towards the sand, while Devenish followed up with the torch presented like a weapon.

'Now wriggle away, sir,' said the inspector.

The surgeon wriggled free, and stopped. 'Stage directions please?'

'It's dark up here. You come forward a yard, and find me coming at you like this,' he strode forward as the surgeon approached. 'Now you jump hurriedly back—have that knife ready to defend yourself, Jones! As Mander, you have the knife in your hand. You trip on the sand. Then the doctor, representing the girl, falls over you, and is accidentally stabbed.'

'It's just possible it did happen in that way,' said Devenish, as the others rose and dusted themselves after the experiment; 'our only trouble is the cry. They must have made the dickens of a noise, and no one seems to have heard it.'

'This place isn't residential,' replied the surgeon, 'and some people don't hear cries when they get to sleep. Besides this is high up. I won't swear it could not happen.'

'Then there was that engine running,' said the other. 'If Jones here would cut down into the flat, and we made the deuce of a squeal, he could hear what it sounded like below. Also he might ask Mander's butler to listen from the servants' premises. But people listening for a sound are twice as sharp as those who are not listening for one and are asleep when it comes.'

Devenish nodded. Jones went below, and the test was made. Jones came up again in ten minutes.

'It didn't sound very loud to me, and I couldn't place the direction well either, sir,' he said. 'The butler heard it faintly, but he says he would have thought it the squeal of a brake.'

'Well, it is a theory that I must try to work out,' said Devenish. 'She could have run back on the knife, or Mander fallen with the knife sticking up in his hand. Would her weight do it?'

'It would,' said the surgeon.

## CHAPTER XIII

WHEN the night watchman turned up at ten, he found the indefatigable inspector waiting for him, and expressed some surprise.

'I was only wondering if this sleepy trouble of yours still bothers you,' said Devenish blandly. 'You see, it is going to be rather awkward for you if we know that you were on the alert all night, and still insist that you saw nothing.'

The man lost colour a little. 'But I didn't see anything, sir.'

'Then you must have been asleep, that is all there is to it.'

The watchman bit his lip. 'What do you mean by my sleepiness anyway, sir?'

'I heard you had been wounded in the head during the war, and it occurred to me that it might have left some unpleasant aftermath. But, of course, if it is not so, I need not question you on that point any further. I will go on to ask you a few more troublesome questions.'

'Am I speaking to you in confidence, sir? This may be a serious thing for me.'

'I hope you realise that. I can only say that I advise you to tell the truth. At the Yard we make it as easy as we can for people who tell what they know without frills. We deal with embroiderers in another way.'

'Well then, you're right, sir.'

'I hope I am. Go ahead. Tell me what is your trouble.'

The man licked dry lips. 'I sleep badly, sir, and in daytime I can't sleep at all. I can't do nothing for it, though I've tried hard enough. A man can't live without sleeping, sir.'

'As a rule, no,' said Devenish, 'but it was a bit of impudence on your part to come here as a night watchman, knowing your disability. You mean to say that not being able to sleep during your off hours, you go to sleep here when you shouldn't?'

'I am afraid that is it, sir. I don't want to sleep, but I do drop off, and can't help it, when I sit down in my box between rounds.'

'I see. But Mr Mander thoughtfully provided you with a means of helping to keep awake.'

The man coloured. 'Yes, I suppose he did, sir.'

'You know he did. And you took a little pains to see that the gadget couldn't do any harm. But you might have turned off the switch instead of cutting the lead, mightn't you?'

The watchman did not notice the trap in the question. 'Suppose I had been startled and forgot to turn it on again, sir, and someone had seen it?'

'Oh, quite so. So you did cut the lead? Well there is nothing like being honest when you have to. Come now! Who was foolish enough to suggest one of the sleepers of Ephesus for the job of night watchman?'

He saw a startled look in the man's eyes, and then that queer expression that suggests a man trying to think of some evasion.

'I saw Mr Mander, sir, and got it. I have a good army record.'

That betraying expression told Devenish that the man was not telling the truth. 'Are you sure that the head of this big business himself engaged all the staff? Come now. Is it likely? I want to be told exactly what happened, and I have means of finding out, you know.'

'Wait a moment, sir. Do you mean who recommended me?'

The inspector knew it was always wise to let a man choose his own loophole of retreat so long as he got the information required.

'Yes, who recommended you?'

'Mrs Peden-Hythe, sir.'

Devenish regarded him for a little with a thoughtful air. Why had he to screw this out of the man? Was there anything behind it? After a weighty pause he began again.

'Any particular reason why she should have recommended you?'

'Well, it was through Mr Peden-Hythe, sir. He wasn't any too fond of Mr Mander, but he told his mother, and she helped, sir.'

'I see. But how do you come to know Mr Peden-Hythe's private views about the dead man? That strikes me as odd.'

The watchman shuffled his feet. 'Well, sir, I was his batman in the war, if you must know, and a better officer I never want to have.'

Devenish repressed his surprise, and put on a grim look. 'Now we are coming to the truth. But surely the war has been over a number of years? Mr Peden-Hythe's dislike for Mr Mander is a matter of months, I had supposed.'

'Longer than that, sir. Mr Mander was managing clerk to those lawyers down in the country.'

'Grant that it was a year or two, or even three years. That is long after the war. Have you kept in touch with Mr Peden-Hythe?'

The watchman nodded. 'He used to send me a fiver every Christmas, sir, but there was no harm in that, though I ought to have done the giving if there had been anything to give.'

'What do you mean by that?'

'It was him rescued me after the building had been bombed, sir, and near lost his life doing it.'

Devenish was getting to the inner wheels of the machine. 'Well?'

'Well, sir, I was in a job steady till my master died, and his son gave up. I thought of Mr Peden-Hythe, and wrote to him. He spoke of me to the lady, as I told you, and I got the job.'

Devenish pursed his lips. 'Then you have seen Mr Peden-Hythe personally since you got the job?'

'Yes, sir, I called to thank him, and a few times since I went to his club to tell him how I was getting on. He asked me to, sir.'

The inspector looked graver than ever, and his intent stare made the watchman more nervous than before.

'Now look here,' he said. 'You might have told me all this before, and your failure to be straight does not impress me greatly in your favour. You found it convenient to ignore some rather important details. How do you expect me to know that you are telling the truth now?'

'I am, sir. I really am.'

'And suppose you really are; how am I to know that you will answer truthfully the next question I am going to ask? Perjury is a serious business, and you may later have to answer an oath.'

'I'll tell you the truth, sir, whatever it is,' replied the other desperately.

'Very well. Did you see Mr Peden-Hythe inside this store on last Sunday night—in any part of the store, or in the lifts?'

'No, sir. I never did. I'll swear to that. What would he be doing here?'

'We are aware that he rang at the outer bell of Mr Mander's flat that night. Think again! Did you see him or did you not?'

The watchman's look was either startled or frightened. It was hard to tell which. 'I did not, sir,' he cried vehemently; 'I swear I didn't! Mr Peden-Hythe wouldn't murder anyone. He's a good man though he does take a glass too much. Why, I'd sooner be charged with murder myself.'

'No one is charging him with murder,' replied Devenish, seeing that the sottish Jameson must have some good qualities hidden under his affectation of raffish cynicism to have inspired such devotion in his batman, but reflecting too that a murderer may be an angel to those he likes. 'That is your considered answer?'

'It is, sir. I can't say anything else.'

Devenish dismissed him, and walked out, and so home. By nine the next morning he was at the house of the doctor, on whose panel the watchman was, and putting some questions to the middle-aged medico.

'Is it possible that the wound in his head could cause such symptoms as he described to me?' he asked, after he had stated his case.

'The insomnia, yes,' replied the other, 'but very few of my patients who suffer from that complaint complain that they are very drowsy at night.'

'Still, if the man is night watchman—'

'He has not been one very long,' the doctor interrupted. 'Habits once formed are very persistent, and the human being has for centuries been used to sleeping at night. Automatically, we weary as night comes on, partly because we have worked during the day, but partly, I contend, because nature and habit have made us sub-consciously regard night as the time for sleep.'

Devenish nodded. 'I see your point.'

'Then I need not labour it, inspector. The habit of a lifetime of sleeping by day and being awake at night might correct the bias, but if a man only became a night watchman fairly recently, I think the inherited habit would make his insomnia that of the normal man. In other words, if he could not sleep, it would be at night that he could not sleep. As insomnia is largely a nervous complaint, he would be more likely too to sleep during the day, since it was not the time his subconscious mind dictated as the wakeful period.'

Devenish was interested in the theory, but he had to get on with his job. 'I think you are right, sir, but now I want to know if the man complained to you of insomnia?'

The doctor shook his head. 'No.'

'But he has visited you on occasion?'

'About twice. On both occasions he was suffering from what most of my panel complain of—indigestion. To the working classes indigestion appears to be cancer, or heart, or anything but what it is.'

'I wondered,' said Devenish thoughtfully.

'But, wait a moment,' said the doctor, as the detective rose, 'I would not swear that the man has not had insomnia. You must remember that men like him rather regard our class as banded together, and likely to confide in each other. Knowing that he was a watchman, he may have been afraid my conscience would prick me, and lead to my telling his employer.'

'I'll bear that in mind,' said Devenish, thanked his informant, and went off to see Mrs Mann, the watchman's wife. He found her a thin but energetic looking woman, who appeared to be the soul of respectability. She was very well dressed for her class at that time of the morning, and her rooms were furnished very comfortably. In some respects she and her husband seemed to have comforts that did not fit in very well with the pay of a mere night watchman.

'Now, Mrs Mann,' said Devenish, 'I have seen your husband, and he complains that he suffers from insomnia—that is, sleeplessness. It is rather important in the case I am working on to prove that Mann was awake and alert that night.'

'If it wasn't for the sleep he gets during the day,' said Mrs Mann earnestly, 'he couldn't carry on, sir. Honestly he couldn't!' They was bombed at night, and he used to worry me before he got this job, what with him sitting up in a chair when I was in bed, or walking about the floor. Dreadful bad insomnia he had, and that's the truth.'

Devenish now had what he wanted to know, but he was anxious that the woman should not tell her husband exactly what she had said.

'A nasty thing,' he agreed, 'but I think the new surroundings may help him at night. I gather that he feels drowsy then. A change of atmosphere does help us all, you know.'

As he walked off, he was rather pleased with the new facts he had elicited, though they were opposed to his judgment of the character of the man concerned. A lying statement in a murder case does not prove that the liar is a murderer, or even that he is shielding the murderer.

But one thing was fairly proved, that Mann did not sleep at night, but did—though he denied it—get some refreshing sleep by day. The man who suffers from insomnia is lucky if he gets three or four hours sleep in the twenty-four. If he has those hours by day, his wakefulness by night is likely to be accentuated.

'The inference,' said Devenish to himself, 'is that he was wide awake, that he saw or heard something, but is afraid to tell. If he was not concerned in the murder himself, the inference is that he saw someone in the store who was guilty of it, or whom he now suspects of being guilty. The man who may have been here, and to whom he is devoted, is Mr Jameson Peden-Hythe!'

# CHAPTER XIV

Sergeant Davis sat listening to what the inspector had to tell him of his recent discoveries. When Devenish had finished, he raised his eyebrows in surprise, and remarked that it looked fishy.

'Though it may be merely fowl or flesh,' replied Devenish, 'the fact is that I consider there must be some sort of connection between Peden-Hythe and Mann other than the five pound notes at Christmas. The ex-officer would send those in memory of old times, the ex-soldier would naturally call to thank him for getting the job. But why should he visit Peden-Hythe several times since at his club to tell him how he was getting on? What would he have to tell him?'

The sergeant was a trained observer, and a notable man in his rank. 'At a venture, sir, since Mr Peden-Hythe suspected that Mander was going to do his mother down, could he have sent in Mann as a spy?'

'That is what I was wondering,' replied Devenish. 'I saw that Mann's rooms looked pretty comfortable ones, and I suspected a subsidy. But there is a puzzle even in that. What would a night watchman know about money affairs, even if he had a chance to hear of them? And what chance would he have at night, in any case?'

'None at all, sir. You might say a trained accountant, who could be there at night and could get at the office safes and books, would be able to look things over. But then Mr Mander wouldn't put wrong entries in the official books. I hear he had a private set upstairs in his flat.'

'Quite so. That is out of the question. Still, here we have a man who does get some sleep by day but not at night, but who says he cannot sleep by day but does sleep at night when he ought not to. Have you interrogated the watchmen in the other parts of the building?'

'I have, sir. There are three altogether, counting Mann, and I have questioned the other two. As you know, this building for greater safety at night is cut into three sections, with fire-proof doors between. If anyone could open the doors and there was a fire, it would be useless to have them at all. But, as it is, the partitions automatically close when the shop is shut, and not even the watchmen could communicate with each other.'

'I know. Well, what is the explanation of Mann's twisting, unless Peden-Hythe planted him here for some purpose? If it comes to the worst, I must frighten the man a bit. I could find a theory to account for this business, only that evidence we have, of a kind, rules against it.'

'May I hear, sir, what you think could account for it?'

'Yes, I'll tell you. I had an impression at first that Mrs Peden-Hythe might be in love, or have been in love, with Mander. It is easier to screw money out of a middle-aged woman when there is some passion on her side as well as the mere hope of profit. We get cases every other day of women being made fools of like that. Mrs Peden-Hythe, on the other hand, gave me the impression of being very keen about money and very little else.'

Davis screwed up his eyes. 'Take it that she wasn't, sir, but really had made love to the man, how does that work in?'

'More or less easily,' replied Devenish, 'If Jameson, the son, suspected not only that his mother was financially backing a man he hated, and regarded as a sharper, but also that she was in love and likely to make a fool of herself over him, he would naturally want to break the connection.'

'That's true, sir. He wouldn't want Mander as a father-in-law.'

'No. Well, he might also suspect or have information to the effect that his enemy was a bit of a libertine. Elderly women are sometimes over-passionate, but they are always exceedingly jealous when they do fall in love, knowing they are up against youth. Suppose Jameson Peden-Hythe put Mann here to let him know of any goings on in the flat above? It was only at night that Mander cut off access to his part of the flat from his household staff, and it was at night that Miss Tumour visited him—and she may not have been the first!'

Davis beamed. 'That does fit, sir, only for the difficulty of anyone outside the flat hearing or getting to know of what was going on there. It would be a hard nut to crack.'

Devenish agreed. 'Yes, but we know that men who were in the R.E. are often skilled craftsmen. I don't say he was capable of it, or did do it, but suppose Mann went up secretly one night and got a "squeeze" of the key-wards or found out the secret of the lock. If he had a duplicate key made he might get in and spy.'

Davis nodded. 'Yes, he could, sir. Mr Peden-Hythe might have told him Mander was up to some hanky-panky.'

'There is one thing makes me pretty sure that there was more than money in this connection between Mander and Mrs Peden-Hythe,' said Devenish, nodding. 'The son I have been told is a kind of snob. His generosity to Mann here does not affect that point; for a man of that type is naturally disposed to be nice to those who do not, and cannot, claim equality. But he hated Mander on his own showing, and that makes me think part of it came from a fear that his mother—who had already climbed to a certain position by marrying his father—was going to lower the family by marrying the "bounder", as he calls him.'

Davis agreed. 'There is something I can't understand about Mann. He looks a sound, honest sort of fellow, but he was taking pay for a job that he didn't do.'

Devenish smiled. 'But who was his paymaster? Nominally, of course, he was Mander's servant, and owed duty to him. But we know now that Mrs Peden-Hythe was the real person behind these stores, and that is the way her son Jameson would look at it. I can imagine him telling the watchman that he needn't bother about conscientious scruples. If anything went wrong when he was spying, the loss would fall on Mrs Peden-Hythe, and he would be responsible.'

'You mean Mr Jameson?'

'Of course. And it would be true. The man who pays ought to call the tune, even if there is a figurehead in between.'

'But if stock was stolen, the insurance companies would have to pay, sir.'

'Of course, but do you think a chap like Jameson would think of that? I don't suppose it ever occurred to him.'

There was silence for a few moments. Both men were thinking, and neither of them was now concentrating on the young man. Davis spoke first.

'Where are the girl's coat and hat and glove, sir?'

Devenish shrugged. 'Ever since the case opened I have been thinking of that. I have no idea whatever. If I had, I should feel well on my way to getting to the core of the case. But now that you have brought it up, what about looking?'

'Where, sir?'

'In this Store, of course. But we shall have to ring up Mr Kephim to see what the girl wore in the way of a coat and hat.'

Davis managed to get through to Mr Kephim, and handed the receiver to the inspector. Devenish put two questions, then listened gravely for a minute. Then he said: 'Thank you, sir, I am much obliged,' and rang off.

'Bit of luck for us, Davis,' he said with a pleased look to his assistant. 'Kephim says she was wearing a smart new coat of Cumberland tweed, which he described to me. She bought it here in the—but wait a moment. Is that department in this section?'

'I think it is, sir. I saw one that sold ladies' tweed coats.'

'Well, it was the first time she had worn it, Davis, and she had a new hat to match—also bought here.'

Davis stared: 'I say, sir, if the hat and coat were left here after the murder, surely we should have found them?'

'If we had looked in the right place, yes. But wait a moment. You got a list on the first day giving the names and addresses of the heads of the various departments.'

'I have them in my note-book.'

'Right. Get that of the head of the department where they sell these tweed coats, and also of the hat shop. See if they are on the telephone, and ask them to come here. If either is not on, get a taxi and bring them round at once.'

He sat down and lighted a cigarette, smoking gustily and excitedly, as his sergeant took up the receiver. Five minutes later, and the business was done. Both the employees asked for were on their way to the Stores.

The policeman at the main door was told to show them when they arrived into the tweed coat department, and twenty minutes later a smartly dressed, middle-aged woman came in, and announced herself as Miss Gay.

'This is your department, Miss Gay?' said Devenish, when he had given her a seat.

'Yes.'

'Do you remember Miss Tumour buying a coat of Cumberland tweed in this department—or would you not know?'

Miss Gay nodded. 'I would not have known, perhaps, with an ordinary customer, but Miss Tumour came to me, and I went with her while she chose the coat—I could tell her which was the best value,' she added blandly.

'No doubt,' he said, smiling. 'Are the articles in your department exclusive, or shall I say standardised?'

She smiled too now. 'She paid twelve guineas for it, and at that price in this tweed it would not be exclusive. Wait a moment, I think I had six of those, or was it only four? I can look it up.'

Devenish accompanied her to the little panelled room that was her office, and she consulted some books, then looked up.

'Half a dozen. Just a moment till I see how many we sold.'

But it was ten minutes before she was able to say, and then she announced that three had been sold, including the one bought by Miss Tumour.

'And the date when the last was sold?'

'Does it matter?'

'It may. You see your assistant might count them or notice what was the date?'

Miss Gay looked puzzled by his remark. 'Miss Tumour bought hers last. That was on Friday. The second sale was on Thursday.'

'Are these coats on stands in the department?'

'Not those in question. They are on hangers hung on a rail in a panelled cupboard. Do you want to see it?'

'That is the only thing I do want to see,' replied Devenish.

Miss Gay nodded and led them down the department to where a long line of cupboards, panelled in stainwood, formed a sort of seven-foot partition. The panelled doors were sliding ones, and she pushed back one and then slid it to again.

'Those are the Narbet tweeds. I am sorry. Here we are.'

She slid back a panel further down, and disclosed a line of closely packed coats.

'These are the Cumberlands in that range of colour,' she began, and then stared, and gasped.

'Which?' asked he, watching her closely.

'The—these four!' she cried excitedly.

Davis suppressed an exclamation of delight. Devenish smiled in mild triumph.

'Sure of that, Miss Gay?'

'Of course,' she gulped. 'Look! I'll take them out for you.'

'Stick them on that counter over there,' said Devenish.

The four coats were taken to the counter and laid out at a little distance apart.

'Now, Miss Gay,' said the inspector, 'I hope you can tell one from the other, or is that too much for you?'

She seemed rather astonished at that. 'Of course. That is quite easy. If one was Miss Tumour's, she wouldn't wear it with the ticket on it.'

Devenish turned to Davis. 'Nice bloomer for one of us, Davis! Of course you are right, Miss Gay. Well?'

Her fingers were trembling as she examined the coats in

turn. When she picked up the third in the line, she dropped it again as if it had burnt her fingers. Obviously she had a feeling against touching anything that belonged to a murdered woman, perhaps some superstition.

'This is it! Good Heavens! What a filthy idea to put it here.'

'A very good idea, from one point of view,' said he. 'It might, if the assistant had been hurried or careless, have been sold to someone else and the evidence disposed of—Hello, constable, what now?'

'Miss Doren to see you, sir.'

A constable had just appeared, bringing in a thin, dark woman of about forty. Miss Gay told the inspector that it was her colleague from the millinery.

Devenish explained what had been found, and the newcomer bit her lip.'

'I call that very clever of you,' she said alertly, 'and I can tell you about that hat at once. It was a model quite unique in its way, though a man might not see anything in it beyond a bit of straw and a ribbon. It may be there now, if it was put back like this coat, for I am sure we were all far too excited and upset last Monday morning to look at the stock. And, of course, we were not allowed to touch anything, once your people took charge.'

Devenish beamed. This was the kind of helper he liked. 'Good! Davis take those four coats into the flat above and lock them up. Now, Miss Doren, we'll see if the hat is where we should like it to be.'

'I don't know that I should like it in my department,' said she, as they moved off, accompanied by Miss Gay.

Again they made a find. The hat Miss Tumour had worn was put away in the place from which it had been taken. Devenish put it in a hat-box, impounded it, and dismissed the women with thanks for their help. Then he sent for a finger-print expert to look for finger-prints on the sliding panels, and to photograph them if found. Finally, he went up in the lift, carrying the hat in its box, and joined Sergeant Davis, who was taking a look at the four coats.

'You got a bull's-eye, sir,' the latter said admiringly. 'It does show this was an inside job, for what could Mr Peden-Hythe know about these departments?'

Devenish laughed. 'But why should anyone try to fake a landing up above, apparently to try to involve Webley? Webley would know even less about the interior of this Store than Peden-Hythe; for the latter, for all we know, may have visited this store many times with his mother.'

'That is true, sir. But if Miss Tumour was killed up above on the roof, why take the trouble to put the hat and coat down here?'

'Unless Mander killed her, which seems unlikely as things stand at present, Davis,' said Devenish. 'By the way, we are still short of a left-hand glove!'

# CHAPTER XV

When Devenish had examined the hat and coat thoroughly, he had them packed up and despatched to Scotland Yard. Then he looked at Davis.

'Obviously she was quite at home here. She arrived, took off her coat and hat to make herself comfortable, and was later killed, either on the roof or in the lift. Now which was which? If one of the two was killed in the lift, was it Mr Mander or Miss Tumour?'

'Was either killed in the lift, sir? If it was Mr Mander, then where is the bullet mark? We found that in the sand, as you told us to look there, so you must have thought—'

'I have too many thoughts, my dear fellow, for my own comfort. I am afraid I shall have a great many more too. This find of mine today unsettles me. That lift, for example, is worth our attention.'

They left Mander's private portion of the flat, locking it up again. The square of heavy pile carpet was still in position on the floor of the lift, and Devenish removed it gingerly and examined the bloodstains on the place beneath.

'It was, the doctor says, largely an internal hæmorrhage,' he murmured, while the sergeant hung on his words. 'The tiny spot in the goods lift, where the dagger was found, might have come from the dagger itself. There was not enough to suggest that anyone had been actually stabbed there.'

'No, sir, there wasn't.'

'But here, granting what the doctor said to be true, there was.'

'But not enough to soak up into the mat, this square, sir.'

'And in any case, would the murderer take up the mat, ask his victim to stand inside while he shot him, or the girl while he stabbed her, and then replace the square?'

'He would not, sir?'

'Where does this square come from?'

'I can ask, sir.'

'Presently. But, in the meanwhile, get me all the squares out of all the lifts, will you, and bring them here?'

Davis was puzzled, but went about his business. When he returned with the first three squares, he found Devenish telephoning to the man who was head of the carpet department, and asking him to come along.

Finally, the lot of carpet squares from the lifts in that section of the Stores was brought in and laid down on the floor of a corridor.

'Notice anything about them, Davis?' asked Devenish, contemplating the long row with an air of great satisfaction. 'When you see a lot of objects separately they look much alike as to condition if they are all pretty new.'

'Yes, sir, but I see it now.'

'That there is a shade of difference?'

'Yes, they are all pretty clean, but the one out of the lift we examined just now is cleaner than the others; looks new in fact, sir.'

'We must wait till the carpet manager comes along,' said Devenish. 'We'll hear from him if they have duplicates.'

It was nearly half an hour before the manager of the carpet department arrived, but when he came, he agreed at once that the square they had picked out looked very new. As he turned it over, he dropped it.

'But it can't be,' he added. 'Surely this is the one where—?'

'Absolutely,' interrupted Devenish, 'but the underside was stained with blood from the lift floor, and that means nothing.'

The manager pursed his lips. 'If it wasn't there, I should certainly say this was not the square laid down when the Stores were opened.'

'Have you duplicates of these, to replace them when worn out?'

'No, not duplicates. But there may be an odd square of this lot that was sent as a sample when the squares were chosen.'

'Let us see that.'

The manager made a movement as if to go to his department, then pulled up short, and scratched his head. 'Wait a moment— let me see. Oh. Mr Mander chose that. He had the last word with regard to most of the fittings and carpets. He was very particular in small points.'

'You mean the sample went to him?'

'Yes.'

'Then where would it go?'

'I could not say. It may be in his flat.'

'We'll go there now, and I shall be glad if you will accompany us,' said Devenish.

But this time when they entered the flat, Devenish rang for the butler, after unbolting the communicating door. The butler came in, and asked what he could do for them.

The inspector had brought the square from below. 'Do you remember this?' he asked, holding it up.

The man stared at it, then nodded. 'That's out of the—out of Mr Mander's billiard-room, sir. He put the stand for cues on it.'

The manager of the carpet department stared. 'No, this is from one of the lifts below.'

Before he had finished his sentence, Devenish was striding off to the billiard-room, and the others followed him hurriedly.

'There is no mat or square under the stand for the cues.'

The butler, who had come in last, wrinkled his brows. 'It was there, sir.'

'We had better look all over the flat to see if there is one like it,' said Devenish.

'There isn't,' said Davis. 'I searched the flat, and saw nothing like that square. I should have noticed it, being like those on the lift, if it had.'

'Oh, well, it's of no importance,' remarked Devenish, winking furtively at his sergeant. 'I need not detain you longer, sir,' he added to the manager, and also dismissed the waiting butler with a gesture.

When they had both gone, he and Davis stared at each other in silence.

Devenish broke the silence first. 'Now we know that one of the two was killed in that lift, Davis. The murderer must have removed the damaged square, and come up here for the one in the billiard-room.'

'Then it must have been someone who knew the flat well, and was aware that the square up here was a duplicate of those below in the lifts.'

'Absolutely, it would seem. But who was killed here? Could there have been two murderers as well as two murdered? Is it possible that the murders were done by two working in collaboration, or independently? Finally, is it possible that there was first a murder, and another in retribution?'

'How do you mean that, sir?'

'I mean was Miss Tumour murdered, and the man who killed her shot in his turn to avenge her?'

'That would be by Mr Kephim?'

'We can't say. I do not see why Mander should murder the girl, but of course I cannot ignore the possibility.'

'And if it was Mr Kephim who killed Mander, he might be so bitter, finding out about them, that he made up his mind to make a show of them in the window.'

'Quite. Well, look here, Davis, I want you to go down to Gelover, and make quite sure that Webley could not have taken out the gyrocopter without anyone hearing it. As you know, it is one of those that you can fold up and wheel into a large garage. Gelover is not a very populous place, and we cannot swear that the plane was not wheeled out of the hanger and pushed along for some distance, where the engine would not be so audible from the manor. That would account too for the muddy tracks. One of the points that Webley made was that the taking-off ground was laid out with hard material, as it is. But if he took the machine to a field and started there, it would be a different matter.'

When Davis had gone Devenish sat down and took out his note-book and pencil.

'Let me make out the hours on Sunday night that the various suspects admitted being out and about,' he said to himself, and promptly wrote them down.

*Mr Kephim.—A quarter to eleven to two o'clock, a.m.*

*Miss Tumour.—Left her flat at a quarter to ten.*

'But she isn't a suspect, by the way,' he added, and erased the entry.

*Mr Cane.—Half-past nine to half-past eleven.*

*Peden-Hythe.—Left Lefort's about ten, back at club midnight.*

He stared at these times and reflected. 'That would make the murder occur between ten and two next morning—if one can believe the men's statements. I am not sure that I can, with the exception of Peden-Hythe, who was seen by the club porter.'

On the whole he thought that he had better go to worry Peden-Hythe again, and promptly rang up the young man's club. He mentioned his name and business to assure a direct reply, and was told that Mr Peden-Hythe was not in the club, but would be back before dinner—at half-past six to be accurate.

So Devenish spent a little time examining the position of the lift, and remarking more significantly on a detail which he already knew but to which he had attached little importance.

This was the fact that, while in each of the three sections of the store, and on all floors, except the top one in the particular section where the crimes had been committed, there was access through the departments, or by means of corridors, from one end of a floor to the other.

On the top floor, where Devenish now was, it was different. Mr Mander had been so anxious for privacy that, save for the one door, he was cut off from the servants' quarters, and the servants' quarters were cut off from the remainder of the top floor by a wall in which there was no door whatsoever.

The space in the remainder of that top floor was taken up by store-rooms, and from it the goods lift descended, but a man in Mander's flat could only reach the store-rooms by descending to the floor below and walking along till he came to the goods lift.

Having made a little sketch, very rough but adequate to his purpose, of this particular feature, Devenish left the Stores and had some food. Then he went to Scotland Yard, had an interview with Mr Melis, who agreed that it would do no harm to frighten Peden-Hythe a little, then left for Jameson's club.

His greeting was subdued, and Peden-Hythe's resentful, but he was invited up to the young man's bedroom again, and sat down to begin his provocative campaign.

'I am not here to worry you this time, Mr Peden-Hythe,' he said in a conciliatory voice. 'I should not have troubled you but for the fact that some evidence has come into our possession which affects a—shall I say protégé?—of yours.'

This innocent remark produced an unexpected result.

Peden-Hythe's eyes almost started out of his head, and his colour ebbed rapidly. 'What the devil do you mean?' he cried.

'I refer to the watchman who was on duty that night.'

This did not appear to reassure the young man, though he tried to look nonchalant. 'What has that to do with me?'

'I understand you recommended him for the post.'

'I believe my mother did, inspector.'

Devenish replied dryly: 'Then I presume that is why he came to thank you for it! Come, sir,' he added severely. 'It does you no good to equivocate. We know that he was your batman in the war. He told us so himself, and also that you had really been behind his appointment.'

The young man pulled himself together. 'Well, that's right enough. But I don't see where I come in yet.'

'I only thought, sir, as you took an interest in him, and his conduct on the night of the murder is so inexplicable that we are very suspicious—'

'Oh, rot! Mann's a good fellow. He wouldn't hurt a fly, and there was no reason for him to hate Mander. In fact, I should say he was a funk; nervous as a cat.'

'And an old regular?'

'Quite, but soldiers years ago didn't expect to be caught up in a big war. Lots of them joined for occupation.'

'The point is this, sir. Not only were there two murders in the Stores that night, but one of them, we have reason to think, was committed in a passenger lift. Then a man either went down or—at any rate used—a goods lift. Now we cannot believe that two lifts were used that night without anyone being seen or anything heard by the watchman.'

'Then why don't you ask him, not me? What excuse does he give?'

'He admits that he suffers from insomnia during the day, and says he is drowsy at night—a serious thing in a man who goes on duty then.

He added an explanation of the gadget installed in the watchman's box, and the fact that the lead had been cut.

'And he says he did that?' asked Peden-Hythe with a look of utter scepticism.

'He would hardly admit it if he didn't do it unless—'

'Unless what, inspector?'

'Unless he invented the insomnia to account for his hearing and seeing nothing.'

'Then you believe he is guilty of the murders—without any motive?'

'We cannot say yet, sir. There is another possible explanation. In a sense that brings me here.'

The young man bit his lip, and looked very much on his guard. 'That he did hear something?'

'And denied it. Yes.'

'But if he hadn't committed the murders, inspector, why should he deny it?'

'It is possible that he is trying to shield somebody,' said Devenish, more dryly than ever. 'I can imagine a case where a man has been befriended and well treated by someone. He sees that someone, but does not like to give him away.'

The sweat broke out suddenly on Peden-Hythe's forehead, and he stared at the detective as if hypnotised.

'I don't like your tone, inspector,' he stammered.

'I am sorry, sir, but there it is. You obtained this job for Mann. Your match-box was found outside in the laneway.'

'But, good heavens! I never got in. I told you I rang the bally bell till I was sick.'

'We have only your word for it, sir.'

Peden-Hythe gasped, then shrugged. 'Wait a moment. I see what you mean. It's all right from your point of view, I see. But I swear I was not in the building. I was a damn fool to go near it.'

'But since you did go near it, sir, it will look very awkward for you if you have to give evidence.'

A drop of sweat splashed on the young man's cheek. 'It looks rotten. I admit that. But what am I to do about it? I can't get any witness to prove I was not inside.'

Devenish fixed him with his eye, and put as much gravity into his look as he could.

'Well, sir, you have to explain it in some way, or stand fire. If Mann was not drowsy, and was not attending to his duties, what was he up to? If he refused to say that he saw something, it is either that he is lying, or speaking the truth. If he is speaking the truth, where was he when the lifts went up and down? I suppose, sir, he did not go to the back door opening on the lane and speak to you?'

Peden-Hythe licked his dry lips. 'No, he didn't.'

Devenish rose.

'Well, sir, since you can't throw any light on these inconsistencies in Mann's explanations, I am afraid I must report to the Yard to that effect. It will then be for them to decide if your evidence will be required at the resumed inquest.'

Peden-Hythe looked at him despairingly, then he hastily volunteered a statement.

'I don't care so much for myself,' he said, 'but I don't want that poor chap to get into trouble if I can help it.'

Devenish sat down again. 'Then, sir, let me hear what you have to say.'

# CHAPTER XVI

'Look here, inspector,' began Peden-Hythe, looking very embarrassed, 'I feel sure you are sportsman enough to leave my mother's name out of this. When I say "Mrs X" perhaps you will understand who I mean.'

'I follow you, sir, go on.'

Jameson licked his lips again. 'Well, er—there's a Mrs X who had pots of money, don't you know. She's a jolly good sort, and so on, but we've all got a weakness. She was a bit impressionable, and she met a bounder—a man who, well, took her fancy. He was a glib blighter, buttered her up no end, and generally looked like getting his nose in front for the matrimonial stakes.'

Devenish nodded. 'I see, sir.'

'The trouble was that she had a son,' went on Jameson, squirming a little in his chair. 'He didn't mind Mrs X having a second husband, but he jolly well did hate the idea of her getting married to a rotten cad.'

'Very natural, sir.'

'I should say so. Anyway, this son did his best to put her off about the rotter, but it was N.G. all the time. I don't know if Mrs X thought he was a bally Galahad, but it looked like it. If she had found him out, you know, she'd have been pretty wild. You see, you don't throw a fortune at a fella's head when you're older without expecting value for it, and exclusive rights, if you take me.'

'Mrs X would have been jealous, no doubt.'

'Absolutely. Well, this son of hers was hoppin' mad about it, what with the idea of the bounder tagging on to his family, and wasting the petty cash in the meantime as well. You wouldn't blame him for wanting to forbid the banns, if you know what I mean.'

'I should understand it at least.'

'Quite. Well that's the way it was. But the son didn't quite know how to set about it, and he had no evidence about Man—about the fella, except his face. It struck him that the fella's face was the kind that's had practice ogling pretty girls, and there were rumours goin' about too, though not direct enough to give a handle.'

'He never thought of an inquiry-agent, I suppose?' Devenish prompted, more or less convinced now that Jameson Peden-Hythe was speaking the truth.

'Jolly well did, if you ask me. But those inquiry fellas seem such cads, and he didn't like to tell them about Mrs X, as you can imagine, having some sort of respect for the old lady.'

'No. What then?'

'Well then, a chap turned up and wanted a job, and it happened that he was a fella who was under some kind of an obligation, or thought he was, and was a very decent, sound fella into the bargain.'

'Who could be pitchforked into a job at a big Stores, say?'

'Absolutely, and not the sort of chap to go spilling other people's secrets. Whatever he saw he would keep to himself. Well, the idea was this. He was to keep an eye on Mander's flat, and he had a key to the back door on the laneway. It was pretty clear that no one was likely to visit that bounder before ten, for the butler might be in and out before that.'

'I see.'

'In any case, if anything had happened, I—I mean the watchman would have been excused, and any damage done would have been made good, so there was no harm in putting him on the job.'

'But rather a dirty business spying, sir,' said Devenish quietly. 'We do it because it is our duty, and we have some public interest to serve.'

'You're quite right,' said Jameson. 'I oughtn't to have said that to you the other day. I take it back, and apologise. But to get down to tin tacks, Mann wasn't able to get anything very definite, for he couldn't be out in the lane all the time. It wasn't his fault, but this son chap got a bit peeved about it, and had an idea that things would move fast before he could interfere—'

'Apparently Mander contemplated a bolt with Miss Tumour,' said Devenish.

'But I couldn't know that. I mean to say Mrs X's son wasn't feeling in the best of tempers Sunday evening, and he determined to barge round to see for himself. He rang the bell of the back door into the Stores, not the door to Mander's private staircase, and Mann came out. Mann had been on the watch after he arrived for his turn of duty, and he had seen a girl let in by the private door.'

Devenish started. 'Oh, he saw that?'

'Yes. Well, this X chap thought he would catch Mander on the hop, and he had had just enough to make him think of the silly plan of ringing at the private bell and making old Mander answer for his deeds. Whether old Mander was dead at that time, or could get a squint from above at the caller, no one can say, but he didn't show up. So Mrs X's son tootled back to his club when he got tired of ringing. Later on he got the wind up, because he had dropped his match-box in the lane and couldn't find it.'

'And finally tried to fool the police into believing he knew nothing about the case.'

'Well, he didn't really, did he? Not from what he says,' pleaded Jameson.

'Has he seen Mann since then?' asked Devenish.

'Yes, he did, but Mann said he knew nothing. After he had reported to X at the back door, he went on with his job—I believe him too. You know, inspector, Mann is really a most respectable fella.'

Devenish studied the young man's face very thoughtfully. It wore an expression which did not seem evasive, and on the whole the detective was inclined to believe that he had told a true story. If he had really thought his mother was going to marry Mander, and suspected that the man was not only mercenary but a secret libertine as well, he might have excused his rather tortuous course of conduct with the reflection that he was saving his mother from an unhappy future.

'What time was it that you rang?'

'I should say it was about just after eleven.'

'Very good, sir,' said Devenish, as he rose to go. 'Your story must of course be tested, and you must not leave town on any account until you get permission from us. But if I find that you have told me the truth, I shall endeavour to keep Mrs X's name out of it.'

Jameson put out his hand. 'I've been a damn fool, inspector, in more ways than one. But I am going to put a padlock on it. I hope you'll have good luck.'

Devenish went away very thoughtful. He wanted to see Mr Melis next, which was fortunate, for Mr Melis was very anxious to see him. When he entered the assistant-commissioner's room at the Yard, he was greeted with a murmur of satisfaction.

'Come in, inspector. You're the very man I want to see. One of our cheerful experts has upset your latest apple-cart, and I want to see how you propose to set it up on its wheels again.'

He motioned Devenish to a seat, and lit a cigarette for effect.

'That bullet,' he began, gesturing with his cigarette as he was wont to do on the amateur stage. 'It isn't the right one.'

'I wondered,' said Devenish.

Melis laughed. He did not think it likely that Devenish had wondered, but thought he was trying to cover up a very natural error.

'It was fired, no doubt,' he continued, 'and fired from that Mauser. But it was fired into the sand, not into Mander. That does make a difference, I must say. For example, it gives us two shots fired instead of one.'

Devenish nodded. 'So Mander may really have been shot in the lift, sir.'

'With a magic bullet which flew into tiny fragments, and so could not be found, I suppose!' Melis rallied him. 'And the blood flowed upwards from under the carpet on the floor? Must be unique that!'

We haven't found the carpet from the lift, sir,' said Devenish, and went on to explain what he had done that day. 'Not yet.'

Mr Melis looked both startled and puzzled. 'Jove! So this alcoholic young man was hanging about that night, and now comes at us with a fairy tale.'

'I am not sure of that, sir.'

Melis forgot to gesture with his cigarette. 'Really? And you're not a bad judge of character either. But what is on now? I suppose you don't still suspect Kephim or Cane, or Webley?'

Devenish knitted his brows. 'I don't know that I suspected Webley much at any time, but Kephim is a possibility, and Cane.'

'What have we against Cane?'

'We have only hypotheses, sir, but that applies to them all. If Cane is concerned at all—and I admit I didn't like him very much—it has something to do with this gyrocopter. Webley is a bit of a genius, it seems, at mechanics proper, but Cane gave me to believe that a man who could invent the thing must have had high technical knowledge.'

'The science of the thing—higher mathematics, and so forth?'

'That is what I mean, sir. There are people who can do anything with machines but do not understand the scientific theories on which they are based. Now Cane is a highly educated man.'

'You think he may be the inventor?'

'He was very bitter about the rewards inventors get, though he talked more or less impersonally. If there is any case against him at all, his invention was stolen by Mander and worked up by Webley, or else he was taken on because of the gyrocopter and agreed not to claim as the inventor, but got discontented when he found it was selling so fast. Why did he go to see Webley at all? Had he heard that the man was to be put forward by Mander as the real inventor? Did he see Mander at the flat on that Sunday night, and find him determined to stick to the original arrangement that we are postulating?'

'It's barely possible.'

'Quite so, sir. In that case he may have shot Mander and discovered that the Tumour woman was an eye-witness. Disposing of her with the dagger that was in Mander's drawing-room, he might have faked evidence which would involve Webley (who was, by this theory, in the plot against him) or alternatively Kephim, with whom he was on bad terms. I don't really believe that, but we may have to work it out if other ways fail.'

'I wanted to know,' said Mr Melis, 'because Inspector Hemp has got a curious side-light, or what may be a side-light, on the case. It does not touch Cane or Kephim, but it may give us a new view of the rather strange girl who was killed.'

Devenish pricked up his ears, 'I shall be glad to hear what he has to say, sir.'

Melis picked up his desk-telephone and asked that Inspector Hemp should come to his room, then he turned again to Devenish.

'I float about a good deal in various sorts of society, you know,' he remarked conversationally, 'and, of course, people know who I am. Now and again I am asked to solve little social problems unofficially. In cases, I mean, where the social status of my acquaintance makes secrecy very necessary. The other day I was approached by the niece of an old friend of mine, Lady X, I shall call her.'

'Not my Mrs X, sir?'

'No. There is a marquisate in the offing, but, in the middle distance, a bit of wreckage that it would not do to let drift into the marquis's gaze. I had a talk with the young thing, found her very contrite and dreadfully frightened. If I could have kept the thing to myself, I would. But it was rather beyond me, so I put Hemp, our blackmail expert, on the job.'

'Couldn't have had a better man, sir,'

'No. I don't think I could.' There was a knock at the door, and he looked up and called out: 'Come in, inspector.'

A very well dressed and bland person came in. He saluted Melis, nodded to Devenish, and was waved to a chair.

'Hemp, I believe that case I gave you bears some similarity to two other cases which had rather puzzled you?'

'Yes, sir. Looked like the same hand to me.'

'Both of those flummoxed you, but my little lot gave you a pointer, I understood you to say.'

'Yes, sir. I suppose it was because she got away with it so easily in the two other cases, and forgot to take all the precautions.'

'Very likely. Are you sure now?'

Hemp pursed his lips. 'Very nearly—in my own mind, quite.'

Devenish was much interested, he leaned forward. 'Any of my birds involved?'

'One of your witnesses,' was the reply. 'Mrs Hoe, a woman who does society pars, and, by virtue of her job, gets to know some secrets.'

Devenish slapped his knee. 'Mrs Hoe? You surprise me, and yet you don't. But can we suppose that she and Miss Tumour would be friends, if Mrs Hoe was blackmailing her?'

'Mrs Hoe might have heard of the prospective bolt to South America, and used that as a handle to extract money,' suggested Melis.

Hemp was studying his colleague. 'Any objections to that, Devenish?'

'Several,' Devenish replied promptly. 'I cannot see a woman keeping her blackmailer's telephone number on her pad. But there are other reasons.'

Hemp looked sceptical. Mr Melis was interested.

'Then you are not very sure that Mrs Hoe had any connection with this case?'

'I think she did, sir, but I can imagine Mrs Hoe and Miss Tumour being in it together.'

'How do you reason that out?'

'Her character, as borne out by her life, sir. Tumour lets Mr Kephim court her, while she is carrying on an intrigue with Mander at the same time. She is engaged to be married to the manager, and visits Mander's flat after her lover has left her. A woman of that type, with apparently no morals, might be up to anything.'

'I think you may be right,' agreed Melis, while even Hemp looked more approving. 'If Mander was in money trouble, or going to bolt with the dibs, if, at the same time, he was sufficiently fascinated with the Tumour woman to suggest a bolt, he was giving himself right into her hands. She and Mrs Hoe may have even planned the campaign that way.'

'But why engage herself to Kephim?' asked Hemp.

Devenish smiled. 'A man at your branch, and asks us that! She may have had no conscience, and yet been in love with Kephim.'

'You're quite a psychologist, Devenish,' chuckled Melis. 'I am with you all the way. Mander had got himself on toast by procuring the passport for Tumour under another name. But all that doesn't help us to solve the murder problem. Mander couldn't have shot himself, and killed the girl, then settled them both in the window below, and then gone up and fired the Mauser into the sand! And if he could have performed the later stunt to a nicety, what about the wheel tracks, and the missing sparking-plugs, etc.?'

Hemp shrugged. 'Well, sir, our bird is not a bit suspicious. I had the young lady send the money last evening as requested. If I can get a search warrant today, it would be better to execute it as soon as possible.'

'For Mrs Hoe's flat, sir?' asked Devenish.

'Yes—all right, Hemp. I'll see about it at once. Let Devenish know if you get any material bearing on his case, please. I don't think we want you any more now.'

Hemp saluted and went out.

Melis turned to Devenish. 'I think you are making headway, though I am not quite sure of your direction,' he said smiling. 'It is certainly possible that Miss Tumour was in this crook game too. But to go back to our earlier muttons. Even if Peden-Hythe told the truth to you and did pay a call on the watchman at the back door that night, it does not explain the watchman's seeing nothing—unless the lifts were used while he was at the back door talking to the young man.'

'That's our trouble still, sir,' replied the inspector, 'but I'll get that yet. Is there anything more you wished to say to me, sir?'

'Only to look for a second gun, Devenish. There must have been one. And the magic bullet!'

# CHAPTER XVII

THE revelation about Mrs Hoe and her suspected activities surprised Devenish more than he would have cared to own. But he knew very little of the woman, and it was quite possible that the dead girl Tumour had known very little more than he. You may be a friend of a dubious character for years without knowing it. On the other hand it was on the cards that Tumour had known, and that, as he had hinted to Mr Melis, the two were in league to blackmail the dead man, Mander.

After a little cogitation, Devenish decided to see Kephim. He found him at home, and was welcomed readily enough by the manager. Indeed it almost seemed to him that Kephim's gloom had lifted a little during the past few days, whatever the reason might be.

When they had exchanged a little desultory conversation, the inspector accepted a cigarette, and spoke of his former interview with Mrs Hoe. He watched the other's face, and there he saw that Kephim was beginning to be interested in the journalist, and in a matter unrelated to the case itself.

It was not at all improbable, he thought, that the discovery of the intrigue with Mander had killed Kephim's love for the woman, Effie Tumour.

You do not mourn for what you have ceased to love, and if Devenish's interpretation of the affair was correct, the man was already finding some consolation in the company of his new sympathiser, which was natural enough in the circumstances.

'I was wondering,' he said thoughtfully, 'if Mrs Hoe had known the late Miss Tumour long?'

Kephim frowned at the mention of the name. 'A number of years, I think,' he said.

138

Devenish started. 'Are you sure of that?'

The other man stared at him in surprise. 'I am not very sure. I think so. I think they had not met for many years, but I believe they were at school together in the country. Then when Mrs Hoe was engaged to do some press propaganda for the firm, they took up the old acquaintance. Why do you ask?'

'Well, I want to get all the witnesses I can, Mr Kephim. A question is involved here as to Tumour's character. Anyone who had only known her a short time might not understand much about her.'

Kephim scowled and bit his lip. 'Character!'

'You know what I mean. Certain types of people are more likely, even in this law-abiding country, to die violent deaths than others. Women of a certain class always provide a big proportion of the murder victims, and next to them one would think blackmailers would figure next. They don't, as a matter of fact; but, even if they escape, the motive for—'

'Wait a moment, inspector,' cried Kephim, much disturbed. 'I really am surprised to hear you mention blackmail. I have a great deal to blame Effie—Miss Tumour for, but I should never have thought her likely to turn to that.'

Devenish was sure the man was speaking sincerely. 'Perhaps not, but have you considered the peculiar circumstances surrounding Miss Tumour's relation with Mr Mander and with you? You proposed to her and were accepted lately. I presume you took that to mean that she loved you.'

'I thought so,' said Kephim, in a low voice.

'Yet, while she accepted you, she was visiting Mander, and indeed seems to have made arrangements to bolt abroad with him. Why then did she accept you? She was under no compulsion to do that, I suppose?'

'Of course not. How could she be?'

Devenish rubbed his chin. 'Did she seem to be loving, affectionate? I mean to say, did she give you the impression that it was her real wish to marry you?'

'Yes. She was all she could have been to me,' said Kephim, 'at that time,' he added, with something like a groan.

'I see. Now, Mr Kephim, you know as well as I do that a woman may be a thorough-paced rogue in many ways, and yet fall honestly in love with a man. There is just a possibility that Tumour was trying to blackmail Mander, leading him on to believe that she would go abroad with him until he made the final and fatal mistake of applying not only for his own passport but for one in which Miss Tumour figured under a false name. Her photograph was, of course, on the passport.'

'But why? I don't see the connection between that and blackmail.'

'I should think it was obvious. With that passport as a weapon, she could threaten Mander at any time.'

'But I thought it was impossible that this could be murder and suicide, inspector.'

'Well, we have to try out all our theories,' said Devenish, 'but we'll leave that for the moment. Have you seen Mrs Hoe lately?'

Kephim coloured a little. It was easy to see that the pretty little woman had sympathised with him very successfully.

'Oh, yes, several times, inspector. She has been very kind. I saw something of her when Effie was alive, but I never—' he checked himself and coloured still more highly.

'I see. What does she think was behind this intrigue with Mander? Or has she not mentioned it to you?'

'I am afraid he thinks Effie meant to bolt with the man.'

'She has no other theory to account for it?'

'She has not mentioned any, I am sure.'

Devenish felt sure that Mrs Hoe was implicated in the case somewhere. She had not mentioned the fact to him that she and Tumour had been at school together, a vital suppression. Then, why was she following up Mr Kephim? Was it because she suspected him of the murder, or simply because she had fallen in love with him? There was some point in the latter theory, since Mrs Hoe had spoken slightingly of Tumour while affecting to admire her and like her. Jealousy might have been behind that; the inconvenient spectre which lurks uneasily behind many apparent friendships.

But Devenish did not wish Kephim to attach too much importance to that part of their conversation which dealt with Mrs Hoe. He might repeat it to the woman herself, which would be highly inconvenient. He turned the subject abruptly.

'Now, Mr Kephim, I need not tell you that your lack of an alibi on Sunday night, and the fact that your fiancée was carrying on an intrigue with Mander, rather complicates your position. If you had nothing to do with the crime, as I am inclined to believe, it is still possible that a third party knew of the intrigue and would not be averse from throwing the blame on you.'

Kephim stared. 'I don't know anyone who would play me a foul trick like that, I must say so. Why, it would be worse than trying to murder me in cold blood.'

'You have no enemies then?'

'Not that kind, thank God.'

'I understood from Mr Crayte that you were not on good terms with Mr Cane?'

Kephim nodded. 'That is true. Cane is a cad, and a damned snob. I can't stick him at any price. Just because he went to a public school and then into the army—'

Devenish interrupted. 'You feel strongly about him?'

'I do,' Kephim leaned forward, and struck one palm into the other. 'Cane is a swine, but I would never believe him a swine of that kind. I'll never believe that of him.'

Devenish was about to reply when the telephone bell rang. Kephim excused himself, and went out into the hall. He shut the door behind him and Devenish was about to get up and go to the door when he returned hastily, his face white and anxious.

'She cut me off,' he said. 'I can't understand what has happened.'

'Who?' Devenish demanded sharply.

'Mrs Hoe. When I went to the telephone she began to tell me something about the police; would I come over? Then she said in a wild sort of voice: "*They're here!*" and then she rang off, and I couldn't get on again.'

Devenish nodded. 'I'll try again for you in a few minutes,' he said quietly. 'If it is the police, they will give me an answer.'

Kephim rubbed his hands nervously together, and seemed much agitated. It was obvious that, if he was not the murderer of Mr Mander—which would account for his fright—he was anxious about Mrs Hoe.

'But what do the police want with her, inspector? And why should she speak in that frightened way about them? She has less reason to fear your people than I have, since I may be suspected, but I don't cry out wildly when you come.'

'Women are naturally more nervous about the police,' said the inspector. 'Sit down, sir, and don't worry too much.'

'But Mrs Hoe is a great friend of mine. She has been most kind since that terrible thing happened—'

'I know, sir. I quite appreciate your feelings, but our people may merely be anxious to question her about Miss Tumour.'

Kephim, however, was not satisfied. 'That is certainly all they could do. They have no reason to do more.'

Devenish spent a few minutes trying to calm him. At the end of that time, he got up.

'Well, sir, I'll telephone to her flat now, to reassure you. Wait here till I come back, please.'

He had no difficulty in getting through to Mrs Hoe's flat, but the voice which replied to him was the familiar one of his colleague from the Yard.

'Oh, that is you, Devenish? Good! Who was it she rang up a few minutes ago?'

'Mr Kephim,' replied the inspector. 'I know, because he is with me now. This is his flat I am speaking from. I don't suppose you have had enough time to discover anything yet, but—'

His colleague replied jubilantly. 'Oh, yes, we have. She got the wind up when we came in, and, instead of taking it quietly, dashed from her telephone into her bedroom.'

'Silly of her.'

'I should say so. I made a rush, and just managed to prevent her from chucking an envelope on to the lead-flat underneath.'

'Oh, good! Papers in that society case you were on, eh?'

'No. We haven't come on those yet, and I don't suppose she thought that was so pressing. She'd had this envelope under the register of the fireplace.'

Devenish became highly excited. 'Not my case, by any chance?'

The voice replied cheerfully. 'Looks like it I must say! No names named, only the initial M. But I'll put you wise later, or if you would like to come over here—'

'Don't let her get away,' said Devenish. 'Put a man on, back and front, when you leave. I can't get away just now, and we can't hold her. My case isn't complete enough, and in your case the matter is to be hushed up.'

The other detective chuckled. 'Right. I'll see that she doesn't give us the slip. Amazing sort of woman she is too. Carried out a good many callous cases of blackmail, and when we get the goods on her nearly goes into hysterics. Hates taking nasty medicine, but didn't mind giving it. Mean, callous little cat, she is!'

Kephim had not been able to restrain his anxiety any longer. As Devenish hung up the receiver, he came out into the hall.

'I hope it is all right?' he asked hastily.

Devenish led the way back into the room and closed the door.

'It is not by any means all right,' he said slowly. 'Now, Mr Kephim, I want you to promise me that you will not visit Mrs Hoe, or allow her to visit you here until I give permission. I don't think it would do her any good, or you either.'

'But what is up?' Kephim cried distractedly.

Devenish shook his head. 'I am not at liberty to tell you yet. I will be glad to tell you at the first minute possible.'

Kephim seemed thunderstruck. He put his head in his hands, and glared down. Then he looked up again.

'It has nothing to do with the case, of course?'

'It has enough connection with the case to make it inadvisable for you to visit her at present, or have any communication with her,' the inspector replied gravely. 'If you do, it may lead to trouble. Now I must get along,' he added, and rose.

Kephim nodded, but did not get up. Innocent or guilty, he looked utterly crushed by the new development.

# CHAPTER XVIII

ON the following morning, Sergeant Davis came back to London and had an interview with the inspector. He had made close investigations into the conditions at Gelover, and was quite certain that no gyrocopter had left the Manor or its vicinity on the previous Sunday night.

'I don't think Webley is quite as straight as he might be, sir,' he added, while Devenish pursed his lips dubiously, 'but I am sure he was not flying that night.'

'Can you be sure?' asked Devenish.

Davis nodded. 'Well, I think so. He seems to be mixed up in some way with Mr Cane, sir, but unless we can get something against him, and get him into court, he won't talk.'

Devenish considered. 'I think I had better see Mr Cane again, and if I can get a hint from him, I'll see Webley myself. By the way, Mrs Hoe is implicated somewhere, and I want you to watch her. Two men are on the job now, under Inspector Hemp, but I shall tell him you will take over.'

'Mrs Hoe, sir?' cried Davis, with a startled look.

He looked still more startled as Devenish explained the latest development, and added: 'Inspector Hemp's case was unofficial in a sense. He can't bring it into court. So we'll take over.'

Davis went away ten minutes later, and Devenish went to call upon Mr Cane.

Cane had just breakfasted, late as it was, and was preparing to go out into the country. His two-seater was standing outside when the inspector turned up and told him that he wanted a talk with him.

'Shall you be long?' Cane asked, smiling. 'I had planned a circular day's tour in Sussex, and ought to start now.'

'It depends upon you, sir,' replied the detective. 'We never keep people long if they answer our questions readily.'

Cane offered him a chair, lighted a pipe, and looked at him mockingly. 'So the great brains of the Yard haven't solved the problem yet!' he said. 'I am rather surprised.'

'Ah, that is just the question,' remarked Devenish dryly. 'I think we have a bit of evidence here and there, and we should have had more if all the people we had interviewed had told us the truth and kept nothing back.'

He looked hard at Cane, and Cane, after a few moments, looked back at him earnestly.

'Present company excepted, of course, inspector?'

Devenish shrugged. 'I am not at all sure of that. Sergeant Davis had just been down seeing Webley, and he is frankly sceptical about your purpose in visiting the man last Sunday.'

'Is your man bound to accept Webley's version against mine?' asked Cane incautiously.

Devenish raised his eyebrows. 'So there are two versions, are there?'

Cane saw that he had made a mistake. He bit his lip.

'There ought not to be. But you are suggesting that Webley's story of our interview does not agree with mine.'

Devenish shook his head. 'I am not suggesting anything, sir. Webley has made certain statements.' He paused to let that sink in, though he did not say what those statements were. 'It seems to me, sir, that there is some question about the ownership of the gyrocopter—or rather the rights of the inventor. Mr Mander took out the patents, though he did not invent the machine.'

'What has this to do with the murder?'

'That is a question we hope to answer with your help, sir. The rights in this invention may be very valuable—'

'They will be—' began Cane.

'If Webley can prove that he was the inventor,' said Devenish. 'It seems to me that Mander, during his lifetime, took advantage of the man's ignorance of business to cheat him over the terms. That is, if he *was* the inventor.'

'What do you mean?'

Devenish smiled-faintly. 'You don't seem to realise, sir, that your very indefinite alibi on that night, which we have not been able in any way to confirm, together with certain pieces of evidence in the Stores, makes your position a very difficult one. There may have been a conspiracy against Mr Mander's life, and the motive may have been something to do with these patent rights. If you can prove that your visit to Webley was quite an innocent one, I may be able to clear you. If you try to confuse us, then we shall be compelled to take sterner measures.'

Cane did not know what he knew, or, as Devenish would have put it sardonically, the real depth of his ignorance. It seemed to him that Webley might have said something to the detective that contradicted his own statement. He considered for a minute or two, very worried now, and secretly rather alarmed.

'What did Webley say?' he asked at last.

'That, sir, is our business. But you need not tell me that you went on Sunday to see this man with no other reason than the one you gave. I am a busy man, and I can't spare the time to bandy questions and answers. Webley, as I say, has made certain statements. It is your business to make a statement to me. If it squares with Webley's, and satisfies me, then it's all right.'

Cane frowned. 'Did your people come on any papers referring to me when they searched Mr Mander's flat?' he asked, after a long pause.

'No, sir. None at all.'

'Did Webley say he was the inventor of the gyrocopter?'

'You are to make a statement, sir, not me.'

Cane bit his lip.

For all he knew, Webley had explained the thing to the police. It would be dangerous to assume that he had not. In the circumstances, safety lay in perfect frankness.

'Then I admit you are right, inspector,' he murmured. 'I was an ass to tell you what I did. If I had really thought you suspected I had any hand in the murder, I should have told you the truth at once.'

'Perhaps you will tell it now, sir.'

'Do my best anyway,' Cane observed bitterly. 'The fact is that when Mander opened here I was broke to the wide. After I left the Service, I started a flying school. I made some profits out of it, and those I put into an experimental machine.'

Devenish grew tense. He fixed his eyes on Cane's face and nodded to him to go on.

'The gyrocopter, in fact,' Cane added in a low voice. 'I was working two years at it, and when I had put all my money in the job, my flying school bust up, and I did not see where I was going to get the money to carry on. I had cut everything down to the bone, and when I went round to get finance, I found that no one was going to touch an experimental machine unless I practically gave it away—and not very many even proposed to do that.'

'Had you patented it, sir?'

Cane shook his head. 'I hadn't. I am not a business man. I had an idea that people could look up the patent-office journal, and copy or adapt my invention. I hadn't the money to fight a case if my rights were infringed. And I was afraid to show my designs to financiers for the same reason.'

'Did you expect them to buy a pig in a poke?'

Cane shrugged. 'I wanted to get hold of a chap who was honest. Damn it all, inspector, everyone knows what inventors are. A fellow brought up for the army isn't trained to that sort of thing.'

'Go on, sir.'

'Well, I footled about a long time, and then Mander started these Stores. All the papers were talking about the genius he was, and how he saw possibilities that no one else did, and the money he had behind him. Then there was an article by him in one paper in which he talked of the possibilities of the mail-order business (I didn't know what that meant then) and how aeroplanes could be used. I did not know either that it was mostly hot-air, written up for him by a journalist to prove that he was going to be a bally pioneer. But it struck me I had the goods with my folding gyrocopter, which could be used to fly anywhere and land in a place where there was no proper landing-ground.'

'It would be adapted for that.'

'Nothing half as good, inspector. Well, I had hardly a bean at that time, and jobs were sticky; so many fellows being out of work, so I tootled round to see Mander and put my case before him. He struck me as being a bounder, but an honest bounder. I told him all I could, and when it came to brass tacks, he asked me if I thought he was mad. I said I didn't, but I knew what was coming. I had heard the "pig in the poke" jest often enough by then to anticipate it. To my delight Mander stopped short of it and asked me what my record was. I told him, and he seemed a bit impressed. Then he asked me if I realised what a lot of money it cost to put a new machine on the market.

'He had me on the hip, of course, for I was pretty well all in, and he was my last court card, if you know what I mean. When he had gone into figures I didn't understand, I saw that it was all U.P. I had a fine machine, but no damn chance of getting it put on the market unless I was willing to sing small. He asked me then what I thought I would have made out of it. Two years before I should have said a million. As it was I said it ought to bring me in at least a thousand a year for the period of the patent rights. Mander said he was very doubtful about that, for the press propaganda would be very expensive, and everything considered, the machine might flop, as many good things had done before, owing to public apathy. But he was prepared to make me a proposal on different lines.'

Devenish nodded. 'You seem to have had the usual experience of inventors, sir.'

Cane frowned. 'You bet I had. Well, I told Mander to give it a name, and he said he was going to start a department to sell aeroplanes, and might make me manager. But a job like that, with fifteen hundred a year to start, was a plum that many ex-pilots would fight for. As a *quid pro quo* I was to have the gyrocopter flown secretly, and if it was a success, or seemed anything like it, he would patent it, and give me a royalty on sales.'

'But surely you did not give the thing away on his bare word?'

'Not I! But that's where the cunning of the old devil came in. He said whatever happened I should not lose, and if I would put my proposal on paper and sign it, he would make out and sign a contract engaging me for ten years as the manager of the aeroplane department in the new Stores at fifteen hundred a year, rising to two thousand; which sounded as if I was on velvet. I was counting, of course, on the additional royalties from the plane.'

'Did he not mention that in the contract?'

'No. You see he said it would be useless at that time, as the machine might not be a success, but the royalty later would be ten per cent, if it went well. I was so bucked at the chance of getting fifteen hundred a year, and so pleased to meet a man who was giving me a chance to make good after all my disappointments, that I signed like a bird. I never thought of any sharp practice.'

Devenish nodded. 'You are not the only one it seems, sir.'

'Mrs Peden-Hythe, you mean? No, I suppose not, inspector. But let me get on. I signed on for this job, and after a great deal of trouble finding a suitable place, I made a flight in the machine and satisfied Mander that it was O.K. Then he got to work having the designs and drawings done over by an expert, and world-wide patents taken out in his name. He told me that my name would not have the same weight as his. After that he made a contract for a firm to manufacture the planes, and began a press campaign. The Stores opened, and I took over my job. I knew Mander had spent a good deal in booming my gyrocopter, but once it was bought, and proved practical, it practically sold itself. I rubbed my hands, for I knew that it was going to be the plane of the future, and I saw myself making money hand over fist.'

'You hadn't got your second agreement, I suppose?'

Cane scowled. 'What do you think! The trial which had convinced Mander of the value of my invention was conducted by me in his presence. There was only one other witness, that man Webley, and he looked a very stupid fellow, though I was told that he was a mechanic.'

'But what about the men who helped you make the first model, sir?'

'The model? My dear chap, I made it myself, I was so afraid of a steal. That's the damned irony of the affair, spending two years by myself working like a dog to keep it dark, and then giving it away with a pound of tea! Of course I had my screw, but I was earning that as well as any man in the place. Well, about ten days ago, I thought I would see Mander and ask him about getting my agreement put ship-shape. I told him he might as well give me my copy.'

'And did he?'

'Did he? The ruffian laughed, and then looked very hard at me. He asked me what I meant by my agreement. Surely I had had one, and if I would point out the clause I referred to, he would be glad to examine it. Of course I thought he had forgotten, and explained what I meant. He shook his head, and said it was the first he had heard of it. Naturally I saw he meant to do me, and went in off the deep-end. I told him he was not going to sell any more of my machines, and he had the nerve to tell me that Webley was the inventor, and the sooner I got it into my head the better.'

Devenish smiled faintly. 'But that's absurd! You could have gone to law surely?'

'I thought so, and said so. Now that the machine had proved itself, I felt I could get a lawyer to take up my case on spec., and I told the beggar so.'

'What did he say?'

'He challenged me to do it. He said I had no witnesses, and no papers. I could go to any lawyer I liked. He said I ought to be damned glad to be where I was, being on my uppers when I came to him—I was fool enough to tell him that at our first interview. At any rate he made my law case look like a ha'penny a pound, and I went round to a solicitor and asked his opinion; giving no names, but just putting the case as that of a friend. The lawyer agreed with Mander. He said I was an ass if I expected to prove anything without a witness, and without a signed contract from the man who was doing the exploiting.'

He drew a deep breath, and Devenish looked at him sympathetically.

'What did you do then?'

'Well, I saw Mander two or three times, and tried every means to make him do the honest thing. He had wanted to pose as the inventor himself at first, and started tinkering in a workshop upstairs, but he couldn't master the technique of aerodynamics, and when he began to negotiate foreign concessions he saw that he couldn't explain the theory of the machine he was supposed to have designed. So he hit on Webley, who is the devil of a clever fellow at machines, but at nothing else.

'It was last Friday that he told me Webley was the inventor of the machine, and he laughed as he said it. I didn't go off the deep-end that time, though I felt like it, for the simple reason that I did not know of any other job I could get at my present figure. He saw that, of course, and said if I was not a fool I would stay where I was and keep my mouth shut. Then it began to dawn upon me that he might only be bluffing. It was to call his bluff that I went down to Gelover on Sunday.'

'Why didn't you tell me this, sir?'

Cane looked surprised. 'Well naturally it seemed to provide me with a motive for revenging myself on Mander. I didn't want to get into trouble.'

'But you are telling me now, sir, and the trouble is not over yet.'

'Quite. Only if Webley said—' he stopped, changed colour, and stared at the inspector. 'You don't mean to say he never told your man?'

Devenish shook his head. 'Not what you have told me, sir. I am glad you were so frank, but I must say that it does not improve your position—By the way, you are not on very good terms with Kephim?'

'That's not altogether my fault, inspector. I dare say he thinks I'm a snob. I don't think I am. The trouble with Kephim, who is a very decent sort otherwise, I believe, is that he has an inferiority complex. When he heard I had been to a public school, and then in the army, he imagined I looked down on him, and that sort of thing.'

'Can you explain those wheel-tracks on the flat roof? You have heard of those from me,' said Devenish, nodding comprehension.

Cane bit his lip. 'No. Can you? I don't know anything about sleuth work, and am one of the few people who don't profess to understand it. But it strikes me there is something odd about this case.'

'Very,' Devenish agreed dryly, 'but what in particular?'

'Too many clues,' said Cane. 'If the murderer did old Mander in, why should he leave so many signs? Wheel-tracks on the roof, though I bet no pilot could land at night there; automatic out of the sports department, blood in two lifts, more on the roof, a dagger out of the flat—why, it is a regular mix-up!'

'Does that fact suggest anything to you, sir?' asked Devenish regarding him thoughtfully.

'Nothing at all, except that the man had a fine confused mind. And sticking the bodies in the window was the last idiocy.'

Devenish nodded again, and rose. 'Well, sir, I can't keep you any longer. I shall go carefully into what you have told me. Meantime, I have another job in hand.'

# CHAPTER XIX

When Devenish left Cane, he was inclined to believe that he had extracted the truth at last. Unless Cane was a consummate actor, his version was correct, and it only remained to interview the man Webley and discover the exact nature of the proposition Mr Mander had made to him.

He took train at once to Gelover and walked to the Manor. He found Webley cleaning one of the gyrocopters. The man was ill-pleased to see him, but his look of resentment gave way to one of alarm when the detective gave him a grim look and tapped him on the shoulder.

'Now, Webley,' he said peremptorily, 'I want the truth from you, and I have come down to get it. What you told me about Mr Cane's visit here last Sunday evening is a pack of lies.'

'It isn't!' muttered Webley sullenly.

'Oh, yes it is, and if you don't come straight out with it now, I shall subpoena you as a witness at the inquest, and that will be unpleasant for you. I have seen Mr Cane, and he tells me that the late Mr Mander didn't invent the gyrocopter here. Is that true?'

Webley nodded sulkily. 'Him? He was only a fool at engines.'

'Did you invent it?'

Webley looked cunning now. He was evidently wondering if it would be safe to bluff it out, and suddenly decided that it wouldn't.

'No, I didn't, sir,' he mumbled, taking out a packet of cigarettes and withdrawing one.

'Put that away, and give me your attention!' said Devenish sharply. 'Did Mr Mander ever mention to you anything about the man who did invent it?'

'He said I did.'

Devenish shrugged. 'He said you were to pretend that you did.'

'That's it.'

'And what were you to get out of that?'

'Two hundred and fifty quid.'

'Had you any idea who did invent the machine?'

Webley grunted. 'That there Mr Cane said he did, but I don't know.'

'Don't you know that Mr Cane came down here to see you about it, and was very angry because Mr Mander had tried to cheat him out of the rights?'

'That's what he said. I couldn't tell.'

'Could you tell me more exactly what he said?'

'Well, I remember he said Mr Mander had stolen his machine, and was trying to chouse him out of it, and he wanted to know what you wanted to know just now, if Mr Mander had asked me to say I had invented it.'

'And what did you tell him?'

'He said—'

'No, I want what you said.'

Webley looked malevolent. 'I said Mr Mander had, and so I had. Then he cursed and swore, and said he would make it hot for me.'

'What did you take that to mean?'

'I don't know at the time, but it seems to me he was trying to put this murder on me. I see in the papers there were tracks of a machine on the roof.'

There was something sneakingly repellent about the man's manner, and Devenish believed that the last phrase was an afterthought. Of the two men he preferred to believe Cane.

'If it comes into court, are you prepared to swear that the late Mr Mander made this offer to you, and asked you to pose as the inventor?'

'If I have to, I suppose I must.'

'Will you put it on paper now, make a statement and sign it? It can do you no harm and may help you in a way.'

Webley thought it over, then agreed. He went back with the detective to the cottage, wrote out a statement of the facts in connection with the gyrocopter, and signed it. Devenish bid him good-day very dryly, folded up the paper and put it in his pocket. Then he walked back to the station and took the next train to town.

On his return to Scotland Yard, he had an interview with the superintendent, then was called for by Mr Melis and entered the assistant-commissioner's room.

Mr Melis was smoking and drawing diagrams on his blotting-pad. At the moment of the inspector's entry, he had just completed a very bad sketch of an automatic pistol.

'Sit down, inspector,' he said lightly. 'My mind is full of arms today. I see pistols for two, if not coffee for one. I suppose you have not come on any signs of that other pistol yet?'

Devenish shook his head. 'No, sir.'

Mr Melis directed his cigarette pistol-wise at the inspector. 'I have been very energetic myself today; toddled round to see the watchman. He's a funny fellow, don't you think? Is he a lath painted to look like iron, or iron inside and out?'

Devenish looked interested. 'What I was asking myself, sir. On the surface, and even when I saw him after the murder, he looked a stolid sort of chap, but Mr Peden-Hythe says he is a funk, and nervous as a cat. Some nervous people do put on a pose of grimness.'

'Like that species of fly which is got up to look like a wasp,' agreed Melis, smiling, 'but we can't say in this case. Some day the psychologists will have perfected a mechanical apparatus for testing character. They will attach you to an electric machine and discover, infallibly, if you are a brave man or a funk, a steady man or a loose 'un. Lacking that, we must do the best we can with the old routine. What I want to know is this—can we connect Mann with the purchase of a pistol?'

'If we could connect him with a motive, sir, it would be even better. But the thought did cross my mind that Mann, if he is nervous, might have been provided with a pistol when he went on duty.'

Mr Melis took up his telephone. 'Mr Kephim's number, please.'

Devenish gave him the number and he rang up. In a minute he was through and asking Mr Kephim if the management provided the watchman with a weapon at night. 'A revolver or automatic,' he added.

'No,' said Kephim, in a tone of surprise. 'If he had had a pistol, I should have informed the inspector. But Mann, in any case, would have no motive for murdering the—'

'Oh, quite. Thank you very much,' Mr Melis interrupted and rang off, to turn again to Devenish.

'If Kephim is the guilty man he shows few of the usual signs. For one thing, he does not appear anxious to have other people charged.'

Devenish smiled. 'No, sir. I asked him about Cane, to whom he bears a grudge. But he was quite indignant at the idea. He said Cane was a snob, but not a murderer.'

Melis agreed. 'Well, we must make an extensive inquiry to discover if Mann did purchase a gun. In "Signals" he would not, I think, be supplied with small arms, but there is always the chance that he found a war souvenir, or bought a pistol from a soldier who had.'

'Like all the others who might come under suspicion, he was searched when he left on Monday morning, sir. It is true that he had means of getting out during the night.'

'By that back door you mentioned? I know. That is the trouble. See his wife, or have her seen by someone, and ask her if she ever saw a weapon in his possession. My own faint impression is that he is shielding someone—I won't mention any names—but you never can tell.'

Devenish assented. 'Very well, sir. Now I thought of seeing that Mrs Hoe. If I can't get something out of her, it is a strange thing. If she had nothing to do with the murder, then she may be glad to explain the circumstances.'

Mr Melis nodded. 'Get that done right away. Thank you, inspector.'

Mr Melis had ideas at times, as the inspector was the first to admit, but quite commonly they turned out to be of seminal rather than direct value, providing the germ from which his more practical subordinates produced workable theories.

The complete absence of motive, as far as could be ascertained, put Mann out of the question in one sense, but Melis had said that he imagined the watchman was shielding someone, which might suggest that, while he had taken no active part, he knew someone who had.

That was the assistant-commissioner's idea, and Devenish considered it, as he did every suggestion coming from that quarter. It might be a fact too, but at present Devenish thought not. As he went to Mrs Hoe's flat he turned it over on every side, and finally evolved an adaptation which he thought fitted in better with the evidence in his possession.

What if Mann had not been shielding the murderer, but simply thought he had been doing so?

Every detective considers his evidence not only from the point of view of the would-be logician, but also from the standpoint of a practical observer. He might refuse to accept what appeared to be a plain, simple, logical statement from one witness, yet give credence to a stumbling and improbable story from another. Like counsel in court, he is bound to give due value to the demeanour and manner of a witness. If either is a bad hand at physiognomy, he makes mistakes.

Jameson Peden-Hythe would have seemed a twister to the man in the street. He had made lying statements, and disingenuous statements at first, but Devenish allowed for an equation other than the personal, and that was the influence of drink on a man who had taken for some years to overindulgence. Who, for instance, would have believed that a man in Jameson's position would have forced himself into a house where he was not wanted, and remained there for hours in the hope that he might see the daughter of the house on her return? Yet that had proved to be true. Again, the murderer had taken pains to leave confusing false clues, which hinted at a degree of caution and cunning. Jameson had dropped a match-box with his name on it, or at least his initials, and had abandoned the search for it after a short hunt. The man who had left evidence that might involve three other people would have found the match-box before he left the lane at the back.

On the whole he was convinced that Jameson had spoken the truth—that is to say, he had been in the laneway on the Sunday night, had had a short interview with Mann at the back door, and had then rung the private bell of Mr Mander's flat for some time without eliciting any reply. But he had seen the ex-soldier before he rang the bell, and it was quite possible that Mann, coming afterwards upon traces of the crime and unaware what Jameson had done after leaving him, believed his old officer had murdered Mander.

If Devenish's theory was correct, however, Mann had not actually seen Jameson inside the Stores, but postulated his presence there when he came on the body of Mr Mander, and reflected that Peden-Hythe had a feud against the dead man. On the other hand, surely his common sense should have told him that Jameson, even if willing to kill a man he thought his enemy, would hardly be likely to butcher a young woman in addition?

But here again Devenish had to face one of those little psychological problems that crop up in every case. If Mann had made this particular mistake, it went to prove that he was really the nervous, emotional fellow Jameson declared him to be. He must have lost his head altogether for a little. What had ultimately pulled him together later had been his devotion and loyalty to the man who had saved his life in the war. That is not improbable in a case of the kind, for the instinct of loyalty to an individual sometimes rises triumphant over the instinct of self-preservation.

Devenish did not make the mistake of believing all his theories to be solutions of the problem, but he was bound to formulate theories to fit every side of the case and then proceed by the method of trial and error to eliminate those that did not fit. He had as yet none to cover the case of Mrs Hoe, and did not attempt to construct one till he should have questioned her further.

All he knew was that she had been blackmailing or attempting to blackmail Mr Mander, either alone or in association with Effie Tumour. Fresh from easy victories over young and inexperienced society women, with reputations at stake, she had not found it so easy to bluff the astute and cunning Mander; though it was more than possible that Mander's contemplated bolt with the funds was due to the pressure that vicious young woman was putting upon him. In that event either he did not know that Effie Tumour was allied with his tormentor, or it so happened that Mrs Hoe was working alone, using as a weapon some confidences given her as a friend by the dead woman.

Mrs Hoe's complicity in the case, if only in its outer fringes, was not at all helpful to Devenish. His years of experience had taught him that while blackmailers are occasionally killed by their desperate victims, these who live on hush-money are not given to violence. They fade out when the goose ceases to lay the golden eggs.

As Devenish approached the building where Mrs Hoe had her flat, he spoke to a man who was lighting a pipe near a lamp-post.

'In?' he asked quietly.

'In all right, sir,' mumbled the man, fumbling for another match.

# CHAPTER XX

DEVENISH regarded blackmail as one of the most loathly crimes, and he felt no pity for the haggard, white-faced woman with whom he was closeted a minute later.

Fear ravages a face more than any other emotion, more even than grief, and he felt it difficult to believe that the Mrs Hoe who now faced him was the attractive, cheerful, pretty young woman he had seen a few days before.

Her face had not a vestige of colour, and that alarming pallor was thrown into greater contrast by the lavish and reckless use of lipstick. Her eyes and her lips blazed in that waxen face. She looked hag-ridden and desperate, as her victims must have looked when they found themselves in her trap.

A practical man, Devenish had no more admiration for a bold rogue than a cringing one, but he felt a great contempt for this scotched snake, and watched sternly her attempts to wriggle free from his entangling questions.

Whatever nerve she had had was gone. She cowered in defeat, and her voice was obsequious and panic-stricken at once.

'I am so glad you have come, inspector,' she said, when she had given him a seat. 'I know you are very clever, but the other man who came here was extremely rude. He would not listen to what I said. He gave me no time to explain anything. You see, I have been made a fool of by someone I met, who asked me to keep some papers for him and not to let anyone have them on any account—'

She stopped suddenly and bit her lip. Devenish was staring at her intently, the corners of his lips curling down, and his expression was so far from sympathetic or comprehending that it frightened her more than Hemp's vigorous method.

'What papers?' he said curtly.

She went on hastily. 'I had no time to tell him. He wouldn't listen. You see these papers are apparently to do with blackmail, but what I wanted to explain was that I did not know it, I thought them quite another kind of paper.'

He looked less stern. She gathered hope.

'You see, in my job, I go to a good many society functions and some time ago I met a man who told me he was a Russian émigré, a "White" Russian, you know.'

'I know. Well?'

'Well, he was rather attractive, Prince Chavalze he called himself, and I didn't know anything about him, and was perhaps a little flattered that he paid attentions to me, when I was only a professional guest, if you know what I mean.'

'I know what you mean,' said Devenish grimly.

Her voice faltered as she went on.

'Well, like most people, I have always been sorry for the poor Russians who suffered for what was not their own fault, and I was silly enough to say so.'

'And yet you don't look a foolish woman,' he remarked dryly.

'We have all some soft spot, inspector. At any rate I did sympathise with him in a way that would have been impossible if I had known that the man was a rogue.'

'If you will get on, please, without wasting time explaining your emotions, it will be much better,' he said, with calculated brutality.

'I am sorry. I was only trying to show you how—but you are quite right. What I meant to say was this: After a little, he asked me if I would do something for him and his cause, and I said I would. He told me he had many papers dealing with counter-revolutionary plots, and he might be caught with them on him. Would I keep a packet for him, and also keep any letters that came for him? How was I to know that it was all lies, and the blackmail at the bottom of it?'

'But surely the inspector who executed the search warrant told you who he was?'

She hesitated a moment. 'Oh, yes, but the prince told me that his enemies might pretend to be police, and have forged documents. He said his countrymen were using forged documents and instruments. I only tried to throw that packet out of the window before I knew that my visitors were really English police.'

Devenish had not yet seen the papers, but from this attempt to throw dust in his eyes he knew that Mrs Hoe's name was not in them, nor could they be in her handwriting. Possibly they were typed, with symbols or initials to indicate the names of the victim or victims.

He allowed himself to appear slightly impressed. 'Of course I did not know this,' he replied. 'Anyone who undertook such a commission for a strange foreigner might be fooled in that way.'

'I thought you would say so,' she replied, brightening a little. 'You see, scoundrels like that have not come into my experience.'

'Only chickens to be plucked, I expect,' he said to himself, and added aloud: 'Well, that can easily be proved. May I ask where you met this prince—was it Chavalze?'

She forced a smile. 'Well, that was what he called himself, and I am sure he was a Russian. Let me see. I go to so many affairs. Would it be Mrs Paul Worger's musical evening?'

'I am asking you, madam.'

'Then I think it was. There were a great many people there, about five hundred I think. You know how big her—'

'Excuse me,' he interrupted, 'will you be good enough to ring up Mrs Paul Worger, and I shall speak to her?'

'Of course,' she said eagerly, 'I'll do it at once.'

When she came back, she told him that Mrs Worger would speak to him. He thanked her, and smiling faintly, shut the door behind him, and went to the telephone in the little hall. Mrs Worger was surprised to find that a detective-officer was speaking, but she readily replied to his questions, admitted that Mrs Hoe had reported her musical evening but denied knowing any Prince Chavalze.

'Mrs Hoe may be mistaken. Foreign names, especially Russian, are difficult, madam.'

'The only Russian of my acquaintance is an ancient professor of Liberal views,' she replied. 'He does not believe in Bolshevism, but he is against the extreme White Russians too. And his name is Vinoculoff.'

'So you do not know any Russian of that name. Thank you, madam,' he said, his ears alert for any sounds coming from the room behind him, while with his left hand he held a tiny pocket mirror up, so that it gave him a glimpse of the door to Mrs Hoe's sitting-room. As he rang off, he saw that the door had been opened half an inch, and was quickly and noiselessly shut again as he turned.

'What did Mrs Worger say?' she asked eagerly.

He looked at her sternly. 'She does not know any Prince Chavalze.'

Mrs Hoe looked startled, then apparently had an inspiration. 'But, of course. He must have been a gate-crasher. That sort of man would be, wouldn't he?'

'You are sure you saw him at Mrs Worger's?'

'I think it must have been there.'

'Do you know,' said Devenish more sternly than ever, 'that Mrs Worger says she was most particular that night to keep out gate-crashers. I thought of the possibility myself, you see. Every guest had to present a blue card.'

'Yes, but this man was evidently a forger,' she said. 'I told you—'

She stopped, knitted her brows, went to a writing-desk, and came back with a little diary, through which she glanced.

'How stupid I am!' she cried. 'I ought to have remembered. It was at Mrs Baleell's entertainment that I met the man. Do let me ring her up, and then you can speak.'

Devenish nodded curtly, and she put down the diary and went out to the telephone.

A faint smile came to the inspector's face as he sat there. He was determined to give the woman rope enough to hang herself, and he waited for two minutes without moving until she came back to apologise for the delay in getting through, and to inform him that Mrs Baleell would speak to him.

Then he got up and went again to the telephone.

'Inspector Devenish of Scotland Yard speaking,' he said.

'You wished to ask me something, inspector?' said a pleasant feminine voice.

'Yes, madam. I wish to know if you know a Prince Chavalze, a Russian émigré of the "White" persuasion. Also if Mrs Hoe could have met him at your house?'

'Yes, I know the prince. He is rather a mysterious person, and I have only met him once or twice. Mrs Hoe probably did meet him here, if she says so.'

'Thank you, madam, I am much obliged to you,' said Devenish, and rang off.

He went back at once to Mrs Hoe, told her that Mrs Baleell had confirmed her statement, and with apologies for troubling her, left the flat.

The moment he was in the street below, he made for the nearest telephone box and rang up the Central Office.

A mention of his rank and business at once brought him in touch with one of the higher officials, who asked him what he could do for him.

Devenish mentioned two telephone numbers, and added: 'A few minutes ago the owner of the first number rang up the second number. Can you tell me who the owner of the second number was? Perhaps you had better give me name and addresses of both these people so that there shall be no confusion.'

At the expiration of ten minutes he had a reply. 'We don't quite understand, inspector. The owner of the number you gave first (that of the person who rang up) gave two calls: the first was to a Mrs Paul Worger, but the second number was not called at all. It belongs to a Mrs Baleell.'

'Good,' said Devenish, smiling to himself. 'Mrs Baleell was not called at all. Would you be good enough to discover to whom the second message was sent? Mrs Baleell's number I got from the telephone book here.'

He waited again, feeling triumphant now. At last the voice of the telephone official came through again clearly.

'Mrs Hoe rang up on the second occasion a lady called Miss Minna Larder, of 666 Sloane Street.'

'I am much obliged to you,' said Devenish, hung up the receiver, and leaving the telephone box, took a taxi-cab at once to 666 Sloane Street.

# CHAPTER XXI

DEVENISH had a feeling that he had heard the name Minna Larder before. But he could not exactly place it. As he drove, he did not speculate as to the part she might be playing in this comedy of Mrs Hoe's. He preserved an open mind until he should see the woman herself and discover who and what she was.

When he called a few minutes later and was admitted by a maid in lavender, he began to see light. The room into which he was shown provided more illuminating rays. He knew now that he had seen the name of Miss Larder on a theatrical billboard. While he waited, he examined thoughtfully the various photographs in the room, showing Miss Larder in parts from Shakespearian plays, and took stock of her quiet, intelligent face, with its wide eyes, broad forehead and agreeable but firm mouth.

'Of course,' he said to himself, as he resumed his seat. 'She is the actress from that Shakespearian touring company, who made such a hit that she was given the part of the young mother in "Devious Days". But what is that face doing in this business?'

For five minutes he waited, then the door opened, and Miss Larder came in and greeted him.

Physically she was as the photographs showed her, and she had a deep, cool voice and a manner which was calculated to set the most nervous caller at his ease.

'You are Inspector Devenish?' she asked, as she motioned him to a seat.

'Yes, madam.'

'I was rather surprised when my maid told me,' she said, sitting down gracefully and allowing a faint smile to appear on her pleasant lips. 'You are sure that you are entitled to that rank, I suppose?'

He took out his credentials, and she examined the card with some perplexity and an occasional glance at him over the top of it. He read surprise in her manner, and a certain uneasiness.

'Then it was you who rang me up a short time ago?' she asked, fixing her eyes thoughtfully on his face.

'Yes. I asked you a question, madam, and I am afraid I did not get a very truthful answer.'

She smiled again, but not with such confidence as before. 'Well, I meant it as a joke, of course. To tell you the truth, inspector, my friend and press-agent, Mrs Hoe, certainly gave me the impression that it was one.'

He nodded. 'She rang you up at my request, madam. But she spoke to you before I did. It will help me, and relieve you from any responsibility, if you will give me the substance of that short conversation.'

Miss Larder bit her lip. 'I do not know if Mrs Hoe would wish me to do so.'

'I am sorry, but it is necessary that you should. I am engaged on a serious inquiry, and the matter is relevant to that, madam.'

She ruminated for a few minutes in silence, and he did not disturb her. It seemed to him that she was fishing in the wells of memory for something. A look came into her eyes, when they swept back to his face, that told him she had now remembered who he was and on what case he was engaged. But she made no comment on that, only looked grave and concerned as she replied at last.

'Very well. Mrs Hoe rang me up to say that she and two or three others were playing a joke on some friends. She had invented a Russian prince, Chavalze. One of her friends would not believe in this man's existence. Would I mind saying that I knew the prince and that she had met him at my house.'

'I see.'

'She said that the friend, who was an inveterate joker, would probably say he came from Scotland Yard. I was to expect that, and understand that it was all part of the little comedy. Then you rang up, gave your name, and naturally I answered as I had been asked to do. I hope I haven't done wrong?'

'On the contrary, you have been of very considerable assistance to me,' he assured her. 'May I ask if your acquaintance with Mrs Hoe is of long standing?'

'Only six months,' she said. 'When I left the provinces and got my chance in town, I was introduced to her by a woman at my club. I heard she was a journalist and was willing to act as press-agent on occasion. I found her very agreeable, and rather fascinating in some ways. But I know nothing more of her than that implies.'

Devenish believed her. 'And that is all I know really,' he said mendaciously. 'Evidently there has been some misunderstanding, madam. But you have helped to a certain extent to clear it up, and I am much obliged to you.'

He took his leave then and was half way to the front door when he heard the telephone ring above. The maid had come to show him out, but leaving her gasping on the stairs, he hastened up again and into the room he had just left. He sat down and waited. The telephone was in a room just beyond. Presently he heard it ring off, and then the sound of the maid's voice speaking to Miss Larder.

Miss Larder came to him at once. She looked pale and agitated.

'What does it mean, inspector?' she cried. 'Mrs Hoe has just rung me up again and asked, if anyone called, not to tell him what she had said. When I told her you had just been here, she cried out, and then I heard no more.'

'It means, madam, that Mrs Hoe is not a very suitable friend or press-agent for you,' he replied. 'She has been trying to throw dust in my eyes, and has had the impudence to make you a party to the attempt. You will understand that I cannot say any more at present, but just apologise for this second intrusion, and go.'

This time he did go, and finding another taxi, tore back to Mrs Hoe's flat. As he dismounted at the door of the building, the plain-clothes man, to whom he had spoken before, approached him.

'She came out just now, sir, looking desperate. I followed her, and I am afraid I was rather clumsy and let her see I was on her track. So, after going about a hundred yards, she changed her mind and went in again.'

'Bless your clumsiness!' said Devenish, smiling. 'It works out all right for once. But, after this, stick to her like a leech, and it doesn't matter if you are seen or not. Don't let her out of your sight!'

The man nodded and sidled away. Devenish went up to the flat, and rang. There was no answer. Devenish rang for several minutes, and there was still no reply. Officially, he would have found it difficult to justify his next action, but the best officials have to be unorthodox at times. He looked about him to see that he was not observed, then picked the lock of the flat with the speed and technique of an expert, and walked in, closing the door behind him.

But there seemed to be no one in the flat. At the back, where there was a fire-escape, a window was open. He looked out doubtfully, and saw a man dressed as a chauffeur standing in some mews behind, looking up at him. Devenish leaned out of the window, and indicated the escape with a wave of his hand. The man dressed as a chauffeur shook his head, and pointed to the flat with his finger.

Devenish walked back into the room, smiling grimly. If she thought of denying him admittance at this stage, it was obvious that Mrs Hoe hoped to make a getaway as soon as she could. Anyone who did not meditate a flight would realise that the police are not to be stalled off so easily.

Devenish began to whistle '*Where is my wandering boy tonight?*' as he went through the flat, examining it cursorily. Then he stepped back into the bedroom.

A tall wardrobe stood against one of the side-walls. He went over to it and flung the door open.

'Now, Mrs Hoe,' he said grimly. 'It's time you gave up this fooling, and realised your position.'

Mrs Hoe stumbled out of the wardrobe, crying with rage and fear combined. She glared at him, ground her teeth in impotent rage, and finally fell, half collapsed upon a chair.

'You beast!' she sobbed. 'You dirty bully!'

Devenish sat down on another chair and regarded her calmly. 'I like your choice of words,' he said, 'but now we can get down to tin tacks, I think. Do you know that you have been obstructing the police in the execution of their duty? That's your official crime. Your unofficial one is thinking me more of a fool than I am.'

He produced a note-book and pencil, laid the book open on his knee, and continued: 'What I want from you is a voluntary statement of your connection with the late Miss Tumour, also with Mr Kephim, of late. If you prefer to accompany me to Scotland Yard, you can make it there. If you do not, then you will please reply to my questions now, and afterwards write and sign a statement. If you refuse to do either, it is on your own responsibility.'

She trembled from head to foot with rage, but she replied in a venomous voice that she would prefer not to go to Scotland Yard.

'Very well,' said Devenish calmly. 'Now please let me hear where you first met Miss Tumour.'

'I was at school with her in the country. She was a farmer's daughter, and had won a scholarship at the County School.'

'You were friendly with her then?'

'Yes. We were great friends.'

'You came up to town. When did you meet her again?'

'A month before Mr Mander opened the Stores.'

Devenish saw that this time, driven by fear of being involved in the murder, she was going to tell the truth.

'She was then chief, or was it second-buyer, in the millinery department at a smaller shop from which Mr Mander got her?'

'Yes.'

'Do you know if she had met Mander previously? I mean before he gave her this post?'

Mrs Hoe bit her lip. 'Yes. He was studying the other shops before he opened, and he took a fancy to her.'

'Did it go beyond that?'

'She told me he took her out to dinner two or three times, and to the theatre.'

'She confided in you. Was she given to confidences?'

'To me, yes.'

'Can you tell me if her appointment to Mander's Stores was as much the result of her fascinating Mr Mander as her ability at her job?'

Mrs Hoe smiled sardonically. 'He was madly in love with her if you want to know.'

He nodded. 'I have to know. Now is it a fact that she told you all about their relations, and what they did?'

'Yes.'

'Did she tell you that Mr Mander contemplated taking her abroad, and that she was going as a Miss Linkster?'

'Yes, she did, or at least he wanted her to go, and had got the passports. She didn't know he was thinking of bolting though.'

'You knew then that she had allowed herself to be falsely represented on a passport, and also that Mr Mander had procured the passports?'

'Of course. I have just said so.'

He shrugged. 'Did she ever tell you why she allowed herself to become engaged to Mr Kephim when she was already associated with Mander?'

'I suppose she thought she was in love with Mr Kephim,' replied Mrs Hoe bitterly.

Devenish glanced at her. The bitterness in her voice, the look on her face, gave him a strong impression that she was in love with Mr Kephim herself, and had been jealous of the woman to whom he was engaged.

'Why did you say Miss Tumour "thought of going" away with Mander?'

She pursed her lips. 'Well, she was in two minds about it. She liked the things Mander could give her, and she hated to give them up, but she was—more fond of Mr Kephim. Lately anyway.'

'You mean that she was really in love at the last with Kephim, and felt disinclined to go off with Mander?'

'She didn't know what love meant!'

'You are a judge of the softer affections, no doubt,' said Devenish acidly. 'But what hindered her from breaking with Mander if she felt that she could not go on?'

'She was afraid, she said, that Mander would sack Kephim. I don't know if that was true.'

He nodded. 'You have visited or have been visited by Mr Kephim two or three times since the murder?'

Her lips curled. 'I suppose your spies told you that.'

'We received information to that effect. Now, how long have you known Kephim?'

'Don't be a fool!' she cried violently. 'He had nothing to do with the murder. He wouldn't hurt a fly.'

'We will assume it for the present, but how long have you known him?'

'Not many months. Before they were engaged Effie used to bring him to tea here sometimes.'

'Then you did not know him well?'

'Only as a friend of Effie's.'

'Why call on him so soon after the murder?'

She coloured up, and Devenish found his theories confirmed. Whatever she had done, and harpy as she was, she had fallen in love with the man she herself had previously spoken of as weak.

'That is my business.'

'I am waiting.'

'Well, I can't tell you anything more. I thought he had been very badly treated, and I went to sympathise with him. I wanted to make up to him for the bad time he had had.'

'It didn't occur to you that your calls might lead him to be suspected?'

She looked horrified. 'Never! I should never have gone if I had thought that.'

He shrugged again.

'You know, of course, that we examined Mr Mander's flat, and went through all his papers,' said Devenish.

'I assumed you did,' she replied. 'The police always do, don't they?'

He was bluffing again now, but from her expression he judged that Mr Mander had had some letters from her, and that she was not sure if they had been destroyed. As this was the effect he had been trying to produce, he was not ill pleased.

'I am telling that so that you may be careful in your replies,' he returned, dryly. 'We don't want to have any more mistakes in your evidence.'

She was cunning enough to see that the police did not intend to proceed against her on a blackmailing charge, and was now most anxious to clear herself of any implication in the murder.

'No one could prove that I was at the flat that night,' she said hastily. 'I have a complete alibi.'

'More convincing than your story of the Russian émigré, I hope. But I may as well hear it, and check it. Where were you on the Sunday night, from half-past seven in the evening until, say, seven next day?'

She replied at once: 'I was staying with Mr and Mrs Jay at Sundymore, Redhill. Mr Jay is sub-editor of my principal paper—'

'I know of him,' said Devenish. 'That sounds good enough. But when did you go there, and when did you leave?'

'Mr Jay called for me with his car at five. I did not leave Redhill until the 9.05 train next morning.'

'Right. We can confirm that at once. But to go back to Miss

Effie Tumour. Can you form any idea why she went to see Mr
Mander that night after she had spent the day with Mr Kephim?
Did she see you in the interim, or did she by any chance ring
you up to tell you she was going?'

Mrs Hoe reflected. She was well aware that the police could
get a record of telephone calls, and another slip on her part
would lead them utterly to discredit her evidence. At this stage
it could do her no good to throw the blame of complicity in
blackmail upon the dead girl, and she determined that frankness
would pay best. After this last debacle she intended to go abroad,
and she would not be allowed to do that if she fell foul of the
C.I.D.

'Yes, she rang me up on returning to her flat.'

'What did she say to you?'

'She said she had had a lovely day with Mr Kephim, and he
was really an awfully good sort.'

'Anything more?'

'Well, she said she felt sure any of the other firms would
jump at him, and it would not pay Mander to sack him.'

'Did she use these names on a telephone?'

'No, she simply called them by their Christian names.'

'And then?'

Mrs Hoe reflected for a few moments. She was calmer now,
and hoped she was making a good impression on the man who
had it in his power to make things hot for her if he chose.

'Well, I gathered that she thought she was in love really this
time,' she went on, and Devenish noticed with amusement how
she hated using the word without qualification. 'She said she
was fed-up with the other business, and sorry she ever started
it. She was going to see Mander to tell him that she was engaged
to Kephim. I agreed with her that it was wiser from her point
of view.'

Devenish nodded. 'Then she was not a party to the blackmail?'

She bit her lip. It is extraordinary how squeamish some

rogues are about using the plain name for their plain profession.

'Any money she had from Mander was because he was in love with her,' she replied.

'Frankly, did she blackmail him or not?'

'No, she didn't.'

'That is what I want to know. Now, can you tell me if she mentioned that she was visiting Mander that night?'

'No. She simply said she was going, not when she was going.'

Devenish got up. 'Just a last question. Do you think Miss Tumour was in possession of a firearm, or any weapon?'

She shook her head. 'I never heard of it. I don't think so. Of course, she might have bought one lately without my knowing.'

He put away his note-book and pencil. 'Now, will you please repeat that statement on paper, in your own words, sign it, and give it to me. Take your time.'

# CHAPTER XXII

When Devenish had made his report and left in the signed statement given him by Mrs Hoe, he went home, put on a pipe, and sat down to consider the general situation.

He began by getting out some sheets of paper, and trying to summarise the points for and against the suspects and witnesses in the case, taking them in the order in which they seemed more naturally to come.

He headed the first page MR KEPHIM, and wrote:

'No alibi in this case, but its absence, considering the man, is rather in his favour; also my presumption that the murders took place prior to the time at which he admittedly left his flat. Mrs Hoe's evidence, while possibly biased in his favour by the fact (presumption?) that she is in love with him, tends to convince me that he is innocent. The motive of jealousy, the only one for him, is strong, but no proof that he knew Miss Tumour was associated with Mr Mander.

'MR CANE.—The only link here is some knowledge of aeroplanes, his claim that he is the inventor of the gyrocopter, stolen by Mr Mander, and his dislike (this may be partly Kephim's fault) of the manager. The fact that some of the evidence tells against Kephim would not be known to Cane. How, for example, could he know that Kephim would be out alone late on the Sunday night? The use of a steel-jacketed bullet, if this was fired into the sandbank to involve Kephim, who was known as a rifle shot, the bullet which was fired on the roof would hint at manufactured evidence. But we have no proof that Cane manufactured it, or was on the roof at any time after the occasion when the gyrocopter made a forbidden landing earlier in the year.

'WEBLEY.—This man is not very scrupulous, but there is no

evidence that he did land on the roof on the dark of a Sunday night in November, but a great deal of technical evidence against the theory. Still, the man will require watching. If he did not fly to London that night, he lives in a cottage by himself, and may have travelled up to town without anyone being aware of it. He admits having been bribed by Mander to cheat Cane out of his inventor's rights. Mrs Hoe may not have been the only one given a handle for blackmail by Mander's double-dealing.

'Mr Peden-Hythe.—A curious specimen of the man of education gone to seed, and now apparently trying to pull himself up. Childishly cunning in some ways, with a positively infantile way of substituting one story for another when the first is found out. His manner altogether convinces me that he is not the kind of man to commit a murder in cold blood. Against that, I must set the fact that he was to a certain extent under the influence of drink on the Sunday night, did actually turn up in the lane, and admittedly tried to get into Mander's back door. His feeling against Mander is very obvious, though to be easily accounted for by the fact that (1) His mother was fascinated by the man. (2) That he had heard rumours that Mander was fooling about with the capital Mrs Peden-Hythe had supplied him with. As his mother's heir, these facts would hit him hard. There is also the fact that (with the connivance of the watchman, who owes him a debt of loyalty and is in his pay), he could have gained access to the interior of the Stores.

'Mrs Hoe.—She appeared to be a rather more complex type than the average blackmailer of her type, though she is like them in being remorseless, cowardly, and as easily bullied as her victims when it comes to a show-down. There is no doubt that she was confided in by the girl Tumour, and little doubt that Tumour was not aware to what use Hoe intended to put these confidences. She agrees that she heard of the false passports, and, inferentially, that she was beginning to use this knowledge to get money from Mander. (Memo.: Is it possible that Mander suspected Tumour of being in this game as well, and killed her to ensure her silence?) I have rung up Mr Jay at Redhill, and he confirms the woman's alibi for that night.

'MANN.—In some ways this is my most puzzling witness. He looks honest, but then he also looks a normal strong-minded man, though he is said to be nervous and cowardly. His service in the army does not count one way or the other, since the soldier of the old regulars did not necessarily expect to fight, and there were some few peaceful people among them. Obviously he could see little in a dark store, and with the microphone gadget cut off, he might not hear a soft foot, while the lifts work extremely noiselessly. In addition he admits that he neglected his duty at times, to work for Mr Peden-Hythe, accepting the latter's view that, as his family were paying the piper, they might call the tune. This is natural enough reasoning for a simple man.

'Against Mann's complicity is the fact that Tumour's coat and hat were new, and were returned to the department from which they came. It is quite possible that a watchman might amuse himself at night by looking at the various things in the store, but would the man who only came on duty at ten be aware that Tumour had bought the articles mentioned at Mander's?'

Devenish finished his notes and his pipe at the same moment. He sat back in his chair, read the notes through slowly, then put them away, and allowed his mind to play about the various subjects the reading brought up.

One thing struck him forcibly, and that was an omission, if an intentional one. He had not mentioned the missing glove, because he associated it with the missing carpet square and did not wish to attach either object at random to anyone on his list.

If Mann had had a pistol, he had no doubt hidden it. The most ignorant of men is aware that searches will be made, and will make it his first duty to dispose of the incriminating object. If he was concerned in the murder, Mann would also dispose of the square.

The evidence of the expert called in by Scotland Yard with regard to the bullet found in the sandbank on the roof would not have been accepted without question by Devenish but for the corroborative evidence of this little square of thick pile carpet. But the carpet itself imported a new complication into the case. It would not have been removed, and the spare piece substituted for it, if it had not been extensively bloodstained. If it was so damaged, the inference was that at least one of the murders had taken place in that lift.

On the following morning, Devenish paid a visit to the expert who had examined the bullet. He was a Mr Green, a rather dogmatic and positive fellow, as men will be when they are used to giving expert witness on a subject they have made their own.

He listened to what Devenish had to say, then nodded, and looked interested.

'That doctor of yours is like all amateurs,' he said. 'He has a ha'porth of knowledge and a ton of conceit.'

'But I thought it was agreed that the bullet was a high velocity one?'

'That was on the assumption that it had gone clean through the man, and vanished.'

'What about the nature of the wound?'

'That is a doctor's job. I don't worry about what is outside my own line, and it is a pity your doctor doesn't do the same.'

'Have you any idea what kind of bullet may have been used?'

The expert shrugged. 'Well, it wasn't a split-nose or a dum-dum. It is my opinion that it may have been caused by a—I mean the wound, of course—by a bullet from a pistol of say .32 calibre. As you suggest, the fact that the bullet was not found does not prove that it carried on out of sight. It would be slowed by impact with the tissues and muscles, and perhaps deflected by striking a bone.'

'It is possible, you would say, that it would be stopped on emergence by a thick pile square of carpet?'

'That is quite possible, inspector. Put the high velocity idea aside for the present.'

'Our surgeon was at the war, and he does know something of wounds.'

Green smiled. 'You must allow for the influence of what looks like corroborative evidence upon any opinion,' he said. 'A young friend of mine, going in for a medical exam. and asked to diagnose the case of a patient, saw a splint and deduced a fracture. If he had seen nothing, he might have discovered the patient's real complaint. Your surgeon saw a high-velocity small arm on the scene. He thinks he is telling you what he discovered from the wound—actually he was telling you what kind of wound that kind of weapon would cause, if it had been used.'

Devenish smiled too. 'I find myself making just that sort of error at times. Well, you are quite sure the bullet I did find had not passed through a human body? My assumption, of course, was that its passage through the sand had cleaned it.'

'It had only passed through sand,' said Green, with conviction. 'But what about making a test. I have a .32 cal. automatic here. We can go to the Store and try it out.'

'We haven't the necessary body,' said Devenish.

'We can get a sheep sent along,' said Green. 'How long is the Store to be kept shut?'

'We can't say yet. Our people have spoken to Mrs Peden-Hythe about it, or rather her solicitor. She is the real owner.'

Green nodded. 'We'll have to make the sheep do. It will give us a general line on the case. Can you have one sent in, carefully wrapped up, and I'll meet you there with the gun and ammunition in an hour.'

'I will arrange it at once,' said Devenish, and took his leave.

Having made arrangements for the carcass of a sheep to be sent to the Stores and delivered by way of the back entrance, Devenish got hold of Sergeant Davis and walked over. Davis had been busy over the case of the watchman, but had nothing of interest to relate.

'I don't think the fellow had a weapon, sir,' he told Devenish as they went. 'His wife never saw him with one, or heard of him buying one. She thinks he is too nervous to use one.'

Devenish smiled. 'Well, she ought to know, and her evidence given to you independently as to his lack of courage is helpful. But I am not going to accept the conclusion yet.'

When they had reached the Store the carcass had not yet arrived, but Devenish arranged with two of the police on duty that the sheep should be taken up to the roof when it came.

'I don't know the relative resistance offered by the tissues and muscles of a sheep and a man, nor what difference the flesh being that of a dead animal makes,' he told Davis, as they went to Mander's flat and let themselves in, 'but it is the best we can do at present, and may, as Mr Green says, give us a hint. We'll make the experiment in the open, upstairs, in case of a richochet. By the way, I had forgotten the square from the lift—will you go down and get one?'

'But won't it spoil it as one of our exhibits, sir?'

'I mean out of one of the other lifts. They are all the same pattern of thick pile carpet. Bring up the underlying square of lino too. We may as well have the conditions as nearly similar as possible.'

'Then you think Mr Mander was shot in the lift, sir?'

'I don't know. No one does. But we are going to consider the possibility.'

Davis nodded, and went away, to return in a few minutes with the objects asked for. Almost simultaneously, Mr Green turned up with two automatic pistols, one of .32 calibre, and two small boxes of ammunition. He was talking with Devenish and the sergeants when a policeman knocked at the door of the flat and came in to say that the sheep was now on that floor.

'You'll have to bring it in through here, Robbins,' said Devenish. 'I know there is only the one way up to the roof. Put it down near one of the sandbanks.'

On the high roof the sound of shots was not likely to be heard very loudly by those in the streets, and would in any case be mistaken for the sound of a back-firing motor. With some trouble the lino was laid on the rooftop, the pile carpet square on top of that, and the carcass of the sheep laid upon it in such a position that a shot would be likely to strike the carpet, if it penetrated the body, and was not stopped on the way by bone or muscle.

Using the two pistols in turn, with two kinds of ammunition, and firing into the sheep at ranges varying from three feet to ten, Mr Green conducted his rough test while Devenish observed closely and dictated his observations to Davis, who took them down in his note-book. After six rounds, two bullets had failed to emerge, two had struck a bone and glanced out, conveniently burying themselves in the sandbank; one had penetrated both the square and the carpet, the last had merely stuck in the carpet's thick pile.

'That is the sort of result you want, inspector,' remarked the expert, as he exhibited this last bullet, 'but one out of six is not good enough. We must have the sheep in another position and I'll try again.'

'It is just possible that the shot which struck Mander met the same resistance as this single bullet,' observed Devenish, 'but, as you say, it will be better to have another go.'

The carcass was rearranged, and Davis was sent down to the butler below to get a kitchen table. When that was brought up, it was arranged to the side of the sheep, and Green, smiling a little as he did so, climbed on the table and resumed his tests.

A second series of six shots gave two bullets that had got no farther than the pile of the carpet, and Devenish professed himself satisfied for the present.

The table was taken away, the dead sheep removed, and the three men went down to the flat and sat smoking and talking things over.

'If Mander was shot in that lift,' said Green, 'I think you

would find that that thick carpet was thoroughly soaked. There might be enough blood to make a slight stain on the underside.'

'But how was Mander shot in the lift, sir, when the woman was killed up here?' asked Davis.

'You are sure she was killed up here?'

'The stains on the sand couldn't come from Mander, if he was below,' said Devenish, 'and the bruises on her upper arms suggest to me that she was gripped from behind and pushed before someone up the stairway that leads to the roof.'

Green shrugged. 'But she would cry out?'

Devenish smiled. 'She might. But I doubt if she would be heard, or would bring anyone to her aid. If you shout as high up as this, your voice sounds pretty thin below.'

'And if you hear a distant cry, you would hardly look up in the air to locate it on a dark November night, sir,' added Davis. 'It's strange how hard it is to locate any sound at night. Then everyone would think the Stores was closed on Sunday and they would only look for the person who screamed in the streets about them, not up on top of this building.'

Green agreed. 'I hadn't thought of that.'

# CHAPTER XXIII

THE report had come in with regard to the soil which had made the wheel marks on the roof, and with it a few notes made by the expert.

It had been easy enough to analyse the dried mud, but a much longer business to discover certain districts from which it had come, and there was a remark in one of the notes that puzzled Devenish considerably.

'It appears to me,' said the writer, 'that this soil has a certain admixture of soot and sulphurous matter that does not suggest a recent deposit on the roof of the Stores. I am inclined to think that this dried clay was deposited on the roof of the building for some time, alternately dried by the sun and wet by the very slight precipitation which has distinguished this year. In its damp state, it would catch and be contaminated by the products of city smoke. The clay itself occurs in a good many districts, but certainly over a fairly large area between London and Gelover. There is, for example, a tract near the village of Humbleby, in a cup-like depression on the reverse slope of the hill under which the village is built. Confirmation of this can be obtained from the geological survey.'

'That sooty stuff couldn't be from the cinder laid taking-off place at Gelover, I suppose?' the inspector said to himself as he read. 'Our people work much closer than that. Besides, if the tyres were already muddy, fine particles of cinder would be certain to show.'

He had been studying this report while he ate his breakfast. Now he looked up a timetable to see how he could get to Humbleby, and found that the village was not on the railway map, being a tiny hamlet with about sixty inhabitants. In the end he took a police car down, Sergeant Davis accompanying him, left it in the village, and walked over the low hill towards the depression on the reverse slope, or rather at the bottom of it.

Here there was a sort of pan, fairly flat and marshy in places, with little herbage towards the centre, and patches of exposed clay. Devenish got out a map, took compass bearings, and discovered that the spot lay nearly in the direct route between Gelover and London, being but slightly to the south-east of it.

Without much hope of finding anything, the detectives quartered the ground carefully over an area of perhaps half a square mile, going right beyond the borders of the pan at times. At the end of an hour they drew together again, but could report nothing.

'Not that I expected to find much,' said Devenish, as they adjourned to a grassy bank, sat down, and began to smoke. 'Now, let me see. I have got the newspapers which gave an account of the flight of the gyrocopter. I'll read you out any salient points.'

He read for some minutes in silence, then began aloud: "'Taking off like some great, lazy moth, rising in an almost vertical line, and appearing for a moment to hover like a hawk above the Manor, the epoch-making machine drifted south, and after a perfect flight landed on the flat roof of the new mammoth Stores. The indignation of our hide-bound and red-tape strangled bureaucracy knew no bounds. 'Let progress perish!' they said in effect, 'but observe the laws.' But, in spite of them, the gyrocopter had triumphed. Slow but sure, it had made its way to London, and landed in a space hardly bigger than a tennis-court.'"

Devenish looked up and laughed. 'A giant's tennis-court that roof,' he said. 'It would take two Tildens to reach the baseline with their hottest drives. Still, you notice the remark, "a perfect flight," qualified by "slow but sure," eh? Nothing to help us there. We had better get along to the village, and inquire at the pub. I bet the flight is talked of now, and will be for ten years. A small sensation is a long topic in a small place.'

They returned to the village over the hill, and had a talk with the landlord of the 'Snig and Spear' ('Snig' meaning a small eel, which accounted for the strange sounding name). Borlas, who kept the place, was a fat man with a cheery expression, and they found him immediately interested in their queries.

'Flight, gentlemen,' he observed. 'Why, I saw it proper. I heard a great shouting and screeching, and out I ran, to see the thing like a whirrling bum-bee overhead. It didn't look like any aeryplane I ever saw, and most of them here was out staring too, till it went over the hill, like.'

'And vanished from view,' said Devenish, smiling.

'That it did,' said the landlord. 'It wasn't so high neither, and old John Higgs, who does mostly no work, but a bit of poaching, he came in that evening, and said he saw it come down over the hill and get up again. But no one else saw it, and he's reckoned a great liar; and is too, surely. Anyway, he told one reporter from the local paper so, and that one put it in, and then old John he came down, and said it was made up, and he never saw it come down, but just wanted something to talk about, and perhaps get half a pint for telling of it.'

Devenish thanked him, and he and Davis went off to interview the poacher. But the poacher was surly. He stuck to his amended story, and they had to leave him without obtaining any information of value.

'Did he make it up, sir, do you think?' asked Davis, as they travelled back to town in the car.

'I have an impression that his first yarn was the true one,' Devenish replied thoughtfully. 'I look at it this way: he does not deny that version until it has appeared in a local paper after an interview with a reporter. Why give the news and then deny it—or, more correctly, give the news to the public and then deny it to his cronies at the pub?'

'That does seem odd.'

Devenish nodded. 'Yes, until you reflect that this was to be a record feat for the gyrocopter, and was featured in the London papers as a "perfect" flight. If it had to descend on the way, even for a short time, that would spoil the perfection, and also make the machine appear less safe than it really was. If only the poacher saw it drop, he may have been squared. No doubt Mander gets press-cuttings, or did, about all the stunts to advertise the Stores.'

'And may have had one from this local paper?'

'That's it. He may have sent someone down diplomatically to quash this evidence of an eyewitness. A fiver would go a long way with Higgs. Otherwise he would have been like a single gallery interruptor at a perfect first-night. It is the only way I can explain his sudden change of front.'

'What is the next move then, sir?'

'I am going to call at the Metereological Record Office and get a chart for the day of the flight. We want to know weather conditions between here and town, and here and Gelover, and the prevailing wind in London and *en route* that day. Then I am going to see the butler at the flat again.'

'Shall you want me with you, sir?'

'No. I shall drop you at the Yard. I have no time to spare there, but you might see the superintendent and tell him what we have discovered today.'

Davis got down later, and when Devenish resumed his journey afoot, and had studied the weather charts supplied him by the experts at the Record Office, he looked a little happier.

'Unless there is a snag in the butler's statement, I have cleared that point up,' he said to himself, and hurried away to the Stores and went up to Mander's flat. Here he interviewed the butler.

'I am anxious to know if the roof above was much used,' he said to the man.

'I couldn't say that it was, sir,' replied the butler. 'You see, Mr Mander meant it for a place for aeroplanes to land, and when there was that trouble over it, he kind of lost heart. But he may have gone up there in the summer evenings, without me knowing.'

'I remember that he tried to get the place legalised, pointing out that the gyrocopter had reversed all the views with regard to the safe landing of a plane on confined spaces.'

'Yes, he did, sir. He was much put out when they wouldn't agree. But then I don't know much about the roof, sir. I never go up there, and there isn't any way from our quarters.'

Devenish saw that point. He knew that Mander had really expected to create a sensation, and make wonderful sales by beginning a mail-order business to be conducted by gyrocopters flown from the roof of the Store, but he had not allowed for the conservatism of the authorities. It was quite likely that he had taken little further interest in the roof, which had been designed for one purpose only, and was not even accessible from the Store, save through the flat.

'Who was responsible for keeping the roof clean?' he asked after a moment.

The butler shook his head. 'We were never asked to see to it, sir, and I don't think anyone else did.'

'Perhaps some of the cleaners of the Stores?'

'Not that I heard of, sir. They would have had to be let in, and I never saw any of them up here, or heard of them coming either.'

Devenish thanked and dismissed him, and went up on the roof alone. Here he leaned against one of the parapets and studied a weather chart with intent interest.

'By Jove! The wind was wrong for a landing on the Sunday of the murder, but right on the day of the first landing,' he mused. 'On that first occasion Webley could have landed as these wheel-tracks show. The only points against it are: first, that it is a question if the mud would have remained here all that time—though there was little rain this year—and, secondly, how is it that the tracks are narrower than the tyres fitted to the gyrocopters in the department below? The edges of the mud may have weathered off, of course, but I am not sure of that.'

He made a further examination of the tracks on the roof,

and saw that the clay was of a peculiarly clinging kind. Further, he descended to the ironmongery department, and brought up a large watering-can which he filled with water, and carried to the roof. Selecting a small section of the tracks, he watered it steadily, and then left it to dry a little in the cool easterly breeze that was now sweeping across the roof, and visited Mander's flat again, where he looked in the study until he came upon some bound numbers of *Flight*. Here he discovered a pretty full account of the marvellous roof landing, and, at the end of the article, a specification of the machine, as far as details had been allowed to leak out.

'I believe that settles it,' he said, as he took a note of the size of the tyres, and went up again to the roof. 'That day was dry, but the previous day there had been heavy rain in the home counties. I'll just see how the tracks look, then ring up Cane.'

To his gratification, the watering had not removed much of the clinging clay on the section he had watered. Most of it had dried again in the cold air. To a certain extent, of course, the flat of the roof was protected by the parapets from anything but a gale.

'Naturally I thought this roof would be regularly cleaned and swept, or I should have thought of it before,' he mused, as he descended for the last time that day to the flat, 'but better late than never.'

A minute later he rang up Cane and told him his views. Cane laughed. 'I could have told you that we found it better to put larger tyres on the landing-carriages of the later machines,' he replied. 'I did not mention the fact, because I thought you were referring to a flight made on the Sunday night when Mander was murdered.'

'And I never looked for it, because I fully believed that the machine on its first flight here came straight across from the hard landing ground at Gelover, Mr Cane. I see now that Webley must have made a forced landing, and the matter was hushed up when it leaked out in that country paper. I'll see Webley again, make sure of that, and then know where I am. The evidence of those wheel-tracks has been one of the complicating features of the case. Once it is cleared away, I shall be able to state that the murderer, however he came here, did not come by air.'

'I felt sure he couldn't, at night, and without landing lights,' said Cane.

Devenish rang off, went to the street, and at once hurried to Gelover. He returned in a more leisurely way, having got what he wanted. When Webley heard that this evidence would exculpate him, he at once admitted the truth of the theory. On the day of the sensational flight, he had landed near Humbleby, but, finding the trouble was not as serious as he thought, had put it right, and managed to rise again within twenty-five minutes. Only the help of the gyrocopter lift, he said, enabled him to rise off that soft clay. He had communicated the fact to Mr Mander, and Mr Mander had told him to say nothing about it.

'But someone else did,' said Devenish. 'Did you go over to Humbleby?' Webley nodded. 'Yes, the guv'nor gave me a fiver, and I saw an old man called Higgs, who told the reporter he had seen me come down, and got a promise from him to say he made it up. It wouldn't have done the machine any good, sir, if it was known it had come down the first time.'

# CHAPTER XXIV

Mr Green had a gun-shop in New Bond Street, and Devenish called upon him next day and had a short talk. He was emerging from the shop when someone touched him on the shoulder, and he turned to face Jameson Peden-Hythe.

Jameson was all smiles. For the first time since Devenish had met him he looked buoyant, almost virile. He had a little colour in his face, and his eyes were clearer, his manner less languid.

'Hello, inspector, you're the very man I wanted to see,' he remarked. 'Old Hay is getting busy, and he wants to know when the bally Stores can be opened again. He wrote to my mother about it this morning.'

Devenish reflected. 'That I cannot say. I hope soon.'

'Soon, eh? Getting on the track at last, I suppose. By the way, what about a coffee? There's a bun-shop close by.'

He grinned a little as he said that, and Devenish also smiled. 'Thank you.'

'Fact is,' remarked Peden-Hythe, confidentially, 'I am one of the neck-or-nothing kind. Got to cut it right out, or swim in it, don't you know. But I'm getting used gradually to soft drinks; though cocoa has me beat before the race starts. By the way, did I tell you you might congratulate me?'

Devenish shook his head, as they turned into the fashionable tea-shop in Jameson's wake. 'No,' he said, scenting the origin of the new radiance and that spirited attempt to 'put a padlock on it'. 'I hadn't heard, sir.'

Jameson led the way to a quiet corner and ordered two coffees. 'Have a cigar,' he said, and added: 'I don't take much stock of proverbial philosophy, inspector, but, by Jove, patience is rewarded this time. Funniest thing in the world, you know.

I mean me getting a bit tight and camping in Sir William's house for simply hours.'

'You think that produced an impression, sir?' said Devenish, laughing as he lit his cigar.

'Must have done,' said Jameson, also lighting up. 'Sort of thing I wouldn't have dreamed of doing in my sober senses, but it worked. I thought I would tell you, since you knew what an ass I had made of myself.'

Devenish nodded. 'Same lady, sir?'

'Absolutely. Fact is, I wrote to her, and did a crawl. I owed her that. So the thing is arranged; witness this coffee. I'm a damned lucky man, inspector!'

Devenish congratulated him heartily. There was, he saw, something fundamentally decent and attractive in his companion; something that helped to explain Mann's loyalty to his former officer.

'Sir William's been very decent about it too,' resumed Jameson, 'though I don't know that he would have taken a fancy to me in a neat prison suiting, as the tailors call it—I suppose I am definitely off your list, inspector?'

'I think I can reassure you on that point, sir. I imagine you will be able to have the usual "morning-coat and striped". But, talking about Mann, there are just one or two little points that I would like cleared up.'

Jameson narrowed his eyes a little, then nodded. 'Carry on.'

'I want to know the time when you actually spoke to Mann at the back door of the Stores—as near as you can make it.'

Jameson told him. 'Anything else?'

'How long were you there talking, do you think?'

'Ten minutes to a quarter of an hour, I should say. It is difficult to say exactly.'

'Then did he leave you, lock the door, and not come out again?'

'He went in, and I heard him lock the door, but I can't say

if he came out again. He may have done later, for all I know.'

'He didn't ask you to take anything for him? I do not suppose for a moment that he did, but I must ask.'

'No. You can be bally well sure of that. I hate carrying beastly parcels, even if they are no bigger than a bee's knee, and Mann would certainly not have thought of handing me one.'

Devenish nodded. 'While you were in the lane you did not hear a shot, or a cry?'

'None at all. I say, you are still dithering on about old Mann. It seems to me sheer waste of time. He wouldn't do it; he had no reason to do it, and wouldn't have done if he had had a reason.'

Devenish finished his coffee, took a pull at his cigar, and fixed his eyes on Jameson's rather indignant face.

'Did it ever occur to you, sir, that you had a grudge against the dead man, that the watchman knew of it, and may have exaggerated its bitterness?'

'Mann? Well, by Jove, he may. I used some pretty hot language about the bounder.'

'Then he knew that you were in the lane when he locked up again, and that you were within a few yards of Mander's private staircase. He might have said to himself that you had got in and, not being in your sober senses, committed the crime.'

Jameson rubbed his head. 'He really is a bit of a bonehead, but surely he doesn't think I go Woolly West-wise round London, armed with a gun, or gat, or whatever the pictures call it? I don't say he wouldn't go a good length to shield me, if he took me for an amateur gunman, for he's the most embarrassingly grateful fella I ever met. But if he thought I did kill the man, why did he imagine I stuck the girl up in the window? Did he think I was a disappointed lover too, like that fella Kephim?'

Devenish laughed. 'You are interested in him, sir?'

'I have to be, my dear chap. He insists on it! Gelert's faithful hound is nothing to Mann when he's on the job. Seriously, though, I should be very sorry if anything happened to him.'

He looked earnestly and inquiringly at Devenish as he said that, and the detective shrugged.

'He is in very considerable danger of being arrested at this moment, sir, and I was wondering if you would have any influence with him.'

Jameson stared. 'Don't be an ass! Arrested, what for?'

'He knows more than he has told,' said Devenish sternly. 'If he had the sense of a blind mouse, he would come out with it.'

'But it's a waste of time to go at him. What about all the evidence, all those clues you fellows found?'

'What about his still being in the Stores that morning at nine, when his turn of duty is over and he usually goes off at eight?'

'What about it? He would not hang about if he was guilty?'

'He would not run away if he was guilty.'

'And give himself away, no. But he would go home at the usual time.'

Devenish shook his head. 'And stay at home wondering if he was suspected? That type of man would want to know the worst. If he is as nervous as you and other people make out, that is what he would do.'

'That may be. But what about the clues?'

The inspector replied slowly. 'Those confused and confusing bits of evidence suggest to me a man who did not contemplate murder, but was eventually determined that the issue should be fogged, and the suspicion so diffused, that we should not get at the real criminal.'

Jameson looked interested. 'Surely a murderer's idea is to get away safely? If he leaves faked evidence, it must be to involve somebody else, and remove the suspicion from his own shoulders. A callous fellow like that wouldn't care who got in for it.'

'Quite so, sir, if he had committed a murder and was callous.'

'But you talk of arresting him for murder.'

'I did not say for murder, sir. The fact is that one or two puzzling bits of evidence have been cleared away. I know that there was no landing of a gyrocopter on the roof that Sunday night. I know why Miss Tumour called to see Mander, and I am of opinion that there was only one murder.'

'My dear fella!'

'And two bodies,' added Devenish grimly. 'Well, perhaps that is a bit too much to say. I mean I am convinced that there was only one murder.'

'Murder and suicide. I see what you mean.'

'Not exactly. But I must not say anything more at present.'

Jameson nodded. 'Right. Will you have another coffee?'

'No, thank you. But I shall be glad if you can make it convenient to go with me to see Mann. I want to assure him that you are in no danger of being implicated, and I want you, if you will be so good, to convince Mann that he had better tell the truth.'

Jameson beckoned to the waitress, and got up. 'Righto! We'll get a taxi outside, and tootle over at once. I should feel no end of a swine if I let that chap in. His wife is a very decent little woman too. But I doubt if I can make the dumb speak.'

They left the café and took a taxi to Mann's. He was just getting up, his wife said, and they sat in the little parlour and waited for five minutes when Mann came down and greeted Jameson with great pleasure. Devenish he greeted respectfully, but with no great cordiality.

'Have a gasper, Mann,' said Jameson, holding out his cigarette-case. 'The inspector here and I have come round to hold a sort of inquest on you, and we begin with the joyful news that my own inquest is over, and the verdict, "Not proven". I am still a free man, as my friend here will tell you.'

'I am glad to hear it,' said Mann, nervously looking at the stolid detective, 'but no one could have thought you capable of it, Mr Jameson.'

'They did, my dear fella, they did! But now we are improving, and want to see you with an equally clean bill of health, if you get me. Fact is, Mann, you've been a bit too much of the modest violet in this business, and the inspector isn't fond of violets of that kind. If there is anything you would like to get off your chest, now is the time. The inspector is ready to give you credit for every sort of virtue but loquacity—what about it?'

Mann bit his lip. 'I don't see what more I can say, sir.'

Jameson looked at him hard. 'Think again! This is a nice, informal little party, but you might have to face one of those almighty cross counsel, who would rasp your skin off as soon as look at you. The inspector thought you might be shielding me, but as I have convinced him that I was not in the last nasty little show, you need not be afraid to speak out.'

Mann looked rather piteously at Jameson, opened his mouth, shut it again, and shook his head.

Jameson's chaffing mood turned to anger. 'Don't be a damn fool, Mann! I tell this looks serious for you. Are you trying to shield someone outside? You're a double fool if you are, and will get no thanks for it. Do you want to be arrested and put through it at Scotland Yard?'

Mann turned his frightened eyes on Devenish, who met them sternly with his own, and nodded.

'If you are wise, you will do as Mr Peden-Hythe tells you.'

But Mann remained silent, looking from one face to the other in desperate anxiety. Jameson tried again.

'Are you trying to shield someone?'

Mann stammered. 'No, sir.'

Devenish shrugged impatiently. 'Now, sir, you have had a shot at it, but without success, I am sorry to say. I must see what I can do.' He turned his eyes on Mann, and went on: 'Now then, we have been making inquiries about you, and there are one or two things we want to know. Give me your attention!'

'I'm listening, sir.'

'In the first place why didn't you tell me you had a pistol?'

Mann's face lost all its colour. 'What pistol, sir?' he asked hesitatingly.

Devenish saw that he was going to carry his bluff. He had, of course, the advantage that all detectives have; the person he was questioning did not know how much he knew. 'The pistol you bought when you took over this job.'

'But the pistol was one from the sports department, sir—I mean the one the police found.'

'Don't tell me what we found! Confine yourself to replying to my questions. I know you had a pistol, but I am prepared to admit that you merely bought it for your own protection—a .32 calibre automatic, wasn't it?'

Mann was no actor, and had prepared no defences against this sort of examination. He had bought a pistol from a chauffeur, who had been touring in the Balkan States with his master, and he felt sure that the police must have got hold of this man. As he hesitated, Jameson spoke up.

'Out with it, Mann! Inspector Devenish doesn't blame you for buying a pistol. Most of the night watchmen are supplied with them. I don't know why the dickens you weren't.'

Devenish cut in again. 'That's right. Now then?'

'Yes,' said Mann, dismally. 'I had a pistol,' and he told them from whom he had bought it. 'But I didn't murder anyone, sir. Really, I didn't.'

Devenish nodded. 'Very well. You had a pistol, a .32 automatic. Will you let me have a look at it, and the ammunition you use in it? That won't do you any harm, and it may clear you completely. A weapon would make you feel more self-confident at night—but I must see it.'

The blank stare of Mann made them both regard him gravely. He gulped once, then gasped: 'I haven't got it now, sir.'

'Haven't got it? When did you dispose of it?'

'The day of the murder, sir.'

Devenish frowned. 'What did you do with it?'

'Threw it in the river, sir, from a bridge, when no one was looking.'

'For what reason?'

Mann was sweating now, and looked a haggard shadow of himself.

'You see, sir, after the murder being discovered, and me being alone in the Store, I was afraid someone might blame me.'

'For being alone in the Store, where you were on duty? Come now,' Devenish shot a rapid question at him: 'Where did you conceal this automatic as you went out? I want an answer at once!'

'In my waistbelt, sir,' stammered Mann, holding on to his chair with both hands in an extremity of nervous fear.

'And you were searched as you went out. You forgot that!' said Devenish, scathingly. He turned to Jameson, and added: 'I am afraid it is no go, sir. He won't tell the truth. I had better take him to the Yard, I think—I don't require a warrant in a murder case.'

Mann almost collapsed. Then he made a tremendous effort to pull himself together, and appealed to the inspector desperately.

'Don't take me there, sir. I'll tell you the truth.'

Devenish had half risen; he now sat down again. 'Very well. When did you hide the pistol?'

'In the night, sir.'

'The night of the murder?'

'Where did you hide it?'

'If you give me two hours, sir, I'll get it and show it to you.'

'I said where is the pistol?'

'Oh, Lord! Sir, I'm not a murderer!' cried Mann.

'You're acting as if you were. But that's enough. I mean to hear where it is, and now.'

Mann licked his lips again and again, and tried to speak. Jameson turned to the detective.

'Wait a bit. He's going to tell us. Come on, Mann. If you're innocent it will help you, not do you any harm.'

Mann was trembling all over. 'Well, I will tell you, sir, and show you where it is too. But you must hear my story, sir. You really must! I can explain. I'm going to explain.'

Devenish took out his note-book and pencil. 'Are you now

offering a voluntary statement? Do you realise that it may be used against you?'

'I'll make a free-will statement, and sign it, sir,' said Mann wildly, 'if you'll only let me do it before I show you where the things are.'

# CHAPTER XXV

THE tragic nature of the scene and the moving terror of Mann had an extraordinary effect on Jameson Peden-Hythe. He sat transfixed, his eyes staring at the wretched fellow, now doing his best to speak, while his expression had changed from one of impatience to one of pity and horror.

Devenish, more used to such scenes, was not really looking at Mann, or watching his attempts to compose himself. He was concentrating on an expression the witness had used, and not even so much on that as the stress he had put on one particular word in the phrase.

The stress on words is as important in criminal investigation as in reading poetry, or making it. Devenish's practical experience of the psychology of witnesses had told him that stressing a single word may mean the whole difference between a whole lie and a white lie; an intention bluffly and recklessly to deceive, and an attempt to square the witness's conscience (for even criminals have a conscience, if a warped one) by an evasion.

While Mann was licking his dry lips, fidgeting in his chair, and trying to collect his thought, Devenish was repeating the phrase he had used.

'I am not a murderer really!' In a denial which was merely vehement, the stress would have been obviously laid on the word 'not'. But it had not been stressed by Mann, who had cried: 'I am not a *murderer* really!' You may kill a man, and not be a murderer, as everyone knows very well; and in a detective's mind the difference between manslaughter and murder is very clearly defined.

He waited a minute or two for Mann to begin, then looked at him encouragingly. 'Now, don't get excited. We're not a judge and jury, you know, and you are not on trial. Just try to think that your evidence may be as helpful to you as to us. The law doesn't exist to harry people for nothing, you see.'

Mann stared back at him, and gathered courage from the change in the detective's tone. 'I ought to have told at once, sir,' he said. 'It looks so black now.'

'Not a bit of it. Get on with your story. I have an idea I could piece most of it together myself, and it hasn't prejudiced me against you yet. Now then, I'll give you a start. You went to the Stores at ten that night to begin your first round. What happened then?'

Mann found his voice at last, and as he went on he spoke more clearly and with fresh confidence.

'I went round, sir, to see that all was right, and when I had done, I went to sit down. I turned on the microphone as usual, but I didn't hear any louder sounds. I did my best to see what was wrong, but couldn't make out what was the matter—'

'Wait a moment,' interrupted the inspector, 'that is rather important. You are sure the gadget was off then?'

'I am quite sure, sir.'

'But you only fixed it when you came back from your round—I mean tried to put it on—not when you first arrived?'

Mann looked surprised. 'No, sir, not till after I made my round.'

'Did you put it on at once then? I want you to be very sure of that. It fixes the time for us more or less. Could you give me the approximate time at which you tried to fix it?'

'It would be round about twenty past ten, sir.'

Devenish nodded. 'Right. Carry on!'

Mann proceeded: 'I thought it was just some little thing that I did not understand, sir, and it did not worry me, since I intended to report it next day and have it seen to. I didn't think anything was likely to happen that night. But, later on, I remembered it and—'

'Leave that till you come to it,' said the inspector. 'You found that the microphone attachment did not work, so that you would not hear any soft sounds in the more distant parts of the Stores. Now after that?'

'Well, sir, my next round ought to have started at a quarter past eleven, but I had to speak to Mr Peden-Hythe here, and I went out to the back door and found him there. We was quite a time talking, as he was a bit excited, sir,' he paused and looked at Jameson apologetically, 'and rather angry. When I left him and locked up again, I started on my second round. I was near the lift coming down from Mr Mander's flat at that moment, and heard it coming down very quiet.'

Devenish nodded. 'Go on.'

'Well, sir, you may believe me or not, but I remembered that gadget being out of action, felt sure some burglar had done it, and got the wind up. I bent down and took my boots off, and then crept back to my box. I had left my pistol there, and I was sure someone had broken in and was going to rob the place.'

'I can believe that, Mann, but what did you do then—go and tackle the fellow?'

'No, sir,' said Mann, with some hesitation. 'While I was taking off my boots, I thought I heard someone open one of those window panels. I thought I had better go up to Mr Mander's, ring his bell, and get him to help me. But I couldn't get up my nerve to enter the lift on that floor I thought a burglar had come out of, so I took a goods lift as far as the floor below the flat, and then risked it. But when I got to Mr Mander's front door, I found it was open, and it struck me that the burglar must have broken in by the back way. After a moment I went in, but there was no one there—'

'Just a moment,' interrupted Devenish. 'Can the lifts be operated from below? I think they can. I mean you must have brought up the lift the man had used, and he couldn't—'

'He didn't come up in that, sir, but in one of the other lifts. I wanted to go down again, thinking I must do something, and had my pistol, but I admit I was nervous, and didn't go down by the lift he had gone down by.'

'The one you first heard descending?'

'Yes, sir. I only took it as far as the floor below, where I had got in, and then went to the next lift. I got the fright of my life when I heard it coming up towards me.'

'What, the man coming up?'

'Yes, sir, and as that stopped on the floor I was on, I had to make a stand. I am afraid I am a funk, sir, and always have been, but I did try to remember then I was there to guard the shop, and I got out my torch and my pistol in a flash and turned the torch on the lift as it was just coming up to my floor, pointing it down, sir, when the top was just knee-high to me. There was a man in it, and he had a black mask on, and I could see a splash of blood on his arm.'

Peden-Hythe started. 'A splash of blood?'

Mann nodded. 'The moment he saw the torch, sir, he touched the lift button, and it began to go down again. But I was so frightened and angry both, if you know what I mean, thinking he had perhaps got in and killed Mr Mander, that I fired down at him, and shot him. And that's the truth, sir, if you asked me questions all day.'

He hid his face in his hands for a moment, and then removed them, and wiped the sweat from his forehead. Jameson stared at him blankly. The detective seemed impressed.

'Come. No harm done so far by telling the truth,' he said reassuringly. 'It was suppressing it that got you into this fix. You had shot the man in the lift, and the lift was going down. What did you do next?'

Mann seemed more surprised by the apparent credence given to his story than by anything else. 'Why, sir, I went down another way, and had a look at him. Somehow the pistol had made me bolder, and I couldn't leave him there, perhaps dying, without going to look. I went to the lift and opened it, keeping the pistol ready in my hand. Then when I turned my torch on him, it struck me he was dead, and I turned it off again and bolted back to my box. But I knew that was no good. I couldn't leave him there without making sure. I went back and looked at him closer. It seemed to me they couldn't hang me for killing a burglar, so I took off the mask he had on, and then I got the start of my life, for I saw it was Mr Mander.'

'He was wearing a mask? You are sure you're not inventing that?' said Jameson.

Mann shook his head. 'No, sir, indeed, though I couldn't make out why he wore it. If he hadn't had one on I should have seen who it was when the lift came up, and wouldn't have fired.'

Devenish nodded. 'If this story is true, Mr Peden-Hythe, it is natural enough. If Mr Mander killed the young woman, and did it in a premeditated way, as the cutting of the electric lead suggests, then he took some precautions to avoid meeting Mann here on his rounds, but wore the mask in case he was seen. He would be aware that the watchman, seeing him wearing it, would mistake him for a burglar, and would not believe for a moment that it was really his employer. Well, Mann?'

'He would know when I went on my rounds, of course,' said the witness eagerly. 'Anyway, sir, I had such a shock that it sent me right off my balance for a while. I felt sure no one would believe me if I said I had killed him by accident. And if I had explained that he came down to the store wearing a mask I would have been laughed at, for at that time, sir, I did not know why he had come down.'

'Did you discover it?'

Mann licked his dry lips again. 'Yes, sir. I wondered and wondered what he could have been doing, and then I remembered that I had heard a sound like a window panel moving back. I wanted to get away from the sight of him, and I wondered if I could find what had brought him down from his flat so secret, so that it would help me with my evidence.'

'You mean confirm your statement that he came down stealthily, and wearing a mask?'

'Yes, sir. I had a general idea where the sound had come from, but there was only one sliding door-panel that let the window-dresser into the window space, and that was to the window they had fitted up as a fancy ballroom. I suppose Mr Mander must have been bleeding internal, for there wasn't very much, and I left him in the lift and went to that panel. I switched on my torch and made a search. If I got a fright when I saw Mr Mander, I got a double one when I saw Miss Tumour near the back, sitting in a chair behind two dancers, with a mask on too—'

'When had you previously seen Miss Tumour?'

'Twice, sir. The wife and I came round to shop last month, when there was a particular sale on, and she was pointed out to me. I knew it wasn't one of the wax dancers, because she was wearing street shoes, not satin ones like the others, and I slipped her mask up careful, and recognised her.'

'You did not examine her more closely to see if she was dead, and how she had been killed?' asked Devenish.

'I was too frightened, sir, and upset. But I could see she was dead. There was no mistaking that. Well, I was in such a dither, sir, that I left her there too. I thought of giving the alarm, but who would believe what I said and wouldn't they think it was just an excuse to kill Mr Mander? I was a fool, but what with one thing and another, I didn't know what to do.'

'But what did you actually do?'

'I knew Mr Mander's flat was left open, and I thought perhaps I could find how it had happened up there. I went up to have a look round. Then—'

Jameson interrupted. 'I hope, Mann, you are really telling the truth. Inspector Devenish here may think you acted very strangely.'

Devenish smiled faintly. 'If you had as much experience as I have of uneducated and nervous people when they get in a panic, it would not seem so strange to you, sir. They are far more frightened of us than any other type of people, and they have a kind of idea that we twist facts to get convictions at all costs—carry on, Mann! What did you find in the flat above?'

Mann continued nervously: 'Well, sir, I looked round and round, and I saw no signs of a struggle or any blood, the only things I saw being the lady's coat and hat and a glove. Then I knew she had been up there, and I wondered how he had killed her and why. But I could make nothing of it, especially as I heard she and Mr Kephim were sweethearts. At last I came on the door opening to the staircase to the roof, and it was wide open. On a night at that time of year it seemed funny. And it seemed funny it had been left open and the cold coming in cruel.'

'So you decided to investigate the roof too?'

'I did, sir. I went up with my torch and had a look round, and then I saw where someone had fallen on one of the banks of sand and left blood there, and it gave me a start. I went over to one of the parapets and leaned against it till I felt better, then I got an idea. I wish I hadn't, for it made this mess for me, sir, but it seemed clever to me at the time, and the sort of thing would prove I had nothing to do with it.'

'What was that, Mann—the gyrocopter?'

'Yes, sir. I knew one had landed on the roof, once, and I said to myself couldn't I make it look as if some enemy of Mr Mander's had bought one of these machines and landed there, gone down and killed him and the young lady. There were tyre tracks on the roof, and I thought the police would see them, and believe the murderer had flown off again.'

Devenish smiled. 'Very nice, if it had come off.'

'Well, sir, if I could make it out that a criminal could get there and away again, I thought they would not look for anyone below having done it.'

'And having evolved this hair-brained scheme of yours, you thought you would go one better, and provide the kind of noise an aeroplane engine would make?'

Mann looked at the inspector with alarm. 'I never knew you suspected that, sir, but so it was. Down below I had seen the engine on the bench, and I thought if I started it up, it would make a noise and be heard. So I went down from the roof and started the engine and let it run, while I tried to get the bodies out of the way—I mean Mr Mander's out of the lift. The lifts was part of my round, and I would have had to give the alarm when I found the body, and I didn't want to give any alarm but let him be found next day and know nothing about it, so to speak. I put on a pair of gloves I found in the workshop, knowing from the papers that burglars wear them, and I took down the blue overalls Mr Mander was found in. I thought if I could draw them on over the body I could keep my hands from getting stained and carry him away.'

'The bleeding would have stopped some time before you reached the ground-floor again.'

'It had, sir. I felt very sick over the job, but I managed to get him out of the lift, spreading two sheets of brown paper under him, and it took me twenty minutes to draw on the blue over-alls without messing my hands.'

'It was then that you saw the state the square of carpet in the lift had got into?' asked Devenish.

'Yes, sir. I left Mr Mander where he was, and thought and thought what I could do to hide the stain in the lift. I couldn't take one of the carpets out of the other lifts, when I just remembered that I had seen a square upstairs in Mr Mander's billiard-room. I went up for that, cut off the engine in the workshop when I was there—'

'And removed three of the sparking-plugs from the engine?'

'Yes, sir. You see, someone might say it was no flying machine, only Mr Mander tinkering with this engine on the bench. But if three sparking-plugs were missing, it would show the engine couldn't have run.'

'I see. I suspected that. But go on.'

Mann wiped his brow once more. 'I felt a bit better then, for I had plenty of time to work before they opened next morning, and I was sure I could make it all like a murder done by an outsider, and I was going to explain that I couldn't sleep, owing to wounds, at home, and fell asleep at my post, sir. I got a lot of ideas for taking suspicion off of me, and it wasn't my fault, really, seeing I mistook him for—'

Devenish intervened. 'Leave us to draw our own conclusions. You cut off the engine, and brought down the carpet square. You substituted it for the stained square on which Mr Mander had fallen when you fired at him, then—?'

'Then, sir, I wondered what I could do with the body. I couldn't take it upstairs to the flat and leave the other body in the window, and I wouldn't have touched the other corpse for a fortune—one was bad enough to do with. The floor of one section of the Stores was on my rounds, but I wasn't expected to open the window panels and look there. So I decided to put Mr Mander in the window, near the young lady.'

Devenish nodded. 'Did it occur to you that you might make it appear like murder and suicide, with jealousy for a motive?'

Mann started. 'How did you know that, sir?'

'Very simply. You provided a pistol for the scene.'

'Well, sir, when I had gone so far, I got worried again. But it wasn't for myself this time. I kept thinking that, as Mr Mander might have been carrying on with Mr Kephim's young lady, Mr Kephim might be suspected of doing them in. And then I remembered that they would have the names and addresses of the customers who bought these machines, and one of them might be suspected; or the man Webley, who flew the machine over that time there was a fuss about it. I may be a fool, sir, and acted hasty—me being in such a funk and getting the wind up proper when I saw the masked man come up in the lift—but I did not want an innocent person had up for what I had done accident-like. It seemed to me the only thing was to make everything as confusing as possible so no one would be proved guilty.'

'You had that idea at the back of your mind, inspector,' said Jameson to Devenish, when the man paused.

Devenish nodded and fixed his eyes again on the witness. 'You forgot that the weapons which had killed the two people would have perforated in one case the blue overalls, and in the other the fancy-dress, worn by the victims. You simply imagined that we would accept the evidence of the pistol there, and the fact that Mander had been carrying on an intrigue with another man's sweetheart, as proof that Mander had killed Miss Tumour in a jealous fit and then shot himself?'

'Yes, sir. My mind was almost turned as it was. I never thought of all those things at the time. I managed to lift Mr Mander and stuck him up in the window, not so near the front. Then I thought I would get a pistol from the sports department, and I got one that was a small-bore, like the pistol I bought. I had a hunt for cartridges for it, but presently found some under a pile of boxes that hadn't been much moved since they were put in, and I hid the sparking-plugs out of my pocket there in a box.'

Devenish pursed his lips. 'But you had still to fire it, and for that purpose you went on the roof again?'

'Yes, sir. I knew of the sand there, and I had heard how sand stops a bullet. I went to the bank where the blood was and fired the pistol into it.'

'That seems what you did do, Mann, but the banks of sand were not disturbed when I came up, and there was nothing of an impression on them to show that anyone had fallen there.'

'No, sir. I began to think again about those who had bought these machines, so I got to work careful, and smoothed it out again. I didn't want you to think either was killed up there by someone who flew on to the roof that night.'

'I see. You were thoroughly muddled, including your

motives. You began to see that the more clues you laid, the
more people you might involve.'

'That is true, sir,' said Mann, passing a hand over his forehead, and sighing, 'but might I have a glass of water now, sir?
I feel rather queer.'

# CHAPTER XXVI

When Mann had been given a glass of water, and rested for ten minutes, he professed himself able to go on, and Devenish put a further question.

'Did you go to the flat below, after that excursion on the roof, and make sure that there was no sand left in or on your clothes by using the vacuum cleaner?'

'Using a vacuum cleaner, sir?' cried the watchman. 'I wouldn't know where it was, sir. I was never in the flat before that night.'

'But answer "Yes" or "No", please.'

'No, I did not, sir. I don't know what that has to do with it.'

'It may prove that Mr Mander did actually follow or thrust that young woman upstairs to the roof; for certainly someone did use the cleaner for that purpose.'

'But suppose she only fell on the sands?' said Jameson, who could keep silent no longer.

'There is the possibility that both tripped over it in the dark,' replied Devenish. 'At all events, if Mann's story is true, that is a point in his favour—Now get on with your story.'

Mann was a better colour now, and spoke more calmly. 'I never supposed there was any harm in it, sir, so, often when I went my rounds, I had a look at the things in the departments. It passed the time, and I used to tell the missus what there was, and she used to like that—the fashions and all. Anyway, when I went down with the pistol I had fired to put it in the window, I took the young lady's coat and hat and glove with me. I put the pistol down on the floor in the ballroom window—the one I had got from the sports department—and fired, sir, and then I went off to where the coats was.'

'Oh, you did that?'

'Yes, sir. I looked through a lot of cupboards that had sliding panels, and presently I come on one that has a lot of coats like the one I had over my arm. I hung it up with the rest, for it was very new looking, and then I went off to the Hats.'

'The millinery department?'

'I believe that is what they call it, sir. Anyway, I got rid of it there, and had another look round. There was the carpet in the lift, covering up the blood and looking all right, and those two in the window, but I just remembered then I had never found what killed Miss Tumour, and it wouldn't do to leave that for anyone to find. I hunted high and low for it, and then I went last on the roof, and after a bit I saw a sharp-pointed dagger thing there, near the sandbank. I didn't like to carry that off and I didn't know what to do with it. It was still sticky, sir, and I dropped it on the floor of one of the goods lifts. I thought it would make the evidence still more confusing and that no one would think I had been up and down in the lifts, as anyone coming from the upper part of the building would do. By that time, it was getting on, sir. I went back to my box, and thought, and thought. Half a dozen times I made up my mind to wake his servants and tell them I had shot him by accident. And then I didn't know what I would say about the young lady being dead too. The time to have told would have been the moment I fired the gun, but I was so upset that I began all that work, covering up, and I couldn't undo that. At other times I thought I would let myself out and bolt. But I had the missus here, and I didn't know where to bolt to, and I knew it would look like being guilty if I did.'

'That would have been even worse than what you did,' agreed the inspector. 'I expect you had a pretty horrid time, wondering what was going to happen in the morning.'

'You're right, sir. I wonder my hair didn't turn white. It was worse than my bit of the war, sir, and I thought that could not be. Anyway, there I was in my box for a long time, holding my head in my hands and having nightmares, when I remembered that I hadn't hidden my pistol or that carpet square. It did give me a turn, though of course no one would come till the morning.'

'You mean your own pistol this time?'

'Yes, sir, the one I bought for protection; Mr Mander being against firearms, with all the alarm gadgets, as he called them. But those were against outside burglars, not ones in the building all the time.'

'People, not burglars, in the building.'

'Yes, I mean Mr Mander and the young lady, sir. Well, when I did think of them, I thought too of the trouble there would be next day when the police came. I knew I'd be searched, and couldn't carry off the pistol or the carpet. I had a rare time trying to think what I would do with them, but at last I got it.'

Jameson was convinced for the first time that Mann was really telling the whole truth. When he had begun his story his nervous hesitation and the way he mentioned each detail had the air of being false. He appeared to be taking time to make up each fresh statement before he made it. But, as he gained courage, he spoke quickly and confidently, and it was easy to see that he was relating actual facts.

Devenish, who had more experience of frightened witnesses, and knew how often terror may make an innocent man present the appearance of one who is guilty, had been able better to judge the man with whom he was dealing. He knew, too, that Mann was mistaken when he talked of staying on in the Store, unless his tale was true. A murderer would have bolted, not bungled. The very confusion and ill-organised attempts to cover up the shooting proved to the inspector's mind that the watchman had merely taken the part he cast himself for and shot Mander while under the influence of panic.

For, obviously, he had not killed Effie Tumour. To kill her it would have been necessary for him to enter Mander's flat, and the detectives were quite certain that the lock had not been tampered with. In any case, so far as they were able to judge, Mann had no motive for killing either. It was this lack of motive which would clear him if a charge of murder was brought, and ought, if properly handled, to enable him to evade a charge of manslaughter.

'Well, let's hear what you did with the square of carpet,' Devenish said quietly.

Mann replied at once. 'You know, sir, there is one of the walls in the big entrance hall of this section of the Stores with a big picture of some warship called the *Foudroyer*.'

'The old *Foudroyant*—yes.'

'Well, sir, I thought no one would be likely to look up there for anything, so I got a pair of telescopic steps they use for the window cleaning and went up and took the picture down. It hangs where you can't see it from the side, and leans out a little from the top. I laid it flat on the floor, got some small nails, and nailed that carpet to the back of the frame. Then I hung it up again, and if you look now, sir, you will see it.'

'That was decidedly smart,' observed Jameson.

Mann shook his head mournfully. 'I don't know that it was, sir, though I thought so at the time. I ought to have told Mr Jameson, I see that now! But when you shoot a man in a fright, and have nerves like me, you're fairly flummoxed. I've had hard luck. If it hadn't been that someone tampered with the microphone, I wouldn't have got the wind up thinking a burglar had got in, and I wouldn't have fired so sharp if I hadn't had the wind up proper.'

Devenish nodded. 'I suppose the pistol isn't up there too, is it?'

Mann assented. 'Yes, it is. There were two rings for the cords, and I got a bit of string and ran it through the trigger guard, fastened the glove to it, and pulled it taut. You see, sir, there is about five inches clear between the picture and the wall at the top, and quite two inches two feet down. The automatic went in easy.'

Devenish heard him out, then looked at him pleasantly. 'If you think you can put down that statement, more or less as you have told it, in reply to my questions, I think you had better make a start. Take your time, and don't get rattled. If your story is true, and I really think it sounds genuine, then that statement will be put in in your favour.'

'I'll do it, sir,' said Mann eagerly. 'I'll get a bit of paper and do it now, and sign it before you two gentlemen.'

Devenish got up. 'I'll be back in an hour for it,' he said. 'Mr Peden-Hythe and I will have a spot of lunch and come back—at least I shall.'

# CHAPTER XXVII

JAMESON had insisted on the inspector taking lunch with him at a café called the 'Vorrey'. As they sat over their food a quarter of an hour after leaving Mann, they discussed the case, and agreed that there now seemed every prospect of its being cleared up rapidly.

'But what puzzles me is the motive Mander had for killing that young woman,' remarked Jameson, when he had ordered coffees and a liqueur for Devenish. 'He was mixed up with her, of course. But what more was there in it, and why take her up to that damned draughty roof to kill her?'

Devenish looked at him thoughtfully. 'There, sir, we are in no better state than you. The man is dead and the girl too, and the most we can hope for is a theoretical reconstruction of the events of that night that took place in and above the flat. I am pretty certain we know what happened below.'

'I wish you would reconstruct it for me.'

Devenish smiled. 'Well, we shall never know in which of the two possible ways the girl came by her death, but we can safely assume there were but two ways—murder or accidental death.'

'Accidental death, by Jove! How do you make that out?'

Jameson looked eagerly at his companion and offered him a cigar as the waiter came up with their order.

Devenish shrugged.

'I am almost inclined now to think that is the correct theory, and I base that assumption on what we know of Mander. If it were not for two things, I should plump for it at once.'

'What things?'

'The fact that Mrs Hoe declared that the girl knew nothing of'—he paused, and added—'but you know nothing of that. The fact is that a woman, one of Tumour's friends, was

217

blackmailing Mander. That woman, who might easily have alleged that Tumour was in the plot, categorically denied it. But, as long as we have no definite proof that she was not also engaged in blackmail, we cannot say that Mander did not murder her to stop her mouth.'

'Do you think he did?'

'No. My inclination is the other way, as I told you. In the first place, we know that Mander was a clever, calculating fellow. Now, if he killed Tumour with premeditation, he would certainly have made some arrangements for bolting after. We know he misappropriated a large sum of money, and we know from his passport trick that he intended to bolt eventually. But the money was in a private account, under another name at a bank never used by him officially.'

Jameson nodded. 'I see.'

'If he intended to kill her, he would not have left that money where he could not get at it until Monday at least, by which time the murder would have been discovered, and his start far too short to promise escape.'

'That's true.'

'He would not either, I think, have trusted to a stupid weapon like a knife. The knife is what I call the weapon of impulse. It makes such a messy job of it that no one who premeditated murder would use it. It is the sort of thing that may be used in a quarrel or picked up in hot blood. But I cannot imagine Mander doing that. If he had decided to kill the girl, what would be easier than poison? He could pinch that from the chemistry department of the Stores, if he hesitated to go elsewhere and sign the poison-book.'

'That is true,' said Jameson, puffing at his cigar, 'and of course the girl would not suspect him of an attempt of that kind. He could easily have put it in wine and offered it to her.'

'Quite. Then there is another point. If murder was in question, he would know that he had from, say, ten on Sunday night to nine, at the latest, on the Monday morning, to get away. But he had made no preparations for packing, and the closest search failed to give us any sign of his having taken tickets abroad. He might have hoped to go by aeroplane, but he would hardly bring in Webley for that, and if he chartered a special in the early hours of the morning, it would have drawn attention to the direction of his flight when the murder was discovered. These omissions to prepare would not be those of a man who, whatever his faults, was cunning, intelligent and far-seeing.'

'I only see one point against that, Devenish,' remarked his companion. 'Why did he put her in the shop window if he did not intend to fly?'

Devenish shrugged. 'I am merely giving the arguments against *premeditated* murder. If her death was accidental, he would still have to bolt. He would know that it would not be sufficient to clean up the stained sand on the roof. He would know that, even if he managed to eliminate all traces from the roof and the flat, there would still be the fact of her presence in the building to explain. You see, Kephim gave evidence that he took her up-river that afternoon, and then saw her home. The chauffeur would have given evidence that he was in the habit of calling on Miss Tumour with his master. In other words, the intimacy between Mander and Tumour would have come out, and as Mander lived in the building and had obvious access when he wished to the shop below, suspicion would have fallen on him.'

'Naturally.'

'But if her death was the result of accident, or even of a hasty blow, without premeditation, it would be a different matter. The bolt would have to be an improvised one, and as we know, or are convinced, he had no time to arrange anything. Taking the body down to the window, he was shot on his return by the panic-stricken Mann. What he would have done if Mann had not intervened, we do not know. We do know that events prove either accidental death or a hasty murder in hot blood.'

'But, even then, why put her in the window?' asked Jameson.

Devenish drew at his cigar, and put it in an ashtray before he replied. 'I haven't any theoretical knowledge of the workings of the mind, but I have a practical knowledge which suits me as well. Some scientist said that love was a disease, and in certain cases it presents the symptoms of a disease. I can say that without cynicism. There are some people who react so seriously to the influence of certain drugs that the would-be beneficial medicine becomes a positive danger. Some people—most, I should say—fall normally in love, and are all the better for it. But others, as you can see in the papers every day, fall in love and become maniacally jealous, and eventually homicidal in their jealousy. To explain what I mean in this case, I must remind you that Mander was madly in love with Miss Tumour; gave her this highly paid post because he was fascinated by her; and finally proposed to run away with her. Now you know that, ever since this Store was opened, women have been running after Mander and his supposititious millions—daughters of good families, people of poor but aristocratic circles. In other words, he could have married well. Instead of that, he chooses a girl who has nothing but her beauty to recommend her.'

'I admit that he must have been madly in love,' said Jameson.

Devenish nodded. 'Now, we come to the other side of the shield. I know that the girl was a bit of a gold-digger at first. She led Mander on, so that he would give her a good time, but she had an affection for Kephim, who had been courting her for a considerable period. Now, according to my informant, just lately Tumour began to fall in love with Kephim. I think there is no doubt of that. I have a feeling that she was never Mander's mistress, but just one of the girls, common enough nowadays, who will bleed an infatuated man for all they are worth; get jewellery and other things; go out to dinner and the theatre, and so on. But Tumour grew tired of the game. Perhaps Mander was growing pressing; perhaps the fact that she was beginning to love Kephim, who had been loyal all along, made her realise that she was playing an ugly part.'

'I think if she was in love it would,' said Jameson.

'At any rate, I know that, after dillying and dallying, she formally accepted Kephim. But she confided to a friend that she did not like to announce her engagement just then, for fear it might react on Kephim's prospects—it would give Mander a handle against Kephim.'

'And he was the sort of man to use it.'

'Absolutely. Well, to get on, Miss Tumour finally told her friend that she had made up her mind to do the straight thing. She intended to tell Mander. If he fired Kephim, she would stand by it. She imagined that other Stores would be glad to get her lover. In any case, she was going to take the risk.'

'That Sunday night?'

'On that Sunday night. Well, she said good-bye to Kephim when he saw her home, and later set out for the flat. She was admitted by Mander, who was not in the best of tempers, I should think, as the result of the interview he had had with your mother. That interview must have shown him that he was on thin ice. She went in, took off her hat and coat, and then we must assume that she came to the point. From her confession to Mander that she did not love him and would not go away with him, but loved and was engaged to his manager, Kephim, we must merely theorise. But I think I can assume that this staggering announcement sent Mander into a frenzy.'

'Can you assume that?'

'Yes, I can. Whether he killed her or not, there is the fact that he must have used some violence towards her. There were marks on her upper arms that prove she was seized by someone with a strong grip. The surgeon who examined her, and the doctor who conducted the post-mortem, were both agreed on that.'

'I see. Go on.'

Devenish pursed his lips. 'Now, we can assume that they were in the drawing-room at the time, for that is where this dagger-like knife was kept. If Mander's frenzy began there, we can say that she tried to escape him, finally rushed up the passage to the roof, and was stabbed in the back up there, as she tried to evade him. The position of the wound suggests infliction while flying from him—'

'But wouldn't his finger-prints be on the handle of the knife?'

'Unless he had taken pains to clean it thoroughly. Still, I think he had hardly time for that, and I am inclined to believe in the theory of accident. The way I see it is this: Tumour entered the drawing-room with him, in a state of nervous tension. She had an unpleasant confession to make, and could have been under no illusions as to the way he would take it. Mechanically, she takes off her coat and hat, and wishing to get the thing over begins to tell him the state of affairs. She is beginning to draw off her gloves, talking the while, or attempting to reply to his furious accusations. She draws the left glove off first, as everyone does, and then, as I see it, Mander loses his head and either tried to take her in his arms or strike at her. She springs up and evades him. His fury and his despair must have been very obvious. No one can believe that she suggested going, or he either, on the roof at night in November. Her presence up there must have been the result of fright or compulsion.

'Fright seems the most likely explanation.'

'I agree. Well, everything points to the fact that Mander was like a maniac with rage. She was alone with him up there, the Stores below were closed; she knew, or might have known, that the servants' quarters were cut off from the residential portion of the flat by solid walls and a sound-proof door. A girl has no chance in a struggle with a healthy and strong man, and will naturally catch up something with which to defend herself. I suggest that in her attempts to evade Mander, she saw the knife and picked it up. She would pick it up in her right hand, which was still gloved, but having taken it, she would, like every normal person, hesitate to use it—and women do not take kindly to knives. You will see that if you study the statistics of feminine crime.'

'She would want to threaten him with it only?'

'Yes. But he is a madly jealous man. His frenzy has entire possession of him. He ignores the threat and comes on. She sees that she must either stab at him or make a further attempt to get away. She must, in this desperate pass, have thought of the staircase to the roof. She managed to get out of the room and on to this staircase. It seems to me that it was on the staircase that Mander caught her up and seized her from behind by both arms. Now, here we have another bit of medical evidence, this time relating to Mander. He had, when found, two lateral bruises on the shin in front of each leg. It seemed to me that he had bounded up the stairs after her and tripped as he caught her up, bruising the shins against a step, and temporarily releasing her.'

'So she got away and on to the roof?'

'Undoubtedly. She got free and ran on to the dark roof. He recovered himself and ran after her. He caught up on her where the pile of sand, to facilitate an easy landing for the gyrocopter, was placed. There she may have come to bay, her hands behind her back, one holding the knife; or he may have sprung at her and driven her violently backwards—he would not be able to judge distances in the dark. But, whether as the result of a struggle, or her falling backwards over the invisible sandbank, Tumour fell on the knife, and died as the result of the wound in the spine. Now that is my theory of the event, and I think it is what actually happened.'

'You seem to have got jolly close to it,' said Jameson admiringly, 'but would the theory of accident fit in with his making a public show of her in the window, in fancy-dress too?'

Devenish nodded. 'In his abnormal state I think it would. Here he had lavished his affections and his money on a woman who had been cheating him, and now proposed to marry his manager. He couldn't leave her in his flat, and still make the mock of her that his new hatred desired. I can imagine him saying to himself that she had made a tool of him to get money and buy fine clothes and cut a dash. Well, she should have fine clothes, and be as much in the public eye as she wished! Then there was a second motive. If he hated her because she had made a fool of him, he would hate doubly the man who had supplanted him, Kephim. Kephim was manager. He would be called for when the body was discovered in the window.'

'By Jove. You're right, Devenish.'

'That would be a sweet revenge, he must have thought. Kephim would be called, and the first sight he would get would be the dead girl who had promised to marry him.'

Jameson took a deep breath. 'True. It would be a dreadful blow at the other man.'

'Mander had to bolt in any case after that. It was his Parthian shot. Whether he would have got far is a matter of speculation, and we need not go into it. He dressed the girl up in that fancy-costume, then went down quietly when Mann was on his round, and disconnected the microphone attachment. Then he went up and brought the body down in one of the lifts (wearing a mask, in case he should be glimpsed by the watchman), and placed the body in a chair in the window. Going up again, he was seen by our panic-stricken friend, and shot before the lift descended again below the level of the floor on which the watchman was standing. We know the rest, I think.'

Jameson beckoned to the waiter and called for the bill. 'I say, Devenish,' he said curiously, 'have you really got to try that poor blighter?'

Devenish nodded. 'I am afraid it will come to a trial, sir, but, if I know anything of British judges and juries, he won't be sentenced. There is a complete absence of motive; as a murder committed by Mann, there is no sense in the case at all. Then a great deal depends on how Treasury counsel is instructed and how he presents the case. He will have all our notes at his disposal and Mann's signed statement. I must go back for that now, by the way—In other words, the prosecution will not press the case, and Mann, after a little homily from the judge on the question of the danger of possessing firearms, will come off scot-free. I don't think I should worry about him if I were you.'

They got up, and Jameson paid the bill. 'Well, inspector, it was very good of you to tell me what you think,' he said, 'and I am much relieved about that poor devil. It makes me feel a great deal happier. By the way, do come down one day to Parston Court to see us. Just let me have notice, and we shall be very pleased to see you.'

'It is very kind of you to suggest it, sir, and I shall be happy to go when I have a day off,' Devenish replied, smiling. 'Oh, I forgot to say that the Stores might be reopened any day now. Would you be good enough to mention the fact to Mrs Peden-Hythe.'

Jameson stared. 'Reopen the Stores! I'll be ashamed of her if she doesn't sell the beastly place—Why, hang it, man, after this I shall hate to look into a shop window!'

### THE END

# THE DETECTIVE STORY CLUB

"The Man with the Gun."

**THE SELECTION COMMITTEE HAS PLEASURE IN RECOMMENDING THE FOLLOWING NOVELS OF OUTSTANDING MERIT**

### The Terror — EDGAR WALLACE

There are many imitators—but only one EDGAR WALLACE. *The Terror* is a most sensational thriller, and has had a great success both as a play and as a film.

### The Leavenworth Case — ANNA K. GREEN

What did MR. BALDWIN say in 1928 ? He said : "*The Leavenworth Case* is one of the best detective stories ever written."

### The Crime Club
#### By an Ex-Supt. of the C.I.D., SCOTLAND YARD

Here is the real straight thing from G.H.Q. A detective thriller that is different, by FRANK FRÖEST, the Scotland Yard man, assisted by GEORGE DILNOT, author of the *Famous Trials* Series.

### Called Back — HUGH CONWAY

A clever and exciting thriller which has become world-famous.

### The Perfect Crime — ISRAEL ZANGWILL

This very ingenious detective novel, by the distinguished novelist and playwright, is the subject of one of the most successful films of the year.

### The Blackmailers — EMILE GABORIAU

All detective writers worship at the shrine of Gaboriau—master of the French crime story. *The Blackmailers* is one of his best, replete with thrills and brilliantly told.

---

## LOOK FOR THE MAN WITH THE GUN

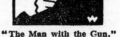

# THE DETECTIVE STORY CLUB

### FOR DETECTIVE CONNOISSEURS

*recommends*

**"The Man with the Gun."**

# THE BLACKMAILERS

## *By* THE MASTER OF THE FRENCH CRIME STORY—EMILE GABORIAU

EMILE GABORIAU is France's greatest detective writer. *The Blackmailers* is one of his most thrilling novels, and is full of exciting surprises. The story opens with a sensational bank robbery in Paris, suspicion falling immediately upon Prosper Bertomy, the young cashier whose extravagant living has been the subject of talk among his friends. Further investigation, however, reveals a network of blackmail and villainy which seems as if it would inevitably close round Prosper and the beautiful Madeleine, who is deeply in love with him. Can he prove his innocence in the face of such damning evidence?

## THE REAL THING *from* SCOTLAND YARD!

# THE CRIME CLUB

## *By* FRANK FRÖEST, Ex-Supt. C.I.D., Scotland Yard, and George Dilnot

YOU will seek in vain in any book of reference for the name of The Crime Club. Its watchword is secrecy. Its members wear the mask of mystery, but they form the most powerful organisation against master criminals ever known. The Crime Club is an international club composed of men who spend their lives studying crime and criminals. In its headquarters are to be found experts from Scotland Yard, many foreign detectives and secret service agents. This book tells of their greatest victories over crime, and is written in association with George Dilnot by a former member of the Criminal Investigation Department of Scotland Yard.

---

## LOOK FOR THE MAN WITH THE GUN

---

# THE DETECTIVE STORY CLUB

### FOR DETECTIVE CONNOISSEURS

*recommends*

**"The Man with the Gun."**

# THE PERFECT CRIME

## THE FILM STORY OF

ISRAEL ZANGWILL'S famous detective thriller, THE BIG BOW MYSTERY

A MAN is murdered for no apparent reason. He has no enemies, and there seemed to be no motive for any one murdering him. No clues remained, and the instrument with which the murder was committed could not be traced. The door of the room in which the body was discovered was locked and bolted on the inside, both windows were latched, and there was no trace of any intruder. The greatest detectives in the land were puzzled. Here indeed was the perfect crime, the work of a master mind. Can you solve the problem which baffled Scotland Yard for so long, until at last the missing link in the chain of evidence was revealed?

# LOOK OUT

### FOR FURTHER SELECTIONS FROM THE DETECTIVE STORY CLUB—READY SHORTLY

---

**LOOK FOR THE MAN WITH THE GUN**